REVIVING IZABEL

Book Two
In the Company of Killers

J.A. REDMERSKI

This book is a work of fiction. Any references to real people, events, or locales are used fictitiously. Other names, characters, places and incidents are products of the author's imagination, and any resemblance to actual events, locales, persons living or deceased, is entirely coincidental.

Copyright © 2013 J.A. Redmerski

All rights reserved, including the right of reproduction in whole or in part and in any form.

Cover photo by Michelle Monique Photography
Cover model: Nicole Whittaker

Table of Contents

CHAPTER ONE 5
CHAPTER TWO 13
CHAPTER THREE 20
CHAPTER FOUR 28
CHAPTER FIVE 40
CHAPTER SIX 47
CHAPTER SEVEN 55
CHAPTER EIGHT 65
CHAPTER NINE 78
CHAPTER TEN 88
CHAPTER ELEVEN 97
CHAPTER TWELVE 105
CHAPTER THIRTEEN 117
CHAPTER FOURTEEN 125
CHAPTER FIFTEEN 137
CHAPTER SIXTEEN 150
CHAPTER SEVENTEEN 166
CHAPTER EIGHTEEN 172
CHAPTER NINETEEN 183
CHAPTER TWENTY 189
CHAPTER TWENTY-ONE 201
CHAPTER TWENTY-TWO 210
CHAPTER TWENTY-THREE 225
CHAPTER TWENTY-FOUR 240
CHAPTER TWENTY-FIVE 249
CHAPTER TWENTY-SIX 262
CHAPTER TWENTY-SEVEN 269
CHAPTER TWENTY-EIGHT 283
CHAPTER TWENTY-NINE 298
CHAPTER THIRTY 305

CHAPTER ONE

Sarai

It's been eight months since I escaped the compound in Mexico where I was held against my will for nine years. I'm free. I'm living a 'normal' life, doing normal things with normal people. I haven't been attacked or threatened or followed by anyone who might still want me dead. I have a 'best friend', Dahlia. I have the closest thing to a mother I've ever known. Dina Gregory. What more could I ask for? Seems selfish to expect anything more. But despite all that I have, one thing has not changed: I'm still living a lie.

I have friends back in California: Charlie, Lea, Alex and...Bri—no, wait, I mean Brandi. My ex-boyfriend, Matt, was abusive and he's the reason why I moved back to Arizona. He stalked me for a long time after we broke up. I got a restraining order, but that didn't keep him away. He shot me eight months ago, but I can't prove it because I didn't actually see him. And I'm just too afraid to turn him in to the police.

Of course, every bit of that is a lie.

They are the pieces of my life that cover up what *really* happened to me. My excuses for why I went missing at fourteen and how I ended up in a California hospital with a gunshot wound. I can never tell Dina or Dahlia, or my boyfriend, Eric, what really happened: that I was taken to Mexico by my own poor-excuse-for-a-mother to live with a drug lord. I can never tell anyone that I escaped that place after nine years and that I killed the man who kept me a prisoner all my young adult life. I mean, sure I *could* tell someone, but if I did that it would only put Victor in jeopardy.

Victor.

No, I'll never be able to tell anyone that an assassin helped me escape, or that I watched Victor kill numerous people, including the wife of a prominent, high-profile businessman in Los Angeles. I'll never be able to tell anyone that after everything I've been through, everything that I've seen, I want nothing more than to pack my bags and go *back* to that dangerous life. The life with Victor.

To this day his name is calming on my tongue. Sometimes while I'm lying awake at night, I whisper his name aloud just to hear it because I *need* it. I need *him*. I can't get him out of my head. I've tried. Dammit I have tried. But no matter what I do I still live every day of my life thinking about him. If he's watching over me. If he thinks about me as much as I think about him. If he's still alive.

I clutch the pillow above my head and shut my eyes picturing Victor. Sometimes it's the only way I can get off.

Eric squeezes my thighs in both hands, holding me still on the bed with his face buried between my legs.

I push my hips toward him, bucking gently against his lashing tongue until my whole body stiffens and my thighs tremble around his head.

"Oh my God...," I shudder as I come and then drop my arms between my legs, spearing my fingers through his dark hair. "Jesus...."

I feel Eric's lips touch my belly just above my pelvic bone.

I look up at the ceiling, just like I always do after an orgasm because the guilt I bear inside makes me too ashamed to look at Eric. He's a great guy. My sexy, dark-haired, blue-eyed boyfriend of twenty-seven who is kind and charming and funny and perfect. Perfect for me if I had never met Victor Faust.

I'm ruined for life.

I wipe the tiny beads of sweat from my forehead and Eric crawls back up the bed and lays down next to me.

"You always do that." He pokes me in the ribs playfully with his knuckles.

Very ticklish on my sides, I recoil and roll over facing him. I smile warmly and run a finger through the top of his hair.

"What do I always do?"

"That moment of silence thing." He fits his thumb and index finger around my chin. "I get you off and you get really quiet for a long time."

I know and I'm sorry, but I have to erase Victor's face from my mind before I can look you in the eyes. I'm a horrible person.

Eric kisses my forehead.

"It's called recuperation," I jest and kiss his fingers. "Perfectly harmless. But you should take it as a good sign. You know what you're doing." I nudge him back in his ribs.

And truly he does know what he's doing. Eric is great in bed. But I'm still too emotionally attached…addicted…to Victor and I have a feeling that I'll always be.

It took me five months after Victor left to try getting on with my life as far as other relationships go. I met Eric at my job at the convenience store. He bought a bag of chips and an energy drink. After that, he made trips to my store twice, sometimes three times a week. I wanted nothing to do with him. I wanted Victor. But I started losing hope that Victor would ever come back for me.

Eric goes to lay his arm across my bare stomach, but I get up casually just before and step into my panties. He doesn't suspect anything, which is good. I don't feel like cuddling, but the last thing I want to do is hurt his feelings. His arms raise up, his fingers interlocking behind his head. He looks across the room at me, grinning seductively. He always does that when I'm not fully clothed.

"Sarai?"

"Yeah?" I slip my t-shirt on and readjust my ponytail.

"I know it's short notice," Eric says, "but I'd like to go along with you and Dahlia to California tomorrow."

Shit.

"But I thought you couldn't get off work?" I pull my shorts up and step into my flip-flops.

"I couldn't back when you asked me if I wanted to go," he says. "But we have some new help at work and my boss decided to give me the time off."

This is not good news. Not because I don't want him around me—I do care for Eric despite my inability to forget about Victor Faust—but my 'vacation' to California tomorrow won't be about sight-seeing, partying, and spending sprees on Rodeo Dr.

I'm going there to kill a man. Or, I'm going to *try* to kill a man.

It's bad enough that Dahlia will be there and that I'll have to keep this from just one person, much less two.

"You…don't seem excited," Eric says, his smile slowly dropping from his face.

I smile big and shake my head, walking back over to him and sitting on the edge of the bed. "No, no, I *am* excited. It just caught me off-guard. We're heading out at six in the morning. That's less than eight hours from now. Are you packed?"

Eric laughs lightly and reaches across my bed, pulling me back over next to him. I sit by his waist, propping one arm against the mattress on his other side, my legs hanging off the edge of the bed at the ankles.

"Well, I just found out this afternoon before I left work," he says. "I know, shitty timing, but all I have to do is throw a few things in a bag and I'm good."

He reaches up and brushes stray hair from my ponytail away from my face.

"Great!" I lie with an equally false smile. "Then I guess it's settled."

~~~

Dina is up before me at four. The smell of bacon is what wakes me. I climb out of bed and hit the shower before planting myself at the kitchen table. An empty plate is already waiting for me.

"I really wish you would've chosen someplace else to vacation, Sarai," Dina says.

She sits down on the opposite side of the table and starts filling her plate. I take a few pieces of bacon from the pile and place them onto mine.

"I know," I say, "but like I told you, I'm not going to let my ex keep me from visiting my friends."

She shakes her ever-graying head and sighs.

I screwed up somewhere along the line with my plethora of lies. When Victor brought Dina to the hospital in Los Angeles after his brother, Niklas, shot me, she had no idea what had happened. Except that I had been shot. It took me a few months to feel confident enough to talk to her about it.

After I figured out what story I wanted to tell her, anyway. That's when I made up the abusive ex-boyfriend story. I should've just told her that I was robbed. By a total stranger. It would've made the lie so much easier to keep up with. Now that she knows I'm going back to L.A. she's worried to death about it and has been for the past two months. I never should've told her that I'm going back there.

I finish off the bacon and a small helping of eggs, washing it down with a glass of milk.

Dahlia and Eric show up together just after I finish brushing my teeth.

"Come on, we need to get on the road," Dahlia urges me out the front door. Her sandy-brown hair is pinned to the top of her head in a sloppy, just-woke-up bun.

I hug Dina goodbye.

"I'll be fine," I tell her. "I promise. I'm not going anywhere near where he lives." I actually picture a man's face this time talking about someone that doesn't exist. I guess I've had to play this role for so long that 'Matt' and all of these 'friends' of mine in L.A. I talk about it to everyone as if they're real, have *become* real on a subconscious level.

Dina forces a smile through her worried face and her hands fall away from my elbows.

"Call me when you get there?"

I nod. "As soon as I walk into my hotel room, I'll call you."

She smiles and I hug her once more before following them to Dahlia's waiting car. Eric puts my suitcase in the trunk with their bags and then hops in the backseat.

"Hollywood here we come!" Dahlia says.

I pretend to be half as enthused as she is. It's a good thing it's so early in the morning, otherwise Dahlia might take my lackluster attitude for what it really is. I stretch my arms out behind me and yawn, resting my head against the seat. I feel Eric's hand on the back of my neck as he starts to knead the muscles there.

"No idea why you want to *drive* to L.A.," Dahlia says. "If we took a plane you wouldn't have to get up so early. You wouldn't be so tired and grouchy."

My head falls to the left. "I'm not grouchy. I've hardly said a word to you yet."

She smirks at me. "Exactly. Sarai not speaking equals grouchy."

"And recuperating," Eric adds.

My face flushes and I reach a hand behind my head and play-slap his hand as it moves in a heavenly motion against my neck. I shut my eyes and see Victor there.

I didn't do it on purpose.

We arrive in Los Angeles after a four hour drive. I couldn't go by plane because I wouldn't be able to carry my weapons along with me. Of course, I couldn't tell Dahlia that. She just thinks I wanted to take the scenic route.

I have seven days to do what I came here to do. That is, if I can pull it off. I've thought about my plan for months, about how I'm going to do it. I knew all along that there's no way I'm getting into the Hamburg mansion. That requires an invitation and socializing in the public eyes of Hamburg's guests and Arthur Hamburg himself. He saw my face. Well, technically he saw more than my face. But I have a feeling that what happened that night when Victor and I tricked Hamburg into inviting us up to his room so that we could kill his wife is something he will never forget, right down to the small details.

Hopefully, a short-cut platinum-blonde wig and heavy dark makeup will hide that long, auburn-haired identity of mine that Hamburg would remember the moment I stepped into the room.

CHAPTER TWO

Sarai

I spend the entire day with Eric and Dahlia playing along to pass the time. We go out to eat for lunch and do a Hollywood tour with a guide and visit a museum before heading back to our hotel, exhausted. At least, I pretend to be exhausted enough that I'm ready to call it a day. Really what I need to do is get ready to go to Hamburg's restaurant tonight.

Dahlia already thinks there's something wrong with me.

"Are you coming down with something?" she asks reaching between our poolside lounge-chairs and feeling my forehead.

"I'm fine," I say. "Just tired after getting up so early. And when's the last time I did this much walking around in one day?"

She leans back against her chair and adjusts the big, round sunglasses on her face.

"Well, I hope you won't be tired tomorrow," Eric says on the other side of me. "There are so many things I want to do. I haven't been to L.A. since before my parents divorced."

"Yeah, it's my first time back in two years," Dahlia adds.

A teenager jumps into the pool several feet away and splashes us a little. I raise my back from the chair and shake the droplets of water from the magazine I had been reading.

I pull my sunglasses off my eyes and rest them on my head. Swinging my legs over the side of the chair, I stand up.

"I think I'm going to head up to the room and take a nap," I announce as I grab my mesh pool bag from beside me on the concrete.

Eric sits up straight and removes his sunglasses, too.

"I'll go with you if you want," he offers.

I gesture toward him, indicating for him not to get up. "No, you hang out here and keep Dahlia company," I say, shouldering my bag. I slide my sunglasses back over my eyes so he can't detect the deceit.

"Are you sure you're feeling all right?" Dahlia asks. "Sarai, you're on vacation, remember? You're supposed to be having a good time, not napping."

"I think I'll be one hundred percent tomorrow," I say. "I just need a long, hot bath and good night's sleep is all."

"OK, I'll take your word for it," Dahlia says. "But don't you get sick on me." She shakes her finger at me sternly.

Eric reaches out and curls his fingers around my wrist. He pulls me down to him. "You sure you don't want me to join you?" He kisses my lips and I kiss him back before rising fully into a stand again.

"I'm sure," I say softly and leave it at that.

I leave them by the pool and head to the elevator.

The second I'm inside the room, I lock the door with the chain so Eric and Dahlia can't walk in on me. I drop my bag on the floor and open my laptop, punching in my password. While it's booting up, I look out the window to see my friends, although small from this height, still lounging at the poolside. I sit down in front of the screen and for probably the hundredth time, I look at every page on the web site for Hamburg's restaurant, double-checking the hours of operation and scanning the professionally-shot photos of the building, inside and out. None of this is really helping me with what I intend to do, but I still find myself looking at it every day.

Feeling defeated, I slam the palm of my hand down on the tabletop.

"Dammit!" I say out loud and slouch against the chair, running my hands over the top of my hair.

I still don't know how I'm going to get Hamburg by himself without being seen. I know I'm in over my head. I have been since I conjured up this crazy idea, but I know if all I do is sit around and think about it I'll never get past that phase.

I came here with a plan: go to the restaurant in a disguise and act as any other guest. Scope the place out for one night. Where the exits are located. The entrances to other areas of the building. The restrooms. But my number one priority was to find the room where Hamburg sits watching the guests from above and listening to their conversations from the tiny mic hidden at every table's centerpiece. Then I would sneak inside and slit the pig's throat.

But now that I'm here, not six blocks from the restaurant, and now that the days I have to do this are ticking away, I'm feeling less confident. This isn't a movie. I'm a stupid girl to think I can waltz into a place like that unseen, take a man's life without drawing attention and escape without getting caught.

Only Victor can pull something like that off.

I hit the tabletop again more lightly this time, close the lid on the laptop and stand from the table. I pace over the red and green speckled carpet. And just as I resolve to head down the hall to the room I secretly rented separate from Dahlia and Eric, the door cracks open but is stopped by the chain.

"Sarai?" Dahlia says from the other side. "You gonna' let us in?"

I sigh heavily and walk over to unlock the door.

"What's with the chain?" Eric asks, walking in behind Dahlia.

"Habit."

I plop down on the end of the king-sized bed.

They both drop their things on the floor. Dahlia sits at the table by the window and Eric lies across the bed behind me, crossing his ankles.

"Thought you were going to take a nap?" Dahlia asks.

She carefully drags her fingers through portions of her wet, tangled hair, grimacing every now and then with the effort.

"Dahlia," I say, looking at them both. "I haven't been up here long. I thought you two were going to hang around the pool for a while?" I hope I hid the aggravation from my voice about how soon they decided to join me. I just can't help it; I'm too stressed out, plus I'm worried about them being here with me at all. I don't want them to get hurt or to be involved in any way with why I came here.

"We can go if you want," Eric says gently from behind.

Instantly I regret my words because it's obvious I didn't hide the aggravation as well as I had hoped.

I tilt my head back and sigh, reaching over and rubbing the top of his ankle.

"I'm sorry," I say and smile up at Dahlia. "You know, I...," then suddenly a perfectly reasonable excuse for the way I've been acting materializes and the floodgates open on the lies. "...I'm just kind of nervous about being back in L.A."

Dahlia gets that oh-I-see look and shoves Eric's feet to the side and sits down next to me in place of them. She drapes her arm around my shoulder and fits her hand around my upper arm.

"I had a feeling that might be what was wrong." I notice her glance back at Eric, giving me the impression that this is what they talked about while they sat down there at the pool together once I left.

I bet it's also why they decided to come up here with me so soon.

"We wanted to check on you," Eric says from behind, confirming my suspicion.

I feel the bed move as he sits upright.

I stand up before he has a chance to wrap his arms around me. It's in this very moment that I realize I've been doing that a lot lately for the past month. How much longer I can keep leading him on, I don't know. I know I should just tell him how I feel, that I'm not as into him as he is into me. But the truth is that I can't tell him the truth. I would just have to make up yet another lie and I'm so deep in lies right now that I'm drowning in them.

At the same time, I've let this go on between us for as long as I have because I really wanted to feel as deeply for him as he seems to feel for me. I wanted to get on with my life, to forget about Victor and be happy with the life he left me with.

But I can't. I just can't....

"He's not going to know you're even here," Eric says about 'Matt'. "And besides, if he did find out, I'd kick his ass if I saw him."

I smile weakly across at Eric.

"I know you would," I say, but I just feel even worse because the only two friends I have in the world have no idea who I am.

I cross my arms and walk to the window, gazing out.

"Sarai," Dahlia speaks up, "I hate to say this to you, but if you're that worried about Matt finding out you're back in town, I don't think it's a good idea to visit your friends here."

"I know, you're right," I say. "I know they wouldn't tell him, but it's probably best I just stuck with the two of you while we're here."

I turn around to face them.

"Sounds like a plan," Eric says, beaming.

It's definitely a plan, because now I don't have to come up with another excuse to not introduce them to my old friends who don't exist.

Dahlia walks over to stand next to me.

"We probably should've vacationed in Florida or something, huh?"

I gaze out the window again.

"No," I say. "I love this city. And I know how much you wanted to come." I smile over at her briefly. "I say we have as much fun as possible this week."

She bumps her shoulder against mine playfully.

"Now that's the Sarai I know." She smiles.

Yes, but I'm not that person....

She walks over and grabs Eric by the elbow, pulling him from the bed.

"Let's get out of here and let the girl rest."

Eric cooperates and then comes over to me, turning me around with my elbows cupped in his hands. He looks into my eyes with his baby-blues and gives me his best pouty face.

"If you need me for anything," he says, "call me and I'll be here."

I nod and offer him a real smile. Because he deserves it for being so kind to me.

"I will," I say.

Then I shuffle them out the door with both hands in front of me.

"I would say don't have too much fun without me, but that would be asking too much."

Dahlia laughs lightly as she steps out into the hallway.

"No, it's not asking too much." She holds up two fingers. "Scouts honor."

"I don't think that's how it goes, Dahl," Eric says.

She brushes him off.

"You just get some sleep," she says. "Because tomorrow you're going to need to be fully charged."

"Agreed." I nod.

"Bye babe," Eric says just before I close myself off inside the room again.

I stand with my back pressed against the door and let out a long, deep breath.

Pretending is so hard. It's far more difficult than just being myself, as abnormal and reckless as I may be.

"I know what I have to do," I say aloud—talking to myself has become my new thing as of late. It helps me to visualize and to figure things out easier.

I walk back to the window and gaze out at the city of Los Angeles, my arms crossed loosely over my stomach.

"A disguise is necessary, but not to hide from Hamburg. Just from the cameras and from anyone else. I *want* Hamburg to see me. It's the only way I'm going to get in."

CHAPTER THREE

Sarai

Dahlia and Eric didn't come back up to the room until a couple hours later, just after sundown. I had made sure to shower and change into a pair of shorts and a t-shirt and to leave the lights off in the room to make it appear as though I had been asleep. The second I heard the card key sliding into the door, I leapt into bed and sprawled out across the mattress, the same way I always do when I'm really sleeping. Eric crept in quietly, trying not to 'wake me', but I rolled over and moaned and cracked my eyelids open to let him know that he had. He apologized and asked if I wanted to go with him and Dahlia to a nearby nightclub and insisted that if I didn't go, he wouldn't, either. But I rejected that idea quickly. I could tell he really wanted to go and I can't blame him; if I were in his position I wouldn't want to hang out in a dark hotel room at barely eight o'clock on a Friday night in one of the most active cities in the U.S.

But the two of them leaving was exactly what I needed. I had spent that entire two hours trying to come up with an excuse to tell them about why I was leaving, where I was going and why they couldn't come.

They solved it for me.

Minutes after Eric leaves, I wait until Dahlia—in her room next to ours—changes out of her swimwear. From the peephole in my door, I watch them walk down the hallway. I count to one hundred, pacing the floor, over and over again. And then I grab my purse and carry it out the door. I walk briskly down the hallway in the opposite direction and make my way to the secret room on the other side of the building.

A little paranoid about getting caught, I fumble around inside my purse, touching just about everything except the key to the room. Finally, I manage to get it into my fingers and I hurry inside, sliding the chain-lock into place afterwards. Throwing open my suitcase on the end of the bed, I take out my short platinum-blonde wig, carefully dragging my fingers through it to straighten the few unruly strands, and then fix it on top of the nearby lampshade so it'll hold its form.

I get dressed in a skimpy Dolce & Gabbana dress, apply my makeup, dark and heavy and perfect after spending a great deal of time at home practicing the technique, and then slip into my strappy heels. Heels. Something else I've spent a lot of time trying to master. My alter ego, Izabel Seyfried, would know how to walk in them and look good doing it, so naturally, I needed to get with the program.

Then I wet my hair and break it into two parts behind me, twist each half and then cross them over one another at the back of my head. Several Bobby pins later, my long auburn hair is fixed tightly against my scalp. I slip the wig cap over the hair and then the wig, adjusting it for a long time until I get rid of any imperfections.

Lastly, I tighten a knife sheath around my thigh and drop the fabric of my dress back over it.

I stand in front of the tall mirror, looking at myself at every possible angle. I feel odd as a blonde. Satisfied, I grab my little black purse and tuck it underneath my arm, the small handgun hidden inside making it bulge somewhat in the center. I reach out for the door handle letting my hand fall back to my side.

"What the hell am I doing?"

What needs to be done.

Why the hell am I doing it?

Because I have to.

I can't get it out of my head. The things this man admitted to, the people he killed because of a sick, sexual fetish. Every night since Victor left me, when I close my eyes, I see Hamburg's face, and that chilling grin he wore when I was bent over that table, exposed in front of him. I see the face of his wife, emaciated and sickly, her sunken eyes glazed over with resignation. I can even still smell the urine that had dried in her clothes and on the ratted cot she slept on in that hidden room.

My chest fills with air and I hold it there for several long seconds before letting the heavy breath out.

I can't let it go. The need to kill him is like an itch in the center of my back. I can't reach it naturally, but I'll bend and twist my arms to the point of pain to scratch it.

I can't let it go…

And maybe…just maybe I'll get the attention of a certain assassin I can't force myself to forget, while I'm at it.

The moment I walk out the door I leave Sarai behind and become Izabel for the night.

~~~

Not having thought beforehand about the importance of at least renting my own fancy car, I have a cab drop me off two blocks from the restaurant and I walk the rest of the way. Izabel would never be seen riding in a cab.

"Table for one?" the host inquires after I make my way inside.

I cock my head to one side and look upon him with a hint of annoyance. "Is that a problem? Am I not allowed to enjoy a meal by myself? Or, are you hitting on me?" I smirk at him and cock my head to the other side. He's getting nervous. "Would you like to eat with me...," I look at the name embroidered on his jacket, "...Jeffrey?" I step closer. He takes an uncomfortable step back.

"Ummm," he stammers, "I'm sorry, ma'am—."

I step back fully and snarl at him.

"Don't ever call me ma'am," I snap. "Just take me to a table. For one."

He nods quickly and gestures for me to follow. Once I'm at my small round table with two chairs situated in the center of the restaurant, I take a seat and set my purse aside. A waiter walks over as the host leaves and presents the wine menu. I reject it with the brushing movement of my fingers.

"Just bring me water with a lemon wedge."

"Yes ma'am," he says, but I let it slide.

As he strides through the room and away from me, I start scoping the place out. There's one exit sign to my left, far off near the hallway. Another one to my right, close to the stairs that lead to the second floor. The restaurant is much like it was the first time I came here: dark, not-so-populated and fairly quiet, except this time I hear the light volume of jazz music playing from somewhere. And while I'm looking around the place, I stop abruptly when I see the booth where I sat with Victor when I came here with him months ago.

I get lost in the memory, picturing everything precisely the way it happened. As I look across the room at the two people sitting there, all I can see is Victor and myself:

"Come here," he says in a gentler tone.

I slide over the few inches separating us and sit right next to him.

His fingers dance along the back of my neck as he pulls my head toward him. My heart pounds erratically when he brushes his lips against the side of my face. Suddenly, I feel his other hand slip in-between my thighs and up my dress. My breath hitches. Do I part them? Do I freeze up and lock them in place? I know what I want to do, but I don't know what I should do and my mind is about to run away with me.

"I have a surprise for you tonight," he whispers onto my ear.

His hand moves closer to the warmth between my legs.

I gasp quietly, trying not to let him know, though I'm positive he definitely knows.

"What kind of surprise?" I ask, my head tilted back, resting in his hand.

"Are you going to have anything this evening?" I hear a voice say and I snap out of my reverie.

The waiter is holding a food menu in his hand. My water with a lemon wedged on the rim of the glass is already waiting in front of me.

A little flustered at first, I just nod, but then shake my head instead. "I'm not sure yet," I finally answer. "Leave the menu here. I may order later."

"Very well," the waiter says.

He sets the menu down and leaves me alone.

I gaze up at the balcony and the tables perched alongside the extravagant railing. Where could Hamburg be? I know he's upstairs because I remember Victor saying that's where he sits. But where? I wonder if he's already seen me and the second that thought crosses my mind, my stomach ties up in nervous knots.

No, I can't look nervous.

I straighten my back against the chair and take a sip of my water, curling my fingers around the slim glass, all except for my pinky finger which makes me look that much wealthier, or just snootier. For a long time I watch the guests come and go, listen to their pointless conversations and find myself wondering which, if any, of the couples here tonight might end up in Hamburg's mansion this weekend making a lot of money to let him watch them fuck.

Then I look down at the reddish-purple flower arrangement sitting in a small glass vase in the center of my table. Reaching inside my purse, I pull out my cell phone, pretend to dial and then gently place it near my ear so no one will think I'm talking to myself.

"This message is for Arthur Hamburg," I say in a low voice, slouching forward a little so the mic hidden in the centerpiece will pick up my voice. "Surely you remember me? Izabel Seyfried. It's been a while, hasn't it?"

Carefully I look to the left and right of me, expecting to see a burly man or two in suits coming toward me with guns.

"I'm not here alone," I go on, "so don't even think of trying anything stupid. We need to talk, you and I."

Gazing up toward the balcony floor I try to get a sense of where he might be, hoping that he's even here. A few tense minutes pass and just when I start to think this night has been wasted and I really have talking to myself, I notice movement stirring on the balcony floor just above the south exit. My heart is drumming rapidly as I watch the tall, dark figure emerge from the shadows and descend the stairs.

I remember this man, broad-shouldered with salt-and-pepper hair and a dimple in the center of his chin. It's the manager of the restaurant, Willem Stephens, who I've met here once before.

He steps up to my table with absolutely no emotion on his face, his big hands folded together down in front of him, his back straight, his chiseled chin solid.

"Good evening, Miss Seyfried." His voice is deep and ominous. "Where, might I ask, is your owner?"

I smirk up at his looming height, take a casual sip of my water and place the glass back on the table, taking my time. Every part of me is screaming, telling me how stupid it was for me to come here, and as much as I know that to be true, I don't care. It's not fear making me tremble underneath my skin, it's adrenaline.

"Victor Faust is not my owner," I say calmly. "But he is around. Somewhere." A faint, sly smile touches my lips.

Stephens' eyes move subtly to scan the area before he looks back at me.

"Why are you here?" he asks, dropping the sophisticated manager act down a notch.

"I have business to discuss with Arthur Hamburg," I say with confidence. "It will be in his best interest that he arrange a private meeting with me. Here. Tonight. Preferably now."

I take another sip.

I notice Stephens' Adam's apple move as he swallows, and the edges of his strong jaw as his teeth grind together. He glances up at the area he came from and I notice a tiny black device hidden inside his left ear. It appears he's listening to someone speak. Hamburg would be my guess.

He looks back at me, his dark eyes cold and hateful, yet he retains his unemotional demeanor as flawlessly as Victor always had.

His right hand unfolds as he holds it out to me and says, "Right this way," and only when I stand up do both of his hands drop to his sides.

I follow Stephens through the restaurant and up the stairs to the balcony floor.

And either this will be my first night as a killer, or my last night alive.

CHAPTER FOUR

Sarai

"If you touch me," I say to the suit-clad guard standing outside Hamburg's private room, "I'll put your nuts in a meat-grinder."

The guard's nostrils flare and he glances at Stephens. "You requested a meeting with Mr. Hamburg," Stephens says from behind. "It's only proper that you be searched for weapons before we allow you inside."

Dammit!

Calm. Just keep calm. Do what Izabel would do.

I breathe in a heavy breath and sneer at both of them menacingly. Then I throw my little black purse at the guard. He catches it as it hits his chest.

"I think it's safe to say I couldn't hide a weapon wearing a dress like this unless I put it up my cunt," I snap, looking back at Stephens. "My gun is in the purse. But don't even think of touching—"

"Let her in," a familiar voice says from the door.

It's Hamburg, still as porky and grotesque as he was before, wearing an oversized suit ready to bust at the buttons if he inhales too deeply.

I smirk at the guard glaring back at me with murder in his eyes. I know that look, I'm all too intimate with it just the same. He takes the gun from my purse and hands the purse back to me.

"Mr. Hamburg," Stephens says, "I should remain with you."

Hamburg shakes his double-chinned head. "No, you mind the restaurant. These people aren't here to kill me or else they wouldn't be so obvious. I'll be fine."

"At least leave Marion outside the door," Stephens suggests, glancing at the guard.

"Yes," Hamburg agrees. "You stay here, let no one interrupt our...," he looks at me once coldly, "...meeting, unless I ask for an interruption. If at any time you no longer hear my voice for a full minute, come inside the room. As a precaution, of course."

He smirks at me.

"Of course," I mimic and smirk right back.

Hamburg steps to the side and gestures me in with an opened hand, palm-up.

"I thought this was over, Miss Seyfried."

Hamburg shuts the door.

"Have a seat," he adds.

The room is generous in size with smooth, rounded walls seamless from one side to the other. A series of large paintings depicting what appears to be scenes of a biblical nature are set near a large stone fireplace, mounted inside enormous glass shadow boxes with lights beaming upward from the bottom like spotlights. The overall lighting is low, like it is in the restaurant, and it smells of incense or maybe scented oil of musk and lavender. On the far wall to my left is an opened door leading into another room where the blue-gray light from several television screens glows against the walls. As I walk in closer to take the leather high-back chair in front of Hamburg's desk, I glimpse inside the small room.

It's just as I thought. The screens show different tables in the restaurant.

Hamburg closes that door, too.

"No, it's far from over," I finally answer.

I cross one leg over the other and keep my posture straight, my chin raised with confidence and my eyes on Hamburg as he moves through the room toward me. I reach down to pull the end of my dress fully over the knife sheathed at my thigh. My purse rests on my lap.

"You've already taken my wife from me." Indignation laces his voice. "You don't think that was enough?"

"Unfortunately, no." I smile slyly. "Wasn't it enough that you and your wife took *one* life? No, it wasn't," I answer for him. "You took *many* lives."

Hamburg chews on the inside of his mouth and takes a seat behind his desk, facing me. He rests his sausage-like hands out in front of him across the mahogany. I can tell how badly he wants to kill me where I sit. But he won't because he believes I'm not alone. No one in their right mind would do something like this, come here alone, inexperienced and reckless.

No one but me.

I just have to make sure he continues to believe that I have accomplices until I figure out how I'm going to kill him and get out of the room without getting caught. Hamburg giving the guard one minute of not hearing his voice before he can burst into the room has further put a serious wrench in the plan that I never really had to begin with.

"Well, I must say," Hamburg changes the tone in the room, "you are stunning no matter what kind of wig you wear. But I admit, I like the red one better."

He thinks my dark auburn hair was a wig. Good.

"You're a sick man, you know that, right?" I tap my nails against the chair arm.

Hamburg smiles creepily. I shudder inside, but keep a straight face.

"I didn't kill those people on purpose," he says. "They knew what they were getting into, that in the heat of the moment, control could be lost."

"How many?" I ask demandingly.

Hamburg narrows his gaze. "What does it matter, Miss Seyfried? One. Five. Eight. Why don't you just get to the reason for your visit? Money? Information? Blackmail comes in many forms and this wouldn't be the first time I was faced with it. I am a veteran."

"Tell me about your wife," I say, stalling, pretending to be the one still holding all the cards. "Before I 'get to the point' I want to understand your relationship with her."

A part of me really does want to know. And I'm incredibly nervous; I can feel a swarm of bees buzzing around in my stomach. Maybe pointless talk will help ease my mind.

Hamburg cocks his head to one side. "Why?"

"Just answer the question."

"I loved her very much," he answers reluctantly. "She was my life."

"*That* is love?" I ask, unbelieving. "You let her memory die with the image of her being a drug addict who committed suicide just to save your own ass and you call that *love*?"

I notice a light move across the floor underneath the door of the surveillance room. There was no one inside before, at least not that I could tell.

"Like blackmail, love comes in many forms." He rests his back against the squeaky leather chair, interlocking his porky fingers over his big stomach. "Mary and I were inseparable. We weren't like other people, other married couples, but because we were so different didn't mean we loved each other less than anyone else." His eyes lock on mine briefly. "We were lucky to find each other."

"Lucky?" I ask, baffled by his comment. "It was luck that two sick people found each other and teamed up to do sick things to other people? I don't follow."

Hamburg shakes his head as if he's some old wise man and I'm just too young to understand.

"People who are different like Mary and I were—"

"Sick and demented," I correct him. "Not different."

"Whatever you'd like to call it," he says with an air of surrender. "When you're that different from society, from what's *acceptable* in society, finding someone just like you is a very rare thing."

Absently I grit my teeth. Not because he's angering me, but because I never imagined that anything this disgusting man could ever say to me would make me think about my own situation with Victor, or that anything he could say I would actually accept.

I shake it off.

The faint light underneath the surveillance room door moves again. I pretend not to have noticed, not wanting to give Hamburg any reason to think I'm anticipating another way out.

"I came here for names," I blurt out, having not thought about it thoroughly.

"What names?"

"Of your clients."

A change flickers in Hamburg's eyes, the shifting of control.

"You want the names of my clients?" he asks suspiciously.

Oh shit…

"I thought you and Victor Faust already had possession of my client list?"

Keep a straight face. Don't lose composure. Shit!

"Yes, we do," I say, "but I'm referring to the ones you never kept a record of."

I think I'm going to be sick. My head feels like it's on fire. I hold my breath hoping I saved myself.

Hamburg studies me quietly, searching my face and my posture for any signs of faltering confidence. He rounds his heavy, double-chin.

"What makes you think there's a ghost list?" he asks.

I breathe a partial sigh of relief, but I'm still not out of the woods.

"There's *always* a ghost list," I say, though I really have no idea what I'm talking about. "I want at least three names that aren't on the list we have a record of."

I smile, feeling like I've regained control of the situation.

That is until he speaks:

"You tell me three names that are on the list you have a record of and then I will oblige."

I have officially lost the control.

I swallow hard and catch myself before I look 'caught'.

"What, you think I carry your list around in my purse?" I ask with sarcasm, trying to stay in the game. "There will be no negotiations or compromise, Mr. Hamburg. You're hardly in any position to be cutting any deals here."

"Is that so?" he asks, grinning.

He's onto me. I can feel it. But he's going to make sure he's right before he makes his move.

"This isn't up for debate." I stand from the leather chair, tucking my purse underneath my arm, more disappointed than before about relinquishing my gun.

I press my fingertips against the mahogany desk, holding my weight up on them as I lean over just slightly toward him.

"Three names," I demand, "or I walk out of here and Victor Faust walks in to blow your brains against that pretty painting of the baby Jesus behind you."

Hamburg laughs.

"That's not the baby Jesus."

He stands up with me, tall and enormous and intimidating.

While I'm running through my mind trying to find the source of how he knows I'm full of shit, he is a step ahead of me and announces it like a kick in my teeth.

"It's funny, Izabel, that you'd come here asking for names that don't appear on a list that you…," he points at my purse, "…don't keep a record of, because then how would you know that the names I gave you weren't already on it?"

I am so dead.

"Let me tell you what *I* think," he goes on. "I think you're here all alone, that you came back because of some vendetta against me." He shakes his index finger. "Because I remember every little fucking thing about that night. Everyfuckingthing. Especially that look on your face when you realized Victor Faust was there to kill my wife instead of me. That was the look of someone blindsided, who had no idea why she was there. It was the look of someone unfamiliar with the game."

He attempts to smile softly at me as if to display some kind of sympathy for my situation, but it just comes off as sardonic.

"I think that if someone was here with you, they'd already be in here to rescue you by now because it's obvious you're in a load of shit."

The door to the main room opens and the guard steps inside, twisting the lock on the door behind him. For a split-second, I had hoped it was Victor coming to save me right on cue. But that was just wishful thinking. The guard is looking across at me with spiteful, grinning eyes. Hamburg nods to him and the guard starts to take off his belt.

My heart falls into the pit of my stomach.

"You know," Hamburg says walking around his desk, "the first time I met you I remember a deal being made between Victor Faust and myself." He points at me briefly. "You remember, don't you?"

He smiles and places his chunky hand on the back of the chair I just abandoned, turning it around to face me.

My whole body is shaking; it feels like the blood rushing through my hands has become acidic. It charges through my heart and into my head so fast I feel momentarily faint. I start to reach for my knife, but they're too close, closing in on me from two sides. I can't take on both of them at the same time.

"What do you mean?" I ask, stumbling over my words, trying to buy myself some time.

Hamburg rolls his eyes. "Oh come on, Izabel." He twirls a finger in the air. "Despite what happened that night, I was really disappointed that the two of you left before fulfilling the deal."

"I would say that after what happened, the deal was void."

He smiles at me and sits down in the leather chair. I see him glance at the guard, indicating a demand with just the look in his eyes.

Before I can turn around fully the guard has both of my hands pinned behind my back.

"You're making a huge fucking mistake if you do this!" I cry, struggling in the guard's grasp.

He forces me over to a square table and shoves me on top of it. My reflexes can't act fast and my chin is stung by the solid marble. The metallic taste of blood springs up in my mouth.

"Let me go!" I try to kick behind me. "Let me go now!"

Hamburg laughs again.

"Turn her head to this side," I hear him say.

Two seconds later my neck is twisted to the opposite side and held there, my left cheek pressed against the cool marble tabletop.

"I want to see the look in her eyes while you fuck her." He looks at me again. "So, we're going to pick up where we left off that night, all right? Does that sound good to you, Izabel?"

"Fuck you!"

"Oh no, no," he says, still with laughter in his voice. "I won't be fucking you. You're not my type." His hungry eyes skirt the guard who is pressing against me from behind.

"I'm going to kill you," I say through spit and gritted teeth; the guard's engulfing hand pressed against my head forbidding me to move it. "I'm going to fucking kill you both! Rape me! Go ahead! But you'll both be dead before I walk out of here!"

"Who says you're going to walk out of here?" Hamburg taunts.

His pants are unzipped; his right hand lingers near the zipper as though he's trying to maintain some kind of self-control by not touching himself yet.

Then he waves two fingers at the guard, who's gripping the back of my hair in his hand.

"Remember that," he says to the guard. "She doesn't walk out of here."

I feel his right hand slide out of my hair and move between my legs. As he's lifting my dress, I use the opportunity to reach back for the knife on my thigh and pull it free, jutting my hand at an awkward angle behind me. The guard yells out in pain, releasing his hold on me as I pull the knife away still wrenched in my fist. My hand is covered in blood. He stumbles backward, holding one hand over the lower portion of his throat, blood gushing between his fingers.

"You fucking bitch!" Hamburg roars, jumping from the chair and coming toward me like a stampeding elephant, his pants falling around his jiggling waistline.

I run straight for him, my knife raised out in front of me, and we clash in the center of the room. The force of his weight knocks me flat on my ass and my knife falls from my hand, sliding across the bloodstained floor. Hovering over me, Hamburg reaches out to grab me but I press my back against the floor and swing my foot out as hard as I can, burying the heel of my shoe in the side of his face. He yelps and stumbles back, his hand pressed over his cheekbone.

"I will cut you up in little fucking pieces! *Godammit!*" he shouts.

I crawl on my hands and knees toward my knife, seeing the guard splayed out in the floor surrounded by a pool of blood. He's choking on his blood; gasping futilely for air to fill his lungs with.

I grapple the knife in my hand and roll over as Hamburg comes toward me, knocking the leather chair over onto its side on his way. I spring up from the floor fast and reach out for the table, pushing it into his path. He tries to shove it out of the way but it wobbles on its base and he trips over it instead. His body crashes against the floor belly-down, the table falling down right next to his head, narrowly missing him. I jump onto his back, straddling his thick body, my knees not even touching the floor. I grab him by the hair, pulling his head backward toward me and I press the knife to his throat, rending him immobile in seconds.

"Kill me! I don't fucking care! You won't make it out of here alive either way." His voice is raspy, his breathing fast and wheezing as if he'd just tried to run a marathon. The smell of his sweat and fear rises up into my nostrils.

With the blade against his throat a vociferous pounding on the door startles me. The distraction catches me off-guard. Hamburg manages to buck underneath me like a bull, rolling onto his side and knocking me over onto mine. I drop the knife somewhere, but I don't have time to search for it as Hamburg scrambles to his feet and charges me. I hear Stephens' voice on the other side of the door as the door vibrates against his beating hands.

I roll out of the way right before Hamburg can get on top of me and I reach for the nearest object, a heavy rock paperweight that had been sitting on top of the table before it was knocked over, and I swing it at him. The sound of his cheekbone crunching under the blow turns my stomach. Hamburg falls backward covering his face with both hands.

The pounding on the door is getting heavier. In a split second I glance over to see the door moving violently in its frame and I know I have to get out of here. Now. My gaze scans the room for the knife, but there's no more time.

I run straight for the surveillance room, weaving my way through debris.

Thank God there is another door inside. I swing it open and dash down the concrete staircase, hoping it's a way out and that I don't run into anyone on my way.

CHAPTER FIVE

Sarai

I take the concrete stairs two at a time, my bloody hands gripping the painted metal railing, until I make it to the bottom floor. A red EXIT sign lies out ahead. I dash across the dimly-lit hallway where just above me a long, fluorescent light flickers making the stairway all the more ominous. Thrusting both hands on the elongated door handle, I give it one hard push and the door opens up fully into a back alley. A man in a suit is sitting on the hood of a car smoking a cigarette when I run out into the open.

I stop cold in my tracks.

He looks at me.

I look at him.

He notices the blood on my hands and then glances at the door and then back at me.

"Go," he urges, nodding toward the dumpster to my right.

I know I don't have time to be confused, time to ask him why he's letting me go, but I do it anyway.

"Why are you—?"

"Just *go!*"

I hear footsteps echoing through the stairwell behind the door.

I thank the man with my eyes and run around the dumpster, down the alley and away from the restaurant. A gunshot sounds seconds after I round the corner and I hope it's just that man pretending to shoot at me.

I stay out of the open, running behind buildings in the cover of darkness, as much as my high-heeled shoes allow me. When I feel far enough away for time to stop, I hide behind another dumpster and step out of the shoes. I take off my blonde wig, chucking it inside the dumpster.

I can't breathe. I feel sick.

Oh God, I feel sick...

I fall against the brick wall behind me, arching my back and planting my hands against my knees. I vomit violently onto the pavement, my body rigid, my esophagus burning.

Snatching my shoes from the ground, I take off running again toward the hotel, trying to hide the fact that my hands and dress are stained with blood, but I realize that's not so easy to do. I get a few suspicious stares as I walk briskly through the front lobby, but I try to ignore them and hope no one calls the police.

Instead of further risking being seen by someone else, I take the stairs up to the eighth floor. By the time I get there and after all of the running I've done, I feel like my legs are going to collapse beneath me. I lean against the wall and catch my breath, both legs trembling uncontrollably. My chest hurts, as if every breath I take I'm sucking in dust and smoke and microscopic pieces of glass deep into my lungs.

The room I share with Eric is locked and I don't have my room key. In fact...

"Oh shit...."

I throw my head back, shut my eyes and sigh miserably.

I no longer have my purse. I lost it sometime during the struggle in Hamburg's room. My room keys. My cell phone. My gun. My knife. It's all gone.

I pound on the door but Eric's not inside. I didn't expect him to be really since it's barely eleven o'clock. But just in case I'm wrong, I try Dahlia's door next.

"Dahl! Are you in there?" I rap on the door quickly, trying not to disturb any of the nearby rooms.

No answer.

Ready to give up, I drop my shoes on the floor and brace both hands against the wall, my head falling forward between my shoulders. But then I hear a faint clicking noise and the door to Dahlia's room opens slowly. I look up to see her standing there.

Not stopping long enough to question the strange look on her face, I push my way inside the room just to get out of the open. Eric is sitting in the chair by the window. I notice his hair is slightly disheveled. So is Dahlia's.

My instincts are kicking me in the back of the head, but I don't really care about what they're trying to tell me. I just stabbed a man in the throat and tried to kill another. I was almost raped. I just ran for my life through the back streets of Los Angeles from men with guns chasing after me. Nothing they could ever do could top that.

"Oh my God, Sarai," Dahlia says stepping up in front of me, "is that *blood*?"

The strange, quiet demeanor she was displaying when I first walked in disappears in an instant when she takes stock of me in the full light of the room. Her eyes are wide and filled with concern.

Eric gets up quickly from the chair.

"You're bleeding." He looks me over, too. "What the hell happened?"

Dahlia's eyes scan my clothes and my oddly pinned hair and wig cap.

"Why—ummm, why are you dressed like that?"

I look down at myself. I don't know what to tell them, so I say nothing. I feel like a deer in headlights, but my expression remains solid and unemotional, maybe a little confused.

"You saw Matt," Dahlia accuses and her voice begins to rise. "Fucking A, Sarai, you did, *didn't* you?"

I feel her fingers curl around my upper arm.

I pull away from her and go to take my hair down from the wig cap, making my way into the bathroom. As I'm taking the bobby pins out of my hair, I notice a condom floating in the toilet.

Eric steps into the bathroom behind me. He knows I saw it.

"Sarai, I-I...I'm so sorry," I hear him say.

"Don't worry about it," I answer and take the last bobby pin out, setting it on the cream-colored countertop.

I push my way past Eric and walk back into the room. Dahlia is looking right at me, shame and regret consuming her features.

"I'm—"

I put up my hand and look back and forth between them both.

"No, I'm serious," I say, "I'm not mad."

"What do you mean?" Dahlia asks.

Eric looks flustered. He raises a hand to the back of his head and runs his fingers through his hair.

"Look, no offense," I say to Eric, "but I've been faking it with you since we got together."

His eyes widen, though he's trying not to let the shock and sting of my admission show too obviously. A huge part of me feels good about the truth, not for vengeance sake, but because I needed to get it off my chest. But I admit, after finding out that the two of them have been fucking each other behind my back, a small part of me is happy to offend him just the same. I guess vengeance always finds a way, even if only in the smallest of gestures.

"Faking it?"

"I don't have time for this." I go toward the door. "You two can have each other. No objections here. I'm not mad. I just really don't care. I have to go."

"Wait…Sarai."

I turn to look at Dahlia. She's so shocked and can hardly pull her thoughts together. After a few seconds of silence I get impatient and give her that yeah-out-with-it look.

"You're really OK with…this?"

Wow, I really *am* unfit for their lifestyle. The *normal* lifestyle. I don't even understand it, all this dating and best friend stuff and the cheating and competition and the head-games. That look on their faces, so blank yet so full of disbelief and question, all over a situation that, to me, really isn't all that important. I have more serious things to worry about than this.

I sigh heavily, annoyed with their confused half-questions.

"Yes, I'm fine with it," I say and then I turn to Eric. "I need our room key."

I hold out my hand.

Reluctantly, he reaches into his back pocket and pulls it out. I take it from his hand and walk right out the door and head to the room next door. Eric follows behind me and tries to talk to me while I'm shoving my belongings into my suitcase.

"Sarai, I never meant—"

I turn around quickly and look him dead in the eyes. "All right, I'm going to say this once, and after that, either change the subject or go back over there with Dahlia. I couldn't care less what the two of you do, but please don't pull that cliché television line about how you never meant for it to happen, because…it's just stupid." I laugh lightly. Because really it is stupid to me. "Next thing you'll be saying is that it wasn't me, it was you. Geez, do you have any idea how that sounds? Is it really so unbelievable that I say I don't care and I actually mean it? No head-games. I'm dead serious." I shake my head and put my hands out in front of me and say, "I. Don't. Care."

I turn back to my suitcase and zip it up, then reach deep inside the side zipper for the key to my secret room, glad I had one extra.

"I have to go," I say making my way back through the room and past him again.

"Where are you going?"

"I can't say, but please listen to me, Eric. If anyone comes here looking for me, act like you don't know who I am. Tell Dahlia the same. Pretend you've never seen me before. In fact, I want you both to go out for the night. Go anywhere, just…don't hang around here."

"Are you going to tell me what happened, why you have blood all over you? Sarai, you're scaring the shit out of me."

"I'll be fine," I say and soften my features. "Just promise me that you and Dahlia will do exactly as I said."

"Are you ever going to tell me?"

"I can't."

The silence thickens between us.

Finally, I open the door and step out into the hallway.

"I guess I should be the one apologizing," I say.

"For what?"

Eric stands in the doorway, his arms hanging loosely at his sides.

"For being with someone else in my head the whole time I was with you." I glance down at the floor momentarily.

We look at each other for a short moment and nothing else is said between us. We know we're both at fault. And I think we're both relieved that everything is out in the open.

There's nothing more to say.

I walk away down the long stretch of hallway in the opposite direction of my private room and double around the back so he doesn't know where I'm going. When I close myself off inside the room, the only thing I can manage to do is fall over onto the bed. The exhaustion and pain and shock of everything that has happened tonight catches up to me as soon as that door closes, rushing over and through me like a wave. I fall hard against the mattress on my back. My calves hurt so bad I doubt I'll be able to walk in the morning without limping.

I stare up at the dark ceiling until it blinks out and I drift quickly off to sleep.

CHAPTER SIX

Sarai

A hard *thud!* jolts me awake sometime later in the night. I rise up from the bed like a catapult.

I see two men in my room: one I've never seen before lying dead on the floor, and Victor Faust standing over his body.

"Get up."

"*Victor?*"

I can't believe he's here. I must still be dreaming.

"Get up, Sarai, NOW!" Victor grabs me by the elbow and jerks me out of the bed and to my feet.

He doesn't stop long enough for me to even grab my things and he's opening the door and pulling me out into the hall alongside him, my hand wrenched within his.

We run down the hall and another man rounds the corner with a gun in-hand. Victor raises his suppressed 9MM and drops him in the center of the hall before the man can get a shot off. He pulls me past the body, his strong fingers digging into my hand as we rush toward the stairwell. He swings the door open, pushes me in front of him and we hurry down the concrete stairs. One floor. Three. Five. My legs are *killing* me. I don't think I can walk much more. Finally on the fifth floor, Victor pulls me out into another hall and toward a back elevator.

When the elevator doors close and we are the only two inside, I finally get a chance to speak.

"How did you know I was here?" I can barely catch my breath, winded from the constant rushing and the adrenaline, but I think mostly because Victor is standing beside me and he's holding my hand.

My eyes start to burn with tears.

I force them back.

"What were you *thinking*, Sarai?"

"I—"

Victor grabs my face in both of his hands and shoves my body against the elevator wall, closing his lips fiercely over mine. His tongue tangles with my own, his mouth stealing my breath in a passionate kiss that is what ultimately makes my knees buckle. All of the strength I had been using to keep my body upright before vanishes when his lips touch me. He kisses me hungrily, *angrily*, and I wilt into his arms.

Then he pulls away, his strong hands wrapped around my biceps as he keeps me pushed against the elevator wall. We stare at each other for what feels like an eternity, our eyes locked in some kind of deep contemplation, our lips inches apart. All I want to do is taste them again.

But he doesn't let me.

"Answer me," he demands, the corners of his dangerous eyes narrowing with censure.

I've already forgotten the question.

He shakes me. "Why did you come here? Do you have any idea what you've done?"

I shake my head in a short, rapid motion, part of me more concerned with that precarious look in his eyes than what he's saying.

The elevator door opens on the basement floor and I don't have time to answer as Victor is once again grasping my hand and pulling me to follow. We weave our way through a large storage room with boxes piled high against the walls and then down a long, dark hallway that leads into an underground parking garage. Victor finally releases my hand and I follow him to a car parked between two black vans with the hotel's logo on the sides. Two beeps echo through the space and the headlights on the car flash as we approach, illuminating the concrete wall in front of it. Wasting no time, I jump inside the passenger's seat and shut the door.

Seconds later, Victor is driving casually through the parking garage and out onto the street.

"I wanted him dead," I finally answer.

Victor doesn't look over.

"Well, you did an excellent job," he says with sarcasm.

He turns right at the light and the car picks up speed as we get on the freeway.

Stung by his words, I know he's right and so I don't argue with him. I screwed up. I screwed up bad.

But I don't realize just how much until Victor says, "You could've gotten your friends killed. You could've gotten *yourself* killed."

I feel my eyes widen beyond their limits and I turn around further to see him. "Oh no...Victor, what...are they OK?"

I feel like I'm going to be sick again.

Victor glances over at me briefly.

"They're fine," he says. "The first room Hamburg's men went into was empty," he adds and looks back out at the road. "I arrived as they were leaving it. I followed one of them to the room you were hiding in, let him unlock it and then I made my move."

The room keys. Both of my extra room keys were in the purse I lost at Hamburg's. And the room numbers were written on the little paper sleeves the keys had been tucked into when the front desk clerk presented them to me. I was so worried about keeping my gun and knife hidden that I didn't think to hide the keys.

"Shit!" I look out at the road, too. "I-I lost my purse at the restaurant. My room keys were in it. I left them bread crumbs!"

Thankfully I didn't have an extra key to Dahlia's room, or else she and Eric might be dead right now.

What in the hell was I thinking?!

"No, you literally left them the keys to your rooms with the hotel name emblazoned on them. Sarai, I should've killed you and saved you and *myself* all of this trouble, a long time ago."

I swing my head around to face him, anger and hurt weighing heavily in my chest.

"You don't mean that," I say.

He pauses and glances at me. He sighs. "No. I don't mean that."

"Don't ever say that to me again. Never say anything like that to me, or I'll kill *you* and save *myself* anymore trouble."

I look away.

"You don't mean that," he says.

I glance back over into those dangerous greenish-blue eyes that I've missed so much.

"No. But it would probably be the wise thing to do."

"Well, you're not exactly scoring wisdom points tonight, so I can feel safe for another twenty-four hours at least."

I hide the smile in my face.

"I missed you," I say distantly, looking out at the road.

Victor doesn't respond, but it would be odd if he did, I admit. Despite his lack of emotions though, I know he missed me, too. That kiss in the elevator said things that words never could.

Victor takes an exit and pulls the car underneath an overpass bridge. He puts the car in Park and the area fades to black when the turns the headlights off.

"What are we doing here?" I ask.

"You need to call your friends."

"Why?"

He reaches into the console between us and retrieves a cell phone.

"Tell them to go back to Arizona," he instructs. "Do or say whatever you have to to get them to leave Los Angeles. The sooner, the better."

He places the phone in my hand. At first, I just stare at it, but he urges me with that look of his, the one that screams hurry-up-already but only someone like me, someone 'close' to him would ever notice it.

Fumbling the phone in my hands, I hold it steady and punch in Eric's number. But then I change my mind, hang up on the first ring and call Dahlia instead.

She answers after the fifth ring.

I take a deep breath and do what I do best. Lie.

"The truth is, you both hurt me. I doubt I'll ever be able to forgive either one of you for what you did."

"Sarai...God, I am *so* sorry. We really didn't mean for it to go that far. I swear to you. I don't know what happened—"

"Listen, Dahlia, please just listen."

She becomes quiet.

I turn on the waterworks. I never knew I could cry on cue and it could be completely fake.

"I want to believe you. I want to be able to trust you again, but you were supposed to be my best friend and you betrayed me. I need time alone and I want you and Eric to go back to Arizona. Tonight. I don't think I can stand seeing either of you again—wait, where are you right now?"

It just dawned on me that if she and Eric were at the hotel then surely she'd know by now that two men were shot to death on the floor where their room is.

"We're at some rooftop party," she says. "A-Are you OK with that? I thought it was messed up for us to go out, but Eric said you insisted—"

"No, it's fine," I cut in. "I *did* insist. Where is he now?"

"I left him on the roof so I could talk. It's really loud up there. What is this number you're calling me from?"

"It's a friend's phone. I lost mine. Did Eric tell you that if anyone comes looking for me—"

"Yeah, he did," she interrupts. "What's that all about anyway? Jesus, Sarai, forget about this issue with me and Eric for a moment and *please* tell me what's going on. The blood. The weird clothes you were wearing and that thing on your head. Was that a *wig cap*? You're in some kind of trouble, I know. I know you hate me and have every right to, but please just tell me what happened."

"I can't fucking tell you!" I scream at her, letting the tears strain my voice. "Dammit, Dahlia, just do what I asked you to do. Give me that much! You fucked my boyfriend! Please, just go back to Arizona, let me get myself together and then I'll be on my way home. Maybe then we can talk. But right now, just do what I ask. OK?"

She doesn't respond for a moment and a long bout of silence passes between us.

"OK," she agrees. "I'll tell Eric that we need to leave."

"Thank you."

I'm only a little relieved. I won't feel good about this until I know they make it back home alive.

I hang up without another word.

"Well, that was convincing," Victor says, slightly impressed.

"I guess so."

"I know your friend believed it," he adds. "But I didn't believe a word of it."

I turn to look at him. He knows me as well as I know him, it seems.

"That's because not a word of it was true."

He leaves it at that and we pull out from underneath the bridge.

~~~

We arrive at a house tucked at the end of a secluded road on the outskirts of the city, perched on a hilltop with semi-perfect views of the cityscape below. An irregular-shaped pool sits to the west side of the house and snakes around behind it, the light blue water lit by underwater lights making it appear luminescent. It's quiet here. All I can hear is the wind brushing through the thick of trees that surround the east side and back of the house, which prevent a full three-hundred and sixty-degree view of the brilliantly-lit landscape of Los Angeles. As we approach the front door, a portly woman in a blue housekeeper's uniform greets us. She has dark, curly hair and olive skin. Her cheeks are plump, encasing her beady dark brown eyes which look at Victor and I with scrutiny.

"Please come in," she says with a familiar Spanish accent.

She closes the front door behind us. The house smells faintly of Windex and an unnatural mixture of sweet scents that can only be attributed to some kind of store-bought air freshener. It seems that all of the windows have been left open, allowing the summer night breeze to filter through the house. It's nothing like the wealthy mansions I've been in, but it's still immaculate and cozy and I feel like I could've at least cleaned up before coming here. My skin and my clothes are still stained with blood...

Victor is dressed in black slacks and a tight long-sleeved button-up shirt that clings to every muscle in his arms and chest, the sleeves unbuttoned and pushed up near his elbows. The shirt hangs freely over his slacks and the top two buttons have been left open. A pair of rich, casual black shoes dress his feet. A shiny silver watch adorns his right wrist and I can't help but notice the single hard, ropy vein that moves along the top of his hand and down the length of his wrist bone. When he follows the housekeeper through the large entryway and briefly turns his back to me, I see the grip of his gun poking from the top of his slacks, the end of his white shirt tucked behind it.

He looks back at me, stops and puts out his arm, guiding me to walk in front of him. My skin shivers lightly when his hand touches my lower back.

Before I have time to feel too out of place next to Victor, Fredrik, Victor's Swedish friend and accomplice whom I met at Hamburg's restaurant long ago, enters the room through the large glass doors overlooking the backyard.

CHAPTER SEVEN

Sarai

"You're early," Fredrik says with a deadly, yet unimaginably sexy smile. He's dressed much in the same way Victor is except that in place of Victor's button-up shirt, Fredrik sports a plain tight white tee that clings to his lean, masculine form. His feet are bare.

The first time I saw Fredrik I found him inconceivably gorgeous with soft, almost-black hair and haunting dark eyes; his facial structure appears sculpted by some renowned artist. But I've always felt there's something dark and frightening that lives inside of him. Something I never personally want to get more acquainted with. I'll settle with the way things were when we met: friendly and charming and mysterious, seeing only the beautiful mask that he wears to conceal the animal that dwells beneath it.

Victor glances at his expensive watch. "Early by only ten minutes," he clarifies.

Fredrik smiles as he approaches, his white teeth semi-bright amid the backdrop of his tanned skin. "Yes, but you know how I am."

Victor nods, but doesn't elaborate. I'm left to wonder what that meant.

"It's good to see you," Fredrik says, looking down at me from his tall height and encompassing presence. He reaches for my hand and kisses the top of it, just above my knuckles. "I hear you killed a man tonight." He raises back up out of his half-bow and releases my hand. A haunting, proud smile lingers on his face, the corners of his eyes warm with something reminiscent or…pleasurable, as if the thought of my killing someone somehow delights him.

I look at Victor to my right. He nods, answering the question that is all over my expression: *Did the guard I stabbed in the neck at the restaurant, die?*

I look at Fredrik and answer matter-of-factly, "I guess I did."

A tiny grin tugs the corners of Fredrik's lips and he glances at Victor briefly with only the movement of his eyes.

"And you're OK with that?" Fredrik asks me.

"Yeah, actually I am," I answer right away. "The bastard deserved it."

Fredrik and Victor seem to be sharing some kind of secret conversation. I hate that.

Finally, Fredrik says to Victor out loud, "You've got your hands full, Faust," and he turns his back to us and heads back toward the glass doors. We follow him outside, passing underneath the covered portion of the patio and descend a set of rock steps that lead onto an enormous rock patio that spreads out in all directions. The patio is decorated by wrought-iron tables and chairs and an outside canopy bed.

I sit down next to Victor on a plush couch.

"How'd you know, anyway?" I ask Fredrik, but then I turn to Victor and say, "And you never did tell me how you knew that I was here." Really, I don't care much, I just want to look into his eyes again. I want to be alone with him, but for now I'll settle with the three-inch space between our bodies sitting next to each other.

"Melinda Rochester told me," Fredrik says with a knowing grin. I start to ask, *Who the hell is Melinda Rochester*, when he says, "Well, she told everyone, actually. Channel 7 news. A man stabbed to death behind a Los Angeles restaurant."

I start to squirm inside my skin. I hope the cameras didn't get a good shot of me.

I turn to Victor, worry heavy on my face. "I wore a white wig," I say, trying to find something, anything that I did right. "I kept my face down...mostly." I give up. I know that what I did is going to continue to dig that grave of mine. I sigh and stare at the bloodstained hands in my lap.

"And finding you was easy," Victor says next to me. "Mrs. Gregory called me after you left Arizona. She was worried about you going to L.A. and thought I should know."

My head swings around to face him. "*What*? Dina knew where you *were*?" I feel the skin around my eyebrows hardening in my forehead.

"No," he says gently, "she never knew where I was, but she knew how to get a hold of me."

His words sting. I swallow down the feeling of betrayal, on both of their parts.

"I told her to contact me only if it was an emergency. If something happened to you."

"You left Dina with a way to contact you," I snap, "but left me with nothing. I can't believe you did that."

"I wanted you to go on with your life. But in case Javier's brothers found you, or if you decided to pull a stunt like you pulled tonight, I wanted to know about it."

I can't look at him. I scoot to put a few more inches of space between us and although I'm bitter and pissed off at him for what he did, I find myself wanting to move back. But I stand my ground, refusing to let him know that the power he holds over me makes my anger towards him feel more like a tantrum.

"I can't believe Dina kept this from me," I say aloud, though more to myself.

"She kept it from you because I told her how imperative it was."

"Well, whatever the case," Fredrik speaks up as he takes the matching chair next to the couch, "it looks like you've gotten yourself into a situation you won't be able to crawl out of easily, if ever."

"Why are we here?" I ask bitterly.

Fredrik laughs lightly under his breath. "Where else are you going to go?"

"I had to get you away from the hotel," Victor says.

"Wait a minute," I say, backtracking. "I didn't kill that man *behind* the restaurant. It happened inside Hamburg's private room upstairs." I remember the man I saw outside behind the restaurant, the one who let me go, and my heart sinks.

"Hamburg wouldn't have let the police believe it happened inside because they would've retrieved the camera footage and saw what *really* happened."

I'm not following him. At all.

"Wouldn't they *want* the police to know what really happened?"

Fredrik leans back against the chair casually and props one bare foot on a knee at the ankle, resting both arms across the length of the chair arms.

Victor shakes his head. "Do I really need to explain this to you, Sarai?"

His faintly aggravated attitude catches me off guard. I look over at him and it only takes a few seconds to understand everything all on my own, without him having to point it out.

"Oh, I get it," I say, looking back and forth between them, "Hamburg doesn't want the police involved because he'll risk exposing himself. What, so he just had the body moved outside? Staged the area to make it look like a random robbery? Not too much different from what he did that night we were at his mansion, I suppose." I don't say any more with Fredrik here. I don't know how close Victor is to him, or if Fredrik even knows what happened the night Victor killed Hamburg's wife.

Victor's eyes smile lightly at me, his way of letting me know how pleased he is that I figured everything out. Still feigning resentment, I don't give him the acknowledgment he's probably expecting.

The housekeeper comes outside carrying a fancy wooden ice bucket with three bottles of beer jutting from the top. Fredrik takes one and then she turns to us. Victor reaches for one, but I decline, barely making eye contact with her, too engrossed in the events of the night still running through my mind.

The housekeeper leaves us shortly afterwards without muttering a word.

"What did you mean by Javier's brothers?"

Victor twists the cap off his beer and sets it on the table.

"Two of them, Luis and Diego, took over Javier's operations just days after you killed him." Briefly, Javier's face flashes through my mind, the shocked, yet proud look on his face, the wideness of his eyes, how his body fell against the floor seconds after I put a bullet in his chest.

I shake it off.

I remember Luis and Diego. Diego was the one who tried to rape me when I lived at the compound in Mexico, the one who Javier castrated as punishment.

"Are they looking for me?"

Victor takes a sip from his beer and then sets the bottle down gently on the table. "Not that I know of," he says. "I've been monitoring the compound for months. Javier's brothers are amateurs. They've no idea what they're doing with power like that. I doubt they even realize that you're a threat."

Fredrik takes a sip of his beer and lets the bottle rest between his legs. "Don't look so relieved," he chimes in. "You would've been better off with amateurs looking for you than Hamburg and that right-hand man of his."

A nervous knot hardens in the pit of my stomach. I glance at Victor momentarily for answers.

"Willem Stephens," Victor says. "He does all of Hamburg's dirty work. Hamburg by himself is as cowardly and only as dangerous as the friendly neighborhood pedophile. He can barely shoot an unmoving target and would crack in two minutes to sell someone out to save himself." He cocks a brow. "Stephens, on the other hand, has an extensive military background, is a former mercenary and was employed by a black market Order back in '86."

"A what?"

"An Order like ours," Victor explains, "only they take on private contracts. They do things that other operatives won't do, sell their services to just about anyone."

"Oh...so basically he kills innocent people for money." I recall what Victor told me months ago about the nature of private contracts, about how hits are carried out on people for petty things like cheating spouses and vengeance. Victor's Order only deals in crime and serious threats to a large number of people or ideas that could have a negative impact on society or life as a whole.

I swallow hard. "Well, he definitely saw me." I reach up with both hands and push my hair away from my face, running my palms over the top of my head. "He was the one who walked me upstairs to Hamburg's room." I look at Victor. "I'm so sorry, Victor. I…I didn't know any of this."

Fredrik laughs lightly. "Something tells me that even if you did know that you still would've gone there."

I look away from Victor's eyes and stare down at my lap again, my blood-stained fingers moving nervously against one another. Fredrik's right. I hate to admit it, but he's right. I still would've gone to the restaurant. I still would've tried to kill Hamburg. But if I had known all of this, I think I would've had a better plan.

Suddenly, it feels like something just reached inside me and stole my breath. "Victor…my phone…," I shoot up from the couch, my long, auburn hair falling about my shoulders, prickling my bare arms where the blood has dried within it, forming a coarse crust-like texture. "Dina's number is in my phone. Fuck. Fuck! Victor, Stephens will go after her! I have to go back to Arizona!"

I start to head toward the back door, but Victor is behind me before I make it across the smooth, intricate rock walkway.

"Just wait," he encourages.

I look down to see his fingers clasped around my wrist. His bewitching green-blue eyes stare back at me with intent and devotion. Devotion. I've never seen that in Victor's eyes before.

Fredrik speaks up from behind, breaking me free from the trance Victor has put on me. "I'll take care of that," he says. I look away from Victor to see Fredrik, who is more important right now considering it's Dina's life on the line.

"How?" I ask.

Victor leads me back over to the couch.

Fredrik takes the cell phone from the table in front of him, searches for a number and touches the screen to call it. He puts the phone to his ear.

Victor urges me to sit back down next to him. I'm too engrossed with Fredrik right now to notice right away that Victor has made sure to sit so close that his thigh is pressed against mine. I want to bask in our moment of closeness, but I can't. I'm worried about Dina.

Fredrik leans against the chair again, shaking his bare foot gently against his knee. The tone in his face shifts alert when someone on the other end answers.

"How fast can you get to Lake Havasu City?" Fredrik asks into the phone. He listens for a second and then nods. "I'm going to text you an address when we end this call. Get there as soon as possible. A woman lives there. Dina Gregory." He glances up at me as if to make sure he got the name right and when I don't correct him, he goes back to the person on the phone. "Get her out of the house and take her to Amelia in Phoenix. Yes. Yes. No, she is not to be questioned. Just make sure that no one harms her. Yes. Call me back on this number as soon as you have her." He nods a couple more times. My heart is about to beat right out of my chest. I hope whoever he's talking to can get to her in time.

Fredrik finally hangs up and then appears to be opening a text screen. He looks up at me, but Victor is the one who gives him Mrs. Gregory's address. Fredrik types it in and then places the phone back on the table.

"My contact is only thirty minutes away," Fredrik says looking at me first, but then he turns to Victor. "What do you want me to do?" He raises his back from the chair and props his elbows on his knees, letting his hands drape between them, a rather casual position, yet he still manages to appear neat and important and dangerous.

"I still need you to check on what we discussed yesterday," Victor says and it's even clearer to me now that Fredrik takes orders from Victor, even though Fredrik doesn't seem the type to take orders from *anyone*. But clearly, they have a strong relationship. "And if you don't mind, I need to borrow your house for the evening."

Fredrik's dark eyes shift to see me and a hint of a grin appears on his face. He stands up and takes his cell phone from the table, hiding it within his rather large fist.

"Say no more," he agrees. "I'll be out of here in twenty minutes. I have someone I'm meeting tonight anyway, so it works out."

Victor's demeanor changes just slightly, but I notice it right away. He's looking across the small patio table at Fredrik with a faint, wary look. "You're not going to do what I think you are?" Victor asks.

I listen closely and I don't try to hide the fact. I *want* them to know that I'm prying because I find it frustrating that neither of them are offering me any explanations for their clandestine comments.

One side of Fredrik's mouth lifts into a grin. He shakes his head subtly. "No, not tonight, I'm afraid. But it's been a while. I'll need you to help me with that soon." His eyes pass over me briefly and it sends a chill through my back. I just can't figure out whether it's a good chill or a frightening one.

"You'll have your opportunity soon," Victor says.

Fredrik walks around the table. "Sorry to cut our visit short."

"It's all right," I say. "Thank you for helping with Dina. Will you let us know when you get that call?"

Fredrik nods. "Absolutely. I will do that."

"Thank you," I repeat.

Victor walks with Fredrik to the glass doors and they step through to the other side. I stay seated, but I watch them from across the stone patio and I listen in as much as I can, but they make sure to keep their voices low. This, too, frustrates me. And I intend to let Victor know it.

CHAPTER EIGHT

Victor

Fredrik reaches out for the sliding glass door and pulls it shut the rest of the way.

"She has no idea about Niklas?" he asks, as I knew he would.

"No, but I'm going to have to tell her. She'll need to be aware of her surroundings at all times. Now more than ever."

"She can't stay here long," Fredrik says, glancing through the glass to see her sitting on the couch outside, watching us. "Neither can you."

"I know," I say. "When Niklas finds out about her involvement in the murder at Hamburg's restaurant, my brother will know right away that I'm involved now, too. My brother is no fool. If Sarai is alive, Niklas will know that I'm helping her."

"And since Niklas suspects that I'm working with you now," Fredrik adds, "she's in as much danger anywhere around me as she is with you."

"Yes, she is."

Fredrik shakes his head at me, a faint smile hidden behind his eyes. "I don't understand attachment," he says. "I respect you as always, Victor, but I'll never understand a man's need to love a woman."

"I am not in love with her," I clarify. "She is just important to me."

"Maybe not," he says and starts to head toward the kitchen, "but it appears that love and attachment both carry the same consequences, my friend." I follow him into the brightly-lit kitchen and he opens a cabinet. "But I'm here for you. Whatever you need me to do to help, I will do it." He points at me briefly from around the cabinet door now with a loaf of bread in his hand.

Fredrik's housekeeper comes into the kitchen, plump and older than both of us, precisely the kind of woman that Fredrik can never be tempted by, which is why he hired her. She asks him in Spanish if she can go home to her family early tonight. Fredrik responds in Spanish, granting her request. She nods respectfully and walks past me into the living room. I watch her from the corner of my eye as she takes a bulky brown leather purse up from the floor beside the leather recliner and shoulders it. Then she makes her way to the front door, shutting it softly behind her.

Sarai is standing in the shadows of the living room when my gaze falls away from the front door. I didn't even hear the sliding glass door open when she entered, and apparently neither did Fredrik.

She steps into the kitchen and into the light, her arms crossed loosely under her breasts, her delicate fingers arched over her girlish, yet toned biceps. She is so beautiful to me, even in the ravaged condition she's in.

"How long did you plan on leaving me outside?" she asks both of us with a trace of irritation in her voice.

"No one ever said you had to stay out there, doll," Fredrik replies.

He likes her, it's obvious to me and he probably knows as much. But he also knows that I'll kill him, too.

Though, I trust him more than I worry if he'll ever revert to his dark side and harm her of all people. Fredrik Gustavsson is a beast of the most carnal kind with a love for women and a love for blood, but he has boundaries and standards and he takes loyalty and respect and friendship very seriously. His loyalty to me is, after all, the reason he betrays the Order every day by helping me.

Sarai walks over to me and looks up into my eyes, cocking her head softly to one side. The smell of her flesh and the gentle warmth emanating from her skin nearly sends me over the edge. I've done fairly well to hold myself back since I kissed her in the elevator. I intend to maintain that control.

When she doesn't say anything, but continues to look into my eyes as if she's waiting on something, I become confused. She cocks her head to the other side and her eyes soften, though with what exactly, I'm not quite certain. It feels expectant and a little mischievous.

I hear Fredrik chuckle under his breath and the refrigerator door closing, but I never look away from Sarai.

"Things are so much easier the way I do it," I hear him say with a smile in his voice.

"Contact me as soon as you get the information on Niklas," I say still looking into Sarai's eyes and disregarding his comment altogether. "And when you hear from your contact that Dina Gregory is safe in Phoenix."

"I will do that," Fredrik says and then walks toward the hall entrance that leads toward his room. But he stops and looks back at us. "If you don't mind—"

I finally look away from Sarai and give Fredrik my full attention. "Don't worry," I interrupt, "I know where the guest quarters are."

He shoves the corner of a sandwich that I barely noticed him prepare into his mouth and bites down, tearing the bread away from his lips. I catch him wink at Sarai just before he disappears down the hall. It was perfectly harmless, directed at what he assumes might happen between us once he's gone, rather than a flirting attempt.

"What information on Niklas?" Sarai asks, her soft features now shadowed by concern.

I reach out and drag my fingers behind a small portion of her hair. "I have a lot to tell you," I announce and I let my hand fall away before I lose control of myself and touch her more than I intended. "I know you must be exhausted. Why don't you shower and get settled in first. Then we'll talk."

A soft grin sneaks up on her lips, but then fails under her blushing cheeks.

"Are you saying I'm disgusting?" she asks coyly. "Is that your way of telling me I need to wash my disgusting ass?"

"Actually, yes," I admit.

For a flinching moment, she appears offended, but then she just shakes her head and laughs it off. I admire that about her. I admire a lot about her.

"All right." Her playful expression shifts into something more serious again. "But you have to tell me everything, Victor. And I know you may have a lot to tell me, but I want you to know that there's a lot I need to say to you as well."

I expected as much. And before she pushes herself up on her toes, leaning her body against mine and kisses me on the lips, I know that by the time she gets out of that shower I'm going to have to figure out what we're going to do. I'm going to have to make some important decisions that will affect both of us.

Because I am sure of only one thing: Sarai can never go home.

Sarai

When I return, Victor is sitting in the living room, perched on the edge of the couch, leaning over the glass coffee table now littered with pieces of paper and photographs. He continues to sift through them without raising his head to look at me as I walk farther into the room. But he's not fooling me, I know he's as aware of my presence as much as I want him to be.

I raided Fredrik's closet for a white T-shirt, which I've slipped down over my bare breasts. Unfortunately, I'm still in the same panties I put on this morning, but Fredrik's boxer-briefs aren't exactly the kind of undergarments I would want to wear to seduce Victor. Just a T-shirt and panties. Of course, I made it a point to wear as little as possible, because I want Victor and I'm not shy in the least bit about letting him know it. Though I'm still having a hard time believing I'm even in the same room as him again after months of thinking he was gone forever.

I think the kiss in the elevator is where my mind is suspended, as though time stopped in that moment and every part of my being is still yearning for the moment to continue, but the rest of the world has still been going on all around me.

I sit down next to him, pulling one bare foot onto the couch and tucking it underneath my thigh.

"What's all this stuff?" I gaze down at the paper and photographs on the table.

He fingers a few pieces of paper, stacking them into a precise spot. "It's a job," he says and then places a photograph of a man wearing a wife-beater tank on the top of the small pile. "I work for myself now."

That takes me aback. "What do you mean?" I think I know exactly what he means, but I'm having a hard time believing it.

He picks up the stack and hits the edges against the table to make all of the pieces fall neatly into place. Then he slides the stack down into a manila envelope.

"I left the Order, Sarai." He glances over at me.

He presses the little flaps of the silver clasp down to seal the envelope.

My thoughts are stuck in the back of my head, my words, hanging precariously on the tip of my tongue. I struggle desperately to believe what he just told me.

"Victor...but...no—."

"Yes," he says and turns his head to face me, looking directly into my eyes. "It is true. I've rebelled against the Order, against Vonnegut, and now I'm a wanted man." He goes back to the other papers on the table. "But I still have to work and so now I work alone."

I shake my head over and over, not wanting to swallow the truth. The thought of him being hunted by the people who made him what he is, by *anyone*, sends a hot flash of panic through my veins.

I let out a long breath. "But...but what about Fredrik? What about Niklas? Victor, I...what's going on?"

He sighs heavily and lets the sheet of paper fall lightly back against the table and then he leans his back into the couch.

"Fredrik still works for the Order. On the inside. He keeps tabs on Niklas and...," his eyes catch mine briefly, "...he's been helping me keep you safe."

Before I have the chance to ask anymore broken questions, Victor stands up from the couch and continues as I sit watching him with my mouth partially agape and both legs drawn up on the cushion.

"As you know, when anyone is suspected of betraying the Order, they are immediately eliminated. But I believe that Niklas has left Fredrik alive and not reported his concerns to Vonnegut for the simple fact that Niklas is using Fredrik to find me. Just as he has left you alive all this time, hoping that one day *you'll* lead him right to me."

It isn't what Victor said that shocks me the most, it's more about what he didn't say that leaves me reeling. I let both of my legs drop from the couch and press my feet into hardwood floor, my hands pushing against the cushions on either side of me.

"Victor, what are you telling me? Are you saying that…Niklas is still with Vonnegut?"

I hope that's not what he's trying to tell me. I hope with everything in me that my decision to let Niklas live that day back in the hotel when he shot me wasn't the biggest mistake of my life.

His eyes stray toward the sliding glass door and I sense a sort of infinite grief consuming him, but he doesn't let it show on his face.

"I told my brother—you were there—that if he decided he wanted to stay with the Order if I chose to leave it, that I wouldn't hold it against him. I gave him my word, Sarai." He walks toward the glass door, folds his hands down in front of him and gazes out at the luminescent blue pool glowing under the night sky. "It is Niklas' time to shine now and I won't take that from him."

"*Bull*shit!" I shoot up from the couch, my fists clenched down at my sides. "He's after you, isn't he?" I grit my teeth and step around the coffee table. "That's fucking it, isn't it, Victor? To prove his worth to Vonnegut, he's been commissioned to kill you. Your piece of shit brother *betrayed* you. He thinks he's taking your place in the Order. I can't fucking believe—"

"It is what it is, Sarai," Victor stops me, turning around to face me fully. "But right now, Niklas is the least of my worries."

Crossing my arms, I start to pace, gazing down at the dark and light swirling patterns in the wood beneath my bare feet. My toenails are still painted blood red from two weeks ago.

"Why did you leave the Order?"

"I had to. I had no other choice."

"I don't believe you."

Victor sighs.

"Vonnegut found out about us," he says and has my undivided attention. "It was Samantha…the night she died. Before I left the Order, I met with Vonnegut in Berlin, the first face-to-face meeting I'd had with him in months. I was in an interrogation room. Four walls. One door. A table. Two chairs. Just me and Vonnegut sitting across from each other with a light blazing in the ceiling above us." He looks back out the glass door behind him and then goes on:

"At first I thought for sure he brought me there to kill me. I was prepared—"

"To die?" If he says yes, I'll slap him for it.

"No," he answers and I feel like I can breathe a little more. "I went *prepared*. I kidnapped Vonnegut's wife before I met with him. Fredrik held her in a room, prepared to do…his thing, if it came down to that."

Immediately I want to ask what Fredrik's 'thing' is, but I skip that for now and say instead, "If Vonnegut intended to kill you, you had his wife as leverage."

With his back to me, he nods.

"Samantha was being watched by the Order. Probably for a long time."

"They suspected her of betrayal? Why didn't they just kill her then, like they did Niklas' mother, or like they wanted to do to Niklas?"

Victor turns around to face me again. "They didn't suspect her of betrayal, Sarai, she was…," he takes a deep breath and presses his lips together.

"She was *what*?" I walk over to stand closer to him. I don't like where this seems to be heading.

"She was more loyal to the Order than I ever could have imagined," he says and it hurts my heart. "As I sat in that room with Vonnegut and the more he spoke, the more I began to understand that Samantha was as much a traitor to me as Niklas has become. Vonnegut told me things that he couldn't have possibly known. He knew I helped you. Sometime before she died that night, she was able to relay information to Vonnegut about us being there."

"I don't believe that." I slash a hand in the air in front of me. "Samantha died trying to protect me. We've already been through this. I don't believe you, Victor. She was a good woman."

"She was a good *manipulator*, Sarai, nothing more."

I shake my head, still not believing it. "Niklas is the one who told Vonnegut about you helping me. He had to have been. Niklas even knew that you had taken me to Samantha's house."

"Yes, but Niklas didn't know that I made Samantha taste-test our food before we ate that night. I knew the second that Vonnegut brought up how distrusting I still was of her after all the years I had known her, that she had betrayed me."

"But that doesn't make any sense." I start to pace the floor again, arms crossed, one arm bent upright, my fingers touching the side of my face. "Why would she protect me from Javier?"

"Because she wasn't loyal to Javier."

I throw my hands in the air above me, washing my hands of this revelation.

"Can't trust anybody," I say, plopping down on the couch again, looking at nothing.

"No, you can't," Victor says and I look up, detecting a hidden meaning behind his words. "Now maybe you can understand why I don't get close to anyone. It's not just the job, Sarai. People generally cannot be trusted, especially in my profession where trust is such a rarity that it's not worth wasting the time and effort searching for it."

"But you seem to trust Fredrik," I point out, looking up at him from the couch. "Why'd you bring me here, of all places? Didn't you learn your lesson with Samantha?"

His expression darkens subtly, stung by my accusation.

"I never said I trusted Fredrik. But right now, Fredrik is my only connection inside the Order and for the past seven months he has done nothing to indicate he is untrustworthy. Quite the opposite, he's done everything to prove that he is."

"But that doesn't make it true," I say.

"No, you're right, but soon enough I'll know one hundred percent if Fredrik can be trusted, or not."

"How so?"

"You'll find out when I do," he says.

"Why bother? You just said that trust is so rare it's not worth the effort."

"You ask a lot of questions."

"Yeah, I guess I do. And you don't answer enough of them."

"No, I guess I don't." He smiles faintly and it melts my heart into a puddle of mush.

I look away from his eyes and swallow down my feelings.

"I'm not safe here," I say looking back up at him.

"You're not safe anywhere," he says. "But as long as you're with me, nothing will happen to you."

"Now who's full of shit?"

He raises an eyebrow.

"You're not my hero, remember?" I remind him. "You're not the other half of my soul who could never let anything bad ever happen to me. Trust my instincts first always, and you, if I choose, last. You said that to me once."

"And it's still as true today as it was then."

"Then how can you say nothing will happen to me if I'm with you?"

His expression becomes vacant as if for the first time in his life someone has rendered him speechless. I gaze across the room into his quiet and emotionless face, only his eyes revealing a trace of numbness. I get the feeling that he spoke before thinking, that he expressed something to me that he truly feels but never wanted me to know: he *wants* to be my 'hero', he will do anything and everything in his power to keep me safe, he *wants* me to trust him fully.

I do.

He walks back over and sits down beside me. The smell of his cologne faint as if he makes it a point to use as little as possible. It makes my head swim with need. I have longed to feel his touch again, to taste his warm lips, to let him ravage me the way he did a few nights before we last saw each other. I've thought of nothing but Victor for the past eight months of my life. While sleeping. Eating. Watching television. Having sex. Masturbating. Breathing. Every single thing I have done since he left me in that hospital with Dina, has been with him in mind.

"Do you think Fredrik will tell Niklas where we are?" I change the subject for fear of breaking into him too much too soon.

"I think if he was going to do that," he says, "he would have told Niklas the little he did know about your whereabouts a long time ago and Niklas would have tried to kill you already."

"There's something…off about Fredrik. Don't you sense it?"

Victor reaches up and touches my wet hair. The gesture causes my heart to speed up.

"You have a good sense of people, Sarai," he says as his hand moves to my chin. "You're right about Fredrik…," the pad of his thumb brushes my bottom lip. A shiver races between my legs. "He is…shall I say…unhinged in a sense."

My breathing picks up and I feel my lashes sweep my face when Victor's lips fall upon mine.

"Unhinged in what way?" I ask breathily when he pulls back. With my eyes closed, I sense him scanning the curvature of my face and my lips, and I feel the breath emitting softly from his nostrils onto my face.

Every miniscule hair stands on end when his other hand pushes up my thigh and finds my naked waist underneath the shirt. His long fingers dance against the flesh of my hipbone and then rests there.

I open my eyes to see him staring back into mine.

"Is something wrong?" he asks and his mouth sweeps mine again.

"No, I...I just didn't expect this."

"Expect what?" I feel his fingers fit behind the elastic of my panties.

My head is swimming, my stomach a fluttering, nervous ball of muscle. "This," I answer, my eyes opening and closing. "You're different," I add softly.

"That's your fault," he says and then his lips devour mine.

He pushes my body back against the couch pillows and falls between my legs.

His cell phone buzzes around on the coffee table and I'm reminded just how human I really am when I curse Fredrik for ruining this moment, even if it's to let me know that Dina is safe.

CHAPTER NINE

Sarai

I'm biting my lip for two reasons: hoping the news is *good* news, and sexual frustration. Victor talks to Fredrik for less than two minutes, hangs up and dials another number. Once he gets Dina on the phone, he holds it out to me.

I take it into my fingers and put it to my ear.

"Dina?"

"Sarai, my *Lord*, where *are* you? What on *Earth* is going on? I was sitting in the den watching TV when this man knocked on my door. I wasn't going to let him in, was suspicious of him right away; was going to get my shotgun. But he said it was about you. Oh, Sarai, I was so scared something had happened!" She finally takes a breath.

"Are you all right?" I ask her gently.

"Yes, yes, I'm fine. As fine as I can be. But he told me we were going down to the station to meet with you. Even showed me a badge. I can't believe I fell for it. The gentleman lied to me." She pauses and lowers her voice as if whispering into the phone so no one else will hear. "He brought me to a *hooker's* house. What is going on? Sarai—"

"Everything'll be fine, Dina, I promise. And don't worry, whoever's house you're at, I doubt she's a hooker."

Victor's eyes catch mine. I look away.

"Where are you? When are you coming home? I know you're in some kind of trouble, but you can always tell me anything."

I wish that were true. More than anything right now. But the bigger truth is that I don't know how to answer her questions. Victor must've caught the look of confusion plaguing my face because he takes the phone from my hand.

"Mrs. Gregory," he says into the phone, "This is Victor Faust. I need you to listen to me very closely." He waits for a second and then goes on. "You need to stay where you are for the next few days. I will bring Sarai to see you soon and we will explain everything, but until then we need you to lay low. No, I'm sorry but you cannot go back—no, it's not safe there." He nods a few times, and I can tell by the vague crinkles forming at the spot between his eyes that he's uncomfortable talking to her, like a man might be if someone else's kid were dropped on his lap. "Yes...no, listen to me." He has lost his patience now and just cuts to the chase, "It is a matter of life or death. If you leave there or make any phone calls to anyone you know, you'll only get yourself killed."

I flinch at those words, not because they're true—I knew that already—but because I can only imagine Dina's reaction to them. I can only imagine what she must be thinking right now, how scared she must be. Scared for me, not for herself and that makes it hurt that much worse.

"Yes, she's fine," Victor assures her once more. "Just a few days. I'll bring her there."

I talk to Dina for a few minutes more, letting her know what I can without telling her too much, to ease her mind. Of course, it isn't helping much at all, considering. We hang up and I stand in the center of the room, feeling very different than I felt before the phone call.

I think it has finally hit me, how badly I screwed up.

Before, when I thought it was mostly me that was in trouble and after I told Eric and Dahlia to get out of L.A., I was worried, but not to this extent. The damage that I've caused runs deeper than my own safety. I've inadvertently put everyone that I know and care for in danger.

The reality of it all, of my actions and their domino effect consequences, the fact that Victor left me, the fact that I tried to live a normal life but failed miserably; I can't bear it anymore. Not any of it. Hell, even the sting of finding Dahlia with Eric is beginning to bother me. Not because of Eric, or because he was my 'boyfriend', but because what they did didn't affect me the way that it should've.

I'm a freak. And right now I can't forgive Victor for putting me through it, for dropping me off into a life that he and I both knew I wasn't fit for and expecting me to conform. I never wanted it to begin with. And that's precisely why it never worked.

The tears begin to well up in my eyes. I let them fall. I don't care.

I sense Victor's presence behind me, but I swing around to face him with anger twisting my features before he has a chance to touch me. And finally, some of the things I've wanted to say to him after all this time come out in a storm of angry words.

"You fucking left me!" I shove the palms of my hands against his form-fitting white dress shirt. "You should've just killed me! Do you have any idea what you've put me through?!" Rage-filled tears shoot from the corners of my eyes.

"I'm sorry...,"

I feel my eyebrows draw inward harshly. "You're sorry?" I let out a quick, short breath. "That's all you can say? You're *sorry*?"

Deep down I know that none of this is Victor's fault, that he only did what he did to protect me. But the bigger part of me, the part that isn't ready to believe one hundred percent that there's no hope for me, wants to blame anyone but myself.

The tears begin to choke me.

"Every single night," I say, pointing sternly at the floor with my index finger, my face contorted with anger and blame, "every hour of every day, I thought about *you*. Only you, Victor. I lived every single day with hope, believing in my heart that you were going to come back for me. Another day would pass and you never showed, but I never lost hope. I thought to myself: Sarai, he's watching you. He's testing you. He wants you to do what he said, to try to be like everyone else, to blend in. He wants you to prove to him that you're strong enough to take on any circumstance, to adapt to any lifestyle, because if you can't do something as simple as live a normal life, there's no way you can live a life with him." I bite down on my bottom lip and try to stifle the tears. I shake my head softly. "That's what I believed. But I was stupid to ever think that you had any intention of coming back for me." A tear-induced shudder rolls through my chest.

Victor, with tormented eyes, which I never thought he could possess, steps closer. I step back, shaking my head over and over, hoping he'll get the hint that I'm not ready for him to be too close. I want to be left alone in my pain.

"Sarai?" he says my name softly.

"Don't," I refuse him and put up my hand. "Please spare me the excuses and the reasons, which I-I know I can't blame you for—I'm selfish, all right? I know this! I already know you did what you had to do. I already know...."

"No, you don't."

I look back up into his eyes.

He steps closer. This time I don't move away, my mind paralyzed by his words regardless of how few or uninformative they were. He cups my elbows within the palms of his hands and unfolds my arms from over my stomach. His fingers brush lightly against the sensitive skin on the underside of my arms, downward until he finds my hands and takes a hold of them.

"I left the Order primarily because of you, Sarai," he says and the rest of me is paralyzed. "When Vonnegut found out that I had been helping you, he knew...," he pauses, appearing to be sifting through his mind for the safest words, "...he knew that I had been compromised."

I throw my hands up in the air. "Speak English! Please just say whatever it is you're trying so hard to tiptoe around! Please!"

"Vonnegut knew that I had...developed feelings for you."

I freeze and my lips snap shut. My heart is beating erratically inside my chest. My tears seemed to have dried up in an instant, only those wetting my cheeks left to linger.

"Being Vonnegut's Number One operative, his 'favorite', the last thing he wanted to do was have me killed. He ordered that I be relieved of duty, taken off the wire for a time until I...came to my senses."

I give him a what-the-hell-is-that-supposed-to-mean look.

"You might call it brainwashing," he says.

He waves it off. "That doesn't matter. What matters is that he was going to give me one chance to prove that my feelings for you were just a fluke and that it would never happen again. Very few ever get second chances in the Order."

"A *fluke*?" I sit down on the edge of the coffee table. I look up at him and say, "Sounds to me like Vonnegut wanted you to prove that you aren't human, that you're still his obedient soldier who's incapable of human emotion. What a deranged bastard."

He nods and crouches down in front of me, interlacing his fingers, his elbows propped on the tops of this thighs.

"Vonnegut ordered me to kill you," he says gently, holding my gaze. "To prove myself. I told him that I would, that I *wanted* to, to prove that I was trustworthy, and he let me go. Of course, I had no intentions of killing you. I left that day and went into hiding. Niklas, knowing only the Order his entire life, decided to stay. I thought maybe he just needed some time to figure things out, to decide what was best for him. I kept out of Niklas' sights as well—if he didn't know where I was, he couldn't deceive Vonnegut or feel that he had to choose between us. But then I heard from Fredrik that Niklas had been contracted to kill me and has been looking for me ever since."

"What a bastard," I say, shaking my head in disbelief and then backtrack. "You said primarily. Other than me, why did you leave the Order?"

"It was a long time coming," he says. "When I had to kill my father to save my brother, I knew then it was time for me to leave." His strong fingers caress my softer ones. "You gave me the final motivation I needed to finally do it."

I reach out and touch his lightly unshaven face with all of my fingertips. He continues to watch me, his eyes probing mine through the small, confined space between us, thick with passion and understanding. I lean in and kiss his lips.

"I'm sorry about your brother," I say softly.

He brushes his lips against mine, his touch spreading through my body and down into my toes like a shot of smooth whiskey.

"I wasn't testing you, Sarai." He kisses me again.

"Then what were you doing?" I kiss him likewise and wilt when I feel his hands move across both of my thighs.

He lifts me into his arms, wrapping my legs around his waist, my ass fitted in the palms of his large hands. My fingers crawl up the sides of his stubbly face and touch his lips before my own lips do.

"I was waiting for when the time was right," he says as his mouth finds my neck.

I wind all ten fingers through his short brown hair, raising my chin as his mouth searches my throat and my jawline. My eyes are shut, the lids heavy with a warm, tingling sensation that I know better than to fight against. He walks with me across the room, though to where I don't know and I don't care. I tighten my bare legs around his waist, the cool, smooth surface of his leather belt pressing against my inner thighs. My fingers are fitted around the buttons of his shirt, breaking them apart with ease.

Victor never answers my question, but I don't care about that, either.

His lips cover mine, the warm wetness of his tongue tangling eagerly with my own. Without breaking the kiss, Victor drops my feet back on the floor to slip my panties off one leg at a time. He raises my arms above me and strips off my shirt, dropping it on the floor. My hands fumble his belt, yanking the prong from the leather hole and sliding the rest of it from the loops in one quick motion. He steps out of his pants and tight, black boxer-briefs. He breathes hot and heavily into my mouth as I'm hoisted back around his waist, and he shoves my back against the wall as if he doesn't want to wait long enough to blindly find our way to the guest bedroom. I don't want to wait, either. We've waited long enough as it is.

I feel his cock enter me and before he slides me all the way down on it, a shot of pleasure races through my thighs and up my spine, turning my neck to rubber, causing my head to fall back against the sheetrock wall. The backs of my eyes tingle and burn. The warm, wetness between my legs inundated by a hot, shivering thrill.

He thrusts once, deep inside of me and holds himself there, grasping my hips, my back pressed against the cool wall. I open my eyes slowly, still having little control over my lids, and I gaze into his staring back at me with the same voracious intensity. Tiny, uneven breaths waver through my parted lips. My arms are wrapped securely around him, my fingers prodding the tight muscles in his back.

"I've wanted this for so long," I say breathily.

"You have no idea...," he says in return and then devours me with a kiss, so forceful that I almost lose control of my muscles. My thighs constrict around his waist when he drives his cock into me again. I shudder and gasp, the back of my head falling hard against the wall. He holds my body in place with his arms fitted underneath my thighs as he drives his hips toward mine, tiny explosions going off inside my stomach with every thrust.

My back arches, my breasts pushed into his view where he covers one nipple with his mouth. I raise my arms above my head, seeking something above me that I might use to hold onto so that I can ride him, but I find nothing. I drape my arms around his neck to hold my weight up and I grind my hips against his, moving like a wave, gasping and moaning, desperate for every hard inch of him as deeply as I can take it. His fingers dig painfully into my back. His tongue tangles with mine, his moans moving through my body.

I come fast and hard, my legs and the sweet spot between them contracting around him, my muscles quivering. He comes seconds later and holds my naked body firmly in place, my ass seized by his powerful hands, as he empties himself inside of me.

In the moment, I couldn't care less about the consequences of what just happened. But only in the moment.

With my head lying on his shoulder, Victor carries me down the hall and into the spacious bathroom across from the guest bedroom. He sets me on the counter and stands between my dangling, naked legs.

"Don't worry about it." He kisses me on the forehead and then opens the tall glass door to the walk-in shower.

Confused, I ask, "About what?"

The faucet squeaks as he turns on the water, moving both hot and cold into position until he finds the desired temperature. I watch him from the countertop, the way his tall, sculpted body moves, the curves along the muscles carved in a poetic pattern around his hipbones, the way his calf muscles harden when he walks.

He comes back over to me and I slip his dress shirt the rest of the way off, sliding it down over his muscled arms.

"You won't get pregnant," he says and urges me to slide off the counter and follow him into the shower. "At least not by me."

A little taken aback, I leave it at that.

He closes the shower door and begins to wash my hair. I bask in his closeness, the way his hands explore my body with such careful precision and need.

For a long time, I forget that he is an assassin, whose hands have taken many lives without thought or remorse or regret. I forget that I, too, am a killer, whose hands took a life just hours ago.

Seems we were made for each other, like two puzzle pieces that at first don't appear to fit, but eventually fall into place when looked at in the most unlikely of angles.

CHAPTER TEN

Victor

Fredrik's housekeeper arrives back at the house early in the morning. I'm awake just after dawn, having my coffee on the rock patio in the backyard when she enters the house. She sees me through the sliding glass door when she makes her way into the living room and then joins me outside.

"Would you like breakfast, señor?" she asks in Spanish.

I set the file consisting of my next job face-down on the wrought iron coffee table.

"Gracias, but I won't be eating," I tell her and then gesture toward Sarai walking through the living room in search of me. "But she will be."

"I will be what?" Sarai asks as she steps through the opened glass door. She walks across the rock patio with bare feet, wearing another one of Fredrik's t-shirts—it bothers me immensely that she's having to wear his clothes rather than mine, but the only ones I have with me are those on my back—and a pair of loose running shorts. Her long, auburn hair is disheveled having just awoken and crawled out of the bed.

She sits on my lap and I fit my right hand between her thighs.

"Breakfast," I answer.

Sarai yawns and stretches her arms above her before laying her head against my shoulder. I fit my left hand behind her at the waist to keep her balanced on my lap. The smell of her freshly-washed skin and hair sends my senses into overdrive.

She makes a subtle face, halfway rejecting the idea.

"You should eat," I urge her.

Raising her head from my shoulder, she looks thoughtful for a moment and then turns her attention to the housekeeper. "Sure, I'd like some breakfast, if you don't mind," she says in Spanish.

For a moment, the housekeeper looks surprised that Sarai speaks to her in her native tongue, but she's over it just as quickly.

The housekeeper nods and heads back into the house.

"I think I've put this question off long enough," she says. "Where do we go from here, Victor? What am I going to do?"

I had been thinking about this very thing since I found out that she was in Los Angeles and after what she had done. I stare off toward the pool, lost in thought, my last desperate attempt to sort out the answers in my head. But they are as broken and unsettled as they ever have been. All except for one.

"Sarai," I say, looking back at her, "you can't go home. I knew this the first time I sent you back to Arizona. The situation wasn't nearly as dire as it has become, but now that things have changed, you can never go home."

"Then I'm staying with you," she says and for the first time in my life, I can't bring myself to protest such an issue. Not with her, or even with myself. The largest part of me, the flawed human part, *wants* her with me and I'll stop at nothing to make sure that it works.

But I know it's not going to be easy.

"Yes," I say, running the palm of my hand across her smooth thigh, "you're staying with me, but there are many things that you must understand."

She gets up from my lap and stands in front of me, one arm crossing her abdomen, the other propped atop it at the elbow. Absently, she brushes her fingertips across the softness of her face as she stares out at seemingly nothing. Then she looks down at me and shakes her head with a perplexed look in her eyes. "I expected you to put up more of a fight. What's the catch? Regardless of what happened between us last night, or what has been going on between us even when we were apart, I still never thought you'd agree to take me with you."

"Would you *like* me to put up a fight?" I give her a wry smile.

She smiles back at me and her arms drop back at her sides. "No. Definitely not. I-I just…."

I bring one leg up and rest my foot on the opposite knee.

"I never imagined that I'd be in a situation like this," I say. "I cannot lie to you and tell you that I think it's going to work. It very likely won't, Sarai, and you have to understand that." Her face falls just slightly, enough that I know my truthful words have discouraged her more than she'll let her expression reveal. "I cannot change my ways," I go on. "Not only because it's all I know, or that it's what I'm best at, but also because I don't want to." I look her straight in the eyes. "I will *never* stop doing what I do."

"I would never *want* you to," she says with a level of intensity. She pulls the nearby empty chair around and places it in front of me before sitting. "All that I'm asking, Victor, is to stay with you. I will do whatever you expect of me, but I want you to teach—"

I put up my hand and stop her right there.

"No, Sarai, I won't do that, either. It won't be like that." Her expression darkens and she looks away from my eyes, stung by my refusal. "I've told you before, I was practically born into this life. It would take you nearly the rest of your life to learn to do what I do, and even still it would not be good enough."

"Then what am I supposed to do?" she asks with a trace of resentment in her tone. "I want to be with you wherever you go, but I don't want to sit by and do nothing, sipping on martinis on the beach while you're out killing people. I'm not useless, Victor, I can do *something*."

"There are many things that you can do, yes," I cut in. "But doing what I do is completely out of the question. Why do you *want* this *so much*?" My voice had begun to rise with the question as I suddenly felt desperate to understand the answer.

The palms of her hands come down on the tops of her bare thighs creating a light slapping noise. "Because it's what I want."

"But *why*?"

She throws her hands up beside her and yells, "Because I enjoy it! All right?! I *enjoy* it!"

I blink a few times, completely stunned by her admittance. Truthfully, that was the last thing I expected her to say. A part of me knew that Sarai was more than capable of taking a human life and be able to sleep soundly every night afterwards, but I never anticipated that she would enjoy killing.

I'm not sure how to feel about this. I need more information.

I lean forward, raising my back from the chair and I come face to face with her. "You enjoy killing?" I ask, though it comes out more like a statement. "So, if you were asked to take someone's life, would you do it without question?"

"No," she says, her brows drawing inward. "I wouldn't kill just anyone, Victor, only men who deserve it."

Men? This side of Sarai is becoming more intriguing. I wonder if she even realizes what she just said. Men. Not people in general, but men.

I pull away from her and rest my back against the chair again, cocking my head to one side thoughtfully.

"Go on," I urge her.

She leans back as well, pulling both of her legs up and resting her feet on the seat, letting her knees fall together to one side.

"Men like Hamburg. Men like Javier Ruiz and Luis and Diego. Men like that guard I killed last night. Willem Stephens, for the simple fact that he works for Hamburg knowing what Hamburg does. Men like John Lansen and all of the others who I met at those rich parties when I was with Javier." Her gaze pierces mine harshly. "Men who deserve to have their throats slit."

The gravity of her words, the determination in her face, it quietly stuns me into submission for a brief moment. Is it possible that I have not one, but now *two* killers in my midst who share a similar penchant for bloodlust? And just as his face crosses my mind alongside hers, I hear Fredrik's car purring into the driveway. It steals the intense moment away and we both look up.

Moments later, Fredrik, dressed casually in a pair of dark-colored jeans and designer shirt, comes outside to join us. He drops the day's newspaper on the coffee table and says, "You might want to have a look at that." Then he glances at Sarai momentarily. "You look nice in my clothes, by the way."

I glare at Fredrik from the side, but bite back my jealousy before either of them notice.

Sarai and I both glance down at the paper, but I'm the one who picks it up. Unfolding the paper, I scan the black text until I find what he is referring to.

> Four bodies were found shot to death in an upscale Los Angeles hotel late last night. Only two of the bodies have been identified and are that of twenty-three-year-old Dahlia Mathers and twenty-seven-year-old Eric Johnson, both of Lake Havasu City, Arizona.

A few sentences down:

> Sarai Cohen, also of Lake Havasu City, is wanted for questioning.

I suppose it doesn't matter which identity she used to check into the hotel, her face is the same on both of them.

Sarai snatches the newspaper from my hands before I can finish.

"No...," she grits her teeth as her darkening face peers down into the tragic news of her friends. She tries to make eye contact with me, but it lasts only a second before the paper seizes her attention again as if her mind hopes to have read it all wrong the first time. "I told them to leave L.A.! Dahlia said they'd *leave*—." Her green eyes bore into mine, full of desperation and fractured by guilt.

I stand up.

Sarai takes the newspaper into both hands and rips it in half right down the center, crushing the leftover halves in both of her fists.

"They fucking killed Dahlia and Eric!" she roars. "They *killed* them!"

The paper falls from her hands and scatters about the intricate rock patio.

Fredrik just looks at me, waiting for whatever I might do or say. He doesn't speak but I can tell that he wants to.

"Sarai." I place my hands on her shoulders from behind. "I will take care of it."

She swings around at me, her hair whirling around her head before falling back against her shoulders, fury burning in her features.

"THEY ARE DEAD BECAUSE OF ME! JUST LIKE LYDIA!"

Trying to calm her down, I forcefully grab her shoulders from the front and I hold her in place.

"I said I will take care of it," I repeat with even more intensity and sincerity than before. I lean forward to keep her gaze fixed on mine. "I will do this for you, Sarai. Hamburg and Stephens will both be dead before this week is over."

I've lost her. She's staring right at me, but it feels more like *through* me instead. Her chest rises and falls with heavy, uneven breaths. Her pupils appear tiny, like pinpricks through a sheet of construction paper, the green of her eyes appears to have darkened.

"No," she argues in an eerily calm voice. "I don't want you to do anything."

Absently she steps backward and my hands fall away from her shoulders.

"I'm going to do this for you," I say. "I want—"

"I said *no!*" She takes two more steps back and then turns around, putting her back to me as she faces the pool.

"*I'm* going to do it," she says quietly, resolutely. "I'm going to kill them and I want you to back off."

"I don't think—"

She turns her head, her dark eyes catching mine. "If you kill either one of them, I'll never forgive you for it. This one is mine, Victor! Give me that much!"

"Sarai, you can't kill them." I walk toward her. "The only person who will end up dead is you. You're not capable—"

"I don't *give* a shit!" Her objective is unshakable. She walks back toward me. "You either help me pull this off, or I figure it out myself. They die by my hands, not yours, or Fredrik's, or anyone else's. Only mine. Teach me. Show me what to do. Whatever the best approach is for someone like me. Help me or I die trying to do it myself. I don't care either way."

"I won't...you can't," I shake my head.

Sarai gives up and starts to push her way past me intent on leaving. But I can't let her go anywhere. I can't because I know that she meant every word of what she said.

I grab her by the wrist, stopping her in her angry march toward the glass door. Fredrik steps out of the way, watching the scene unfold with an odd glint in his eyes that I can only make out as fascination.

"Let *go* of me!"

"You're not leaving." I hold her wrist tight and grab the other one as she begins to struggle against me.

She wants to take all of her anger out on me, to scream into my face, to curse me with words she desperately wants only to say to Hamburg and Stephens before she kills them, but she can't do any of it. The anger, as always, gets the best of her and she bursts into tears.

She told me once that she always cries when she's angry.

The tears roll down her cheeks in rivulets. She tries once more to break free from me, but I hold on tight and put painful pressure on her wrists, hoping to allay her.

"Victor please! Just fucking teach me, goddammit! Even if it's only to kill the two of them! That's all I ask! I'll never ask you to help me again! PLEASE!"

She finally stops struggling and collapses against my chest. I wrap my arms around her small form, cradling the back of her head in my hands and I press the side of my face against the top of her hair. The cries roll through her chest violently, her body trembling in my embrace. These are not cries of sadness and pain, they're cries of guilt and anger and the dire need to avenge the deaths of people—even Lydia—who might still be alive if it were not for her.

Fredrik looks over at me and I know what that calm look on his face reads. He thinks I should give Sarai what she wants.

But it's not Fredrik's opinion that ultimately makes up my mind, it's my need to protect Sarai that decides, even if by doing so she still might end up dead.

I choose the safer of the two ill-fated paths.

"I will help you."

CHAPTER ELEVEN

Sarai

I raise my face from his shirt, sniffling back the damned tears that once again have betrayed me in a weak moment.

"You'll help me kill them?"

He nods. "Yes."

"Thank you," I say softly.

I push up on my toes and kiss him lightly on the mouth.

The housekeeper speaks up behind us in a small voice, standing at the sliding glass door, "Breakfast is ready."

She looks at us through dark and beady curious eyes, surely having heard the commotion while she was inside.

"Marta makes the best scrambled eggs," Fredrik says with a gleaming smile, as though nothing had happened. "Cooks them in bacon grease." He puts all of his fingers against the center of his lips and kisses them. "I love American food."

He follows behind Marta. "Though I understand scrambled eggs cooked in bacon grease is a southern thing?" he asks looking back at us as we follow in behind him.

Victor shrugs.

"Well, Marta isn't exactly from Alabama," he goes on as we all enter the kitchen, "but she can cook like she is."

Fredrik and Victor ramble on about food, I know probably trying to take my mind off what happened. But I don't care about anything right now other than Dahlia and Eric's faces in my memory. I know I'm being punished. By Life. By Fate. I don't know by who or what, all I know is that I'd do anything to give them back their lives.

The three of us sit down at Fredrik's glass-top kitchen table and eat. And I find it almost funny how Fredrik makes Marta taste the food before serving it to us as if he had taken the paranoid technique right out of the Victor Faust Handbook.

During breakfast, which we all take in very slowly due to conversation, Fredrik eventually relieves Marta of duty for the day. It was just after he and Victor began speaking to one another in Swedish. I hate that I couldn't understand what they were saying, but it become clear to me that it had to do with Marta and not me.

Marta grabs her purse and tells us all goodbye, thanking Fredrik for paying her for a full day even though she didn't work it.

"What was that all about?" I ask just after she closes the front door behind her.

I set my fork down on my plate, finished with my breakfast.

"There's a lot to talk about," Fredrik says and takes a drink of orange juice. "And she shouldn't be in earshot of the conversation." He points at me and smiles. "And Marta, though it might not seem like it, listens to everything that goes on around here."

"Then why didn't you just continue in Swedish?" I ask.

"Do *you* speak Swedish?" Victor asks me casually.

"No."

"Well, you're a part of this," he says, setting his glass of water on the table.

I smile. It's in this moment that I feel like a part of *them* for the very first time. Both of them. The three of us sitting around the table, minutes later cleared of plates and glasses, replaced by files and photographs of contract hits. In a sense it's surreal to me, discussing the details of interrogation and murder as casually as if we were discussing the day's weather. But also for the first time in my life, I feel that I belong somewhere. I'm not pushing my way through a dark tunnel with my hands out in front of me searching for the door anymore. The door is right there in plain view and I've already walked through it. I'm finally where I belong in my life. And I'm with Victor, which means more to me than anything.

I'm finally with Victor.

~~~

Victor and I leave Fredrik's house in the hills of Los Angeles late afternoon and drive eleven hours to Albuquerque, New Mexico. On the way, I have him stop at a mall where I pretty much spend a couple thousand dollars on new clothes, shoes, accessories and makeup for myself, seeing as how everything I owned is in Arizona or was left in the Los Angeles hotel. I stuffed the backseat with shopping bags and shoe boxes, but by the ninth hour on the road I wished I had bought less. All I wanted to do was crawl into the backseat and sleep, but I got stuck with being cramped in the front, curled up awkwardly on the bucket seat of his black Cadillac CTS with my head pressed against the window. Since Victor left the Order he no longer has the convenience of flying on private jets to get around. He can still certainly afford them if he wanted to spend his own money, but being a man who the Order wants dead, means staying under the radar and giving up some luxuries that might lead Niklas right to him.

Apparently, giving up such luxuries also includes the extravagant multi-million dollar homes he has always chosen to live in. His house in Albuquerque is far from matching the one he lived in on the East Coast that overlooked the ocean. As we come up the dirt driveway, I see a house of moderate size made of straight, high tan stucco walls with a boxy shape that reminds me of the houses I used to build with Legos when I was a kid. But judging by the elaborate landscape that hugs the smooth white sidewalk leading up to the door and surrounds the east side of the house, it's obvious that Victor hasn't completely given up *all* luxuries. Even more obvious when we step inside as the interior is as beautiful as Fredrik's house had been, though with more of a southwestern style than a modern luxury bachelor pad. Rust reds and browns and yellows are dominant throughout the space, with tall ceilings held up by dark wooden beams and rafters which make the house appear much larger on the inside than it appears on the outside. A cozy stone fireplace is set in the wall in the spacious living room with two metal ornate mirrors mounted above it. The walls are painted yellow, which complement the terra cotta tile flooring that appears to spread throughout the whole house.

"You always manage to get the best housekeepers, that's for sure," I say, setting several of my bags down on the floor in the living room.

"Not this time," he says behind me. He sets the other bags from the car down next to the tawny-brown leather couch. "It's just me."

"Really? But it's so clean in here. I guess you haven't been here long then?"

"About four months." He looks over at me. "Do you like it? I hope so since it is your new home."

A smile breaks in my face.

He breaks apart the buttons of his dress shirt and takes it off, laying it over the back of a brown leather chair. Secretly, I take note of his physique as he walks toward a long, brightly-lit hallway with an arched entrance.

I follow him.

"Of course you know we won't be here forever." We enter a large bedroom. "But it's home for now, at least."

He steps out of his pants and I'm trying really hard not to watch him too intensely, but it's becoming increasingly difficult.

"Come here," he says, standing before me in nothing but his tight black boxer briefs which are doing very little to hide the hard bulge growing behind the fabric.

I swallow nervously, though why I'm nervous all of a sudden, I have no idea, and I walk toward him. A twinge spasms between my legs, and I'm not sure why of that, either. It's as if my subconscious mind is more aware of what's about to happen than my conscious one. Either that, or my mind is just running away from me with thoughts of what I only wish would happen.

I look at him curiously, tilting my head gently to one side.

"I'm not sure what this is between us," he says carefully, "but I *am* sure that I don't want it to stop. Whatever it is."

"I feel the same way."

A little confused about where this is heading, I tilt my head to the other side and ask, "Is something wrong?"

He shakes his head subtly. "No, nothing's wrong."

"Well…if you're worried I'm going to fall in love with you and cling on to your every move, you don't have to worry."

"You're not in love with me?" he asks and it seems like nothing more than a simple inquiry.

"No, I don't love you, Victor."

He nods, completely accepting it. "Good. Because I'm not in love with you, either."

I don't think either of us truly knows what the word means in this kind of situation. We both display the same accepting, yet somehow confused expressions.

"But…I uh…," I clasp my fingers together behind my back and look down at the tile floor, moving my foot about as if I were shuffling my toes nervously in sand. I stop and look him in the eyes. "But I uh would maybe…appreciate it if you didn't sleep with anyone else. I…well, I don't think I'd like that much."

"I agree," he says with another solid nod. "I think if I caught you with another man, I would have to kill him."

I nod a few times, as casually as he had.

"Definitely," I say in return. "The same goes for you."

"Agreed."

There's an awkward bout of silence between us and I glance over at the king-sized bed with tall cherry wood posts at all four corners, just feet away.

I look back at Victor as he approaches me. I lift my arms above me when his fingers slide behind the ends of my shirt and he pulls it off.

"I would also like to say that I don't mind if you cling to my every move." He fits his fingers behind the elastic of my panties. "For the record."

"Really?"

He crouches down before me as he slides my panties over my hips and down my legs. He stays there, looking up at me, his head level with my bellybutton.

"Yes," he answers. "Of course, you can't be getting in my way when I'm trying to do a job."

"Yes, of course," I say and my skin reacts to his lips kissing the area just above my pelvic bone. "I-I would never get in the way of your job," the words shudder from my lips. My hands begin to shake when he lowers himself between my legs, spreading my lips below with the pads of his thumbs.

I move my legs apart just a little, enough to give him access.

"But no leaving me in someplace far away while you travel everywhere to fulfill contracts," I say, my fingers curling within the top of his hair, my breathing uneven and rapid. "I don't want to be a stay-at-home wife, y'know what I mean?"

A sharp gasp pierces the air around my mouth when the tip of his tongue flicks across my clit. I nearly wilt right here and now, the muscles in my thighs deteriorating with every passing second.

"Yes, I am quite aware of the concept," he says and then licks me again, dragging his tongue between my wet petals. I throw my head back and grasp his hair tighter, winding it within my fingers. "You'll go wherever I go. So I can keep an eye on you."

"An eye on me. Of course." It was a poor attempt at a response. All I can think about is his head between my legs and that hot, prickling sensation turning my insides into mush.

Victor hoists me up with my ass planted firmly within both of his hands, my thighs wrapped around his head from the front and he licks me furiously for a moment before tossing me onto the bed on my back.

With my thighs pushed toward me, his mouth falls between my legs and my eyes roll into the back of my head as he sends me into oblivion.

CHAPTER TWELVE

Sarai

Training begins two days later, but it doesn't start off the way I expected it to. I don't know what I expected really, but it certainly wasn't *this*.

"What are we doing here?" I ask as we pull into the parking lot of a physical fitness and martial arts studio an hour away in Santa Fe.

"Krav Maga," he says and I just look at him as though he were speaking to me in another language. He shuts the car door and we walk toward the front of the building. "I won't be able to devote one hundred percent of my time teaching you. So, three days a week I'm going to bring you here for some training. You can learn a lot in Krav Maga in a short time. And it focuses on self-defense—"

"What?" I stop on the sidewalk just before we get to the front door. "I'm not a damsel in distress who just got robbed in a dark parking garage, Victor. I don't need self-defense classes. I need to learn how to kill."

"Killing is the easy part," he says matter-of-factly. He opens the glass door, gesturing me inside ahead of him. "Getting to that point without getting *yourself* killed in the process is the hard part."

I scoff. "So, you want me to learn how to kick a guy in the nuts? Trust me, I'm already perfectly capable of doing that."

A faint grin appears at the corners of his delicious lips.

Just then, a tall dark-haired man with rolling muscles walks toward us through the vast room. Tall windows are set along the top of the wall, letting in the sunlight. Two separate groups of people are training in a turn-by-turn sequence, standing around in a half-circle atop an enormous black mat spread across a large section of the floor.

The man with bulging arms underneath a black t-shirt offers his hand to Victor. "How long has it been? Three? Four years?"

Victor shakes his hand firmly.

"About four, I believe."

The man looks at me momentarily and then Victor introduces us.

"Spencer, this is Izabel. Izabel, Spencer."

"A pleasure," Spencer says, holding out his hand.

Reluctantly, I shake it. They know each other? I'm not sure I like that or not. I suddenly feel like I'm being set up. I smile squeamishly up at the tall, good-natured brute.

Victor turns to me and says, "There's no one better to train you in self-defense than Spencer. You're in good hands."

Spencer smiles so big I feel like if it were any bigger he might bite my head clean off my neck. He stands with his heavily-muscled arms down in front of him, his hands folded. The thick, ropy veins running along his hands and up his darkly-tanned arms reminds me of a body builder, but he's not quite as big as one. He's just bigger than *me*, making him more intimidating.

I put up a finger at Spencer. "Will you excuse us for a minute?"

"Of course," he says.

I catch the quick grin he gives Victor.

I grab Victor by the hand and pull him off to the side. In the background I hear the constant sound of bodies being thrown down on top of that black mat and the voice of an instructor harping repetitive commands and making the students 'do it again'.

"Victor, I think this is a waste of time. I don't understand why you brought me here." I cross my arms. "I want *you* to teach me these things, not some random guy the shape of a bus." I look over my shoulder, hoping Spencer didn't hear that, even though I made sure to keep it at a whisper.

"I have to meet with Fredrik in an hour," Victor says.

"Oh, so you're dropping me off with a babysitter?" Lines deepen around my eyes. I shake my head at him in total disbelief, not to mention, offense.

"No, that's not what this is about."

"But I want *you* to teach me," I repeat, pushing the words harshly through my teeth.

Victor sighs and shakes his head, appearing annoyed and frustrated with me.

"You have no discipline," he says. "None whatsoever. Just like my brother was." That stings my pride. "How am I ever going to teach you anything when you can't even do the simplest things that I ask of you?"

Instantly, I regret acting like such a child.

I let out a surrendering breath. "I'm sorry," I say softly. "I guess I just imagined training with you."

"You will," he ensures me, placing his hands on my shoulders, "but for now, you need to learn the basics. And this is the best way to do it."

"But why can't you teach me the basics?" I ask with the same amount of surrender as before. "Why does it have to be him?"

Victor leans in and presses his lips softly against the corner of my mouth. "Because Spencer isn't afraid to hurt you," he says and it surprises me somewhat. "And I don't want to hurt you if I can help it. The only way you're going to learn is if it's real."

My eyes widen. "Wait…so you're saying this *tank*," I point over my shoulder with my thumb, "is going to hit me for *real*?"

"Yes. It's what I'm paying him for."

I think my mouth just fell on the floor. The air in the room suddenly hits the backs of my eyes.

"You don't have to do this, Sarai, but if you're going to, I want you to go all in. Don't half-ass it. In real life someone attacking you isn't going to go easy on you," he goes on, gazing thoughtfully into my eyes, wanting desperately for me to understand and to trust him. "I'll train with you when the time is right. But when *I* do it, it will be brutal, Sarai. I will come at you with the same force a real attacker would. You learn the basics first, obtain some skills that you can fight me with and then I'll feel better about training you myself. Do you understand?"

I nod. "Yeah, I guess I do." And I'm being honest with him. I totally understand now. And I can't remember the last time I was this nervous to go through with something. But Spencer, the tank, doesn't really scare me that much because I know deep down that even though Victor is paying him to *not* go easy on me, he still won't hit me with everything he's got. If he did, he'd kill me.

"Do you want to stay?" Victor asks.

"Yes. I do."

"Good."

He leans in to my lips again and kisses me deeply, stealing my breath away. Shocked by his unnatural display of public affection, I find myself unable to speak when he pulls his lips away from mine.

"I'll be back here to pick you up in a few hours."

"OK."

We walk back to stand with Spencer who looks somewhat excited to start training with me, as if I were a shiny new toy that he can't wait to play with.

"Are you ready to start learning Krav Maga?" Spencer asks.

"Yes," I answer and my eyes drift toward the people fighting on the black mat behind him.

"Are you sure you can handle it?"

I want to say yes with confidence, because after all, I always imagined that self-defense classes consisted of nothing more than simple blocking and hitting and screaming to let others know of my whereabouts. I always pictured average women who've never fought in their lives all standing around waiting for their turn to take the instructor down with a few 'helpful' moves. But as I watch the group training behind Spencer, the aggressive intensity and violence in some of their moves, I'm beginning to think this kind of self-defense is very different.

"Should be simple enough," I say without the confidence that I wanted.

"If you say so," Spencer chimes in with a knowing grin that frays my nerves further.

But I'm not afraid. Nervous, yes, but not afraid. I'm ready to do this. I'm starting to look forward to it. I want to prove to Victor that I have what it takes.

And I want to prove to him that I'm *nothing* like his brother.

Victor leaves me and before the first hour is over I'm exhausted and so sore that I can hardly walk a straight line without stumbling.

~~~

"Always defend and attack at the same time," Spencer says, standing over me lying beneath him on the mat, wanting to curl into the fetal position. "And never go down. This isn't wrestling, Izabel. If you go down, you're dead."

Out of breath and trying to hold back the intense pain searing through the back of my calf muscle, I bring myself to my feet.

"Come at me," he demands, his voice rising over the shouts of the few students still watching after the second hour. "If you don't come at me, I'm coming after you!"

I'm too exhausted.

"I can't!" I give up and fall against the mat on my butt. "This is too much. It's my first day and I feel like it's my first real fight. What happened to showing me what to do, teaching me how to hit?"

"Going light on you, that's what you really mean, isn't it?"

"Yes! Where are the instructions? The rules?"

My back is *killing* me. I lay against the mat, spreading my arms against it above my head, and stare up at the brightly-lit ceiling. I don't care anymore about Spencer and his dive-in-head-first training. I just want to rest.

The fluorescent lights running along the ceiling move by fast as I'm suddenly being dragged across the mat by my ankle.

"There are no rules in Krav Maga," I hear Spencer say, but I realize a half a second later that it's not Spencer dragging me.

It's a woman, with light brown hair pulled into a ponytail at the back of her head. Confused by the turn of events, I'm too distracted to notice her foot coming down on my stomach. I yell out in pain, doubling forward as my legs and back come off the mat at the same time, my arms crossed over my abdomen. The breath is knocked right out of my lungs.

"STOP!" Spencer says from somewhere behind me.

I feel like I'm going to puke.

The woman stops instantly and takes a few steps back.

"Get up," Spencer says and I decipher through the pain devouring my midsection that his voice is much closer than before.

I look up to see him crouched behind me.

"I'll let you catch your breath," he says gently and offers his hand. "This is Jacquelyn. My wife."

I grab onto his forearm and he grabs mine likewise and lifts me to my feet.

"Nice to meet you," I say to her with a God-awful grimace. "Or at least your foot."

She smirks.

"Your man paid me to pretty much beat the shit out of you," Spencer says. "But since I'm not in the habit of beating on women, I figure I should let my wife do the honors so that I can still get paid."

"It's the best way to learn," Jacquelyn speaks up. "That man of yours knows what he's doing. Brutal? Sure.

Necessary to one's survival in close combat situations? Absolutely. For frail little bitches who do the dance of terror when they see a spider? Absolutely fucking not."

"Well, I'm not one of those," I say icily. "*That* I can fucking assure you."

"Then prove it," she taunts, bending over forward with her hands opened halfway out at her sides. "Remember there are no rules in Krav Maga. Always defend and attack at the same time. Always fight with aggression. And never go down."

"Yeah, I got that much. If I go down I'm dead."

Jacquelyn pretty much beats the hell out of me for the rest of the session. And when Victor finally arrives to pick me up, my nose and lip are bleeding, my right eye is bruised and throbbing, and I think I chipped a tooth.

This goes on every other day for the next two weeks.

And it didn't take long for me to become good at it. Spencer says I'm a natural and that I must've 'skipped the Barbie dolls and dress-up when I was growing up'.

He really has no idea…

I'm getting so much stronger, so much better at my technique. At one point I even managed to hurt Jacquelyn, buried my elbow in her ribs. I think I cracked them, but she won't say so. Not because of her pride, but because she doesn't believe in whining or letting something as petty as a cracked rib stop her from fighting.

It didn't take long for her to grow on me, either. When she's not beating me to a pulp, I actually enjoy her company.

Only two weeks have passed and I've done nothing but train with Jacquelyn and have even started training with Victor in the use of guns. But regardless of enjoying the training and looking forward to it every day, I'm frustrated that's it's taking so long. I expected Hamburg and Stephens to be long dead by now.

And I'm getting impatient.

"Victor, I don't plan to fight Hamburg and Stephens. I just want to *kill* them. That's it. I don't get why you're making me go through all this."

Victor moves the sheet from his body and climbs out of the bed, walking naked across the room.

I quietly admire the view.

"There's more to it than you know," he says as he disappears inside the bathroom just steps away.

That certainly gets my attention.

I raise up from the bed and call out, "Is that right?" I toss the sheet off and follow briskly behind him, stopping in the doorway of the bathroom and leaning against the frame. He's turning on the shower water.

He closes the glass shower door, letting the water run for a moment and then he turns back to me.

"You're not exactly going through the training just to kill Hamburg and Stephens. If you're going stay with me, regardless of what you're doing with your time, you need to learn how to fight. You need to know how to identify, differentiate, load and fire just about every weapon. There is a lot that you need to know and not enough time to learn even half of it." He opens the shower door and reaches inside, letting the water stream into his hand, testing the temperature.

He adds, "This training has little to do with Hamburg and Stephens. I want you to be safe always, so it's vital that you start learning these things now."

I smile faintly, savoring the moment. When we first met, I couldn't imagine Victor having much of a caring or emotional bone in his body. But every day I witness him opening up more to me. And I see that it is becoming easier for him.

I go back to the matter at hand though what I really want to do is kiss him right about now.

"But why is it taking so long? I just want to do this and be done with it."

I come the rest of the way inside the bathroom and hop onto the counter, sitting in nothing but my panties.

"Because while I'm working on a plan to get you close enough to kill them, you need to be training, doing as much with your time as possible." He steps over to me and cups my face in the palms of his hands. "Just being in the same room with me—just *knowing* me, Sarai, is a death sentence every day. Every time you walk out that door you risk being shot. The only reason the Order hasn't found me yet is because Niklas is the only one in the Order looking for me. For now, anyway. He doesn't want anyone else to find me. *He* wants the credit. The recognition. Especially since he was the one contracted to take me out." He presses his lips against my forehead. I shut my eyes softly and reach up with both hands and hold onto his wrists. "But one day, likely very soon, I'll have to face my brother because the Order won't give him forever to pull it off. Either he'll find me, or I'll find *him*. And one of us will die."

With my fingers still hooked halfway around his wrists, I carefully pull his hands from my face. I look perplexedly into his gorgeous green-blue eyes, tilting my head to one side.

"Why not just leave it alone?" I ask. "Victor, I can understand that you'd want to kill him before he kills you, but why risk getting killed by going and looking for a fight?"

Steam begins to fill the room, fogging the large mirror mounted over the counter behind me.

"Because if Niklas doesn't find me, if he can't pull off his first official contract since being promoted an operative under Vonnegut, they'll kill him." He props the palms of his hands on the countertop on either side of me. "No one's going to kill my brother but me. I don't care what he's done, or about our differences, he's still my brother."

I nod, understanding. "OK, so then when is all of this going to happen? This...showdown with Niklas. Me getting to kill Hamburg and Stephens?"

Victor smiles slimly and I reach up and brush my fingertips across his lips. He takes my hand into his and kisses my fingers. "We're going to have to work on this problem of yours, Sarai. You being so impatient, and of course as I said before, undisciplined. We start on that next."

"I can't help it that I'm impatient. Those two evil bastards are out there living the high-life every day, doing God knows what to no telling how many women. Not to mention, they're looking for me. They killed my friends because of me. Dina is still hiding out in some place that isn't her home and she's scared. Her life has been turned upside-down because of them. Because of me. I want them dead so at least Dina can go on with her life."

"What are you going to tell her?" he asks. "When you see her today, what are you going to say?"

I glance away from him and watch the steam coat the tall glass shower walls and billow lightly over the top of the shower in soft puffs. My skin is beginning to sweat lightly, beading off my face, neck and collarbone.

"I'm going to tell her the truth," I say.

"Do you think that's wise?"

I look right at him. "I think it's only fair. She's practically my mother. She's done so much for me. I owe her the truth." I smile and add, "And besides, if you didn't agree with my decision to tell her the truth, you'd have already made that perfectly clear to me by now."

Victor smiles back at me and fits his hands on my waist, helping me off the counter.

"I guess we better get ready then if we're going to get there on time," he says and walks me to the shower. I step out of my panties before stepping inside the shower with him.

Victor had told Dina, and me, that he would take me to see her a few days after Fredrik's contact took her away from Lake Havasu City. But things didn't quite turn out how we planned. Victor and Fredrik both agreed that it was too risky and too soon. I overheard them talking one night about Dina and about how she might have had surveillance on her before Fredrik's contact arrived that night. Victor wanted to be certain that wasn't the case and that if any of us happened to show up where Dina was being hidden, we wouldn't fall right into the trap. But as the days passed and Fredrik continued to monitor the house where Dina has been kept, he and Victor agreed that it is, in fact, safe.

Today, I finally get to see her since I left with Eric and Dahlia for Los Angeles.

CHAPTER THIRTEEN

Victor

Sarai must be prepared, not just for the imminent threats, but for the life which lies ahead of her. She chose her path a long time ago, she chose it the day she met me even if she wasn't aware of it at the time. I wanted to look the other way, as much as I fought with myself and my strange and unnatural need to be near her, I still wanted her to have a normal life.

I did not want her to end up like me…

But I knew the day that I left her eight months ago, I knew before I walked out of that hospital room with Mrs. Gregory at her bedside, that I would one day go back for her. It was never my intention or my plan, I simply knew that it would eventually happen, one way or another.

Twenty-eight years of the thirty-seven that I have been alive I have known only life in the Order. I have known only discipline and death. I have never known friendship or love without suspicion and betrayal. I have been…programmed to defy customary human emotions and actions, but I…It wasn't until I met Sarai that I allowed myself to believe that Vonnegut and the Order were not my family, that they used me as their perfect soldier. They denied me all my life the very elements that make us human. And I cannot let that go unpunished.

One day I *will* kill Vonnegut and take the rest of the Order down with him for what they have done to me and my family. A family which they have destroyed. Sarai is my family now, and hopefully Fredrik will prove his loyalty in *his* final test. They are my family and I will not allow the Order to destroy them, too.

But for now, Sarai is my focus and she will be as long as necessary. She must be trained. She must absorb as much as she can as quickly as she can. It is impossible for her to ever be on my level. She will never be able to live the life of an assassin as I do because that would take half a lifetime to learn. It is why the Order recruits at such young ages. It is why Niklas and I were taken when we were just boys.

Sarai will never be like me.

But she has other skills. She has abilities that even after all of the years of training I have gone through, *I* could never match. Sarai's life in the compound in Mexico gave her a priceless set of skills that cannot be taught in a class or read from a book. She is the perfect liar and manipulator. She can become someone else in two seconds flat and deceive an entire room of people who are not likely to be deceived by anyone. She can make a man believe anything she wants with very little effort. And she doesn't fear death. But she's better than an actress. Because one never knows that it's an act until it's too late. Javier Ruiz was Sarai's *true* teacher. He taught her things that I would never be able to. He was her real trainer in learning the deadly skills that are now beginning to define her as a killer. And like all evil teachers, Javier Ruiz was also his favorite student's first victim.

Like the abilities she already possesses, to learn to fight she must live it, breathe it, to fully understand it. My forcing her to train with Spencer and Jacquelyn is necessary to her survival because she must learn as much as she can as often as she can. But the skills she already has are what will make her a soldier in her own right.

They are what will make us the perfect pair.

But first, Sarai has to understand fully what she is capable of. And she must pass the tests. All of them, even the ones that may cause her to despise me.

I am confident that she will. Pass the tests, anyway. To despise me is still debatable.

We arrive in Phoenix just after dark and are greeted at the door of the tiny white house by Amelia McKinney, Fredrik's liaison. She is a beautiful woman of voluptuous curves and long, blonde hair, though her more *un*attractive feature are her large plastic breasts that must surely give her back pain. And she dresses rather whorish for a woman with a PhD and who has taught a fourth grade class the past five years.

"Hello Victor Faust," she says with a hint of seduction, holding the front door open for Sarai and me. "I've heard a lot about you."

"A lot? Interesting."

Holding the screen door open with one hand she steps aside and ushers us in, a mass of gold bracelets hang from her wrist with dangling gold pendants. Several large rings adorn her fingers. And she smells of soap and toothpaste.

I place my hand on the small of Sarai's back and let her go in before me.

"Fredrik has told me about you," Amelia says, closing the door behind us. "Though I guess 'a lot' is an overstatement in your case, seeing as how he doesn't seem to know much about you himself." She twirls her hand at the wrist out beside her and adds, "But I suppose the fact I know so little about you is what makes you all the more intriguing."

"Don't even think about it," Sarai says, halting our little single-file line and turning back to look at her.

Discipline, Sarai. Discipline. I sigh quietly to myself, but I admit, it makes me hard to see her so overprotective of what belongs to her.

Amelia puts up both hands, thankfully in a surrendering fashion rather than a challenging one. "No problem, honey. No problem at all."

Sarai accepts her white flag and we continue into the house where we find Dina Gregory in the kitchen cooking what appears to be a Thanksgiving meal for about fifteen.

Sarai runs into Dina's open arms and the smiles and heartfelt words of relief and excitement commences. I ignore it all for the moment, turning my attention to the more imperative issues: my surroundings, and this woman I've never met.

I trust no one.

Amelia, like many of the women acquainted with Fredrik Gustavsson, knows nothing of the Order or mine or Fredrik's involvement with any such private organization. She is not like Samantha from Safe House Twelve in Texas was to me. No, Amelia and Fredrik's relationship, though it can no longer technically be called that, is much more…complicated.

I begin to search the house for cameras and weapons, sweeping my fingers along bookshelves and plants and knickknacks and furniture, planting my own concealed surveillance paraphernalia along the way.

"Fredrik said that you might do that," Amelia speaks up behind me, though I'm quite sure she didn't see the tiny device I just stuck to the underside of the television stand. She laughs lightly. "I made sure to clean the house really good before you came. Where are the white rubber gloves?" she jokes.

I never turn around to look at her, or stop what I'm doing.

"Have you had any unfamiliar visitors here since Mrs. Gregory was brought to stay with you?" I ask, leaning over an end table beside a recliner and inspecting a lampshade.

"Wow, you and Fredrik really are the most paranoid men I've ever met. No. Not that I recall. Well, a satellite salesman came once last week wanting me to switch from cable. Other than that, no."

She moves up behind me and lowers her voice, "How long is this woman supposed to stay in my house?" I notice from my peripheral vision she glances toward the kitchen entrance to make certain no one but I can hear. "She's a nice lady and all, but...," she sighs guiltily, "...Look, I'm thirty-years old. I haven't lived with my parents since I was sixteen. She's crampin' my style. I had a man over last week and he thought she was my mother. It was awkward. I haven't been laid since she got here."

I turn around to face her fully. "And how long have you known the man that you brought here?"

"Huh?"

"The man? How long have you and he been sleeping together?"

Her thinly-groomed brows bunch together in the low center of her forehead. "What is that any of your business? Going to ask me how many positions he's fucked me in, too?"

"How long?"

"I met him at a bar last Saturday."

"Well, that constitutes as an unfamiliar visitor."

She wants to argue the point, but she doesn't.

"Fine. Whatever. The satellite man and the *almost*-lay from the bar. That's it."

"Before I leave I'll need his name and anything else you can give me on him, including an accurate description."

She shakes her head and laughs with displeasure. "I don't know why I put up with Fredrik's bullshit." Then she pulls open a tiny drawer underneath the end table and retrieves a notepad and an ink pen.

"Because you can't help yourself," I point out, though not trying to be unpleasant, just simply stating a fact. Something else I need to work on: keeping my mouth shut when women say certain things that are not up for comment.

Her bright blue eyes widen with offense. She scribbles something on the paper, tears it from the notepad and shoves it in my hand. "What's *that* supposed to mean?" But before she gives me a chance to dig myself further into the hole, she changes her tone and leans in toward me and whispers suggestively, "Hey…just how alike *are* the two of you, anyway?"

I know precisely what she's asking—she wonders, probably hopes, that my sexual aptitude is as dark as Fredrik's is—but she's treading very dangerous territory with Sarai being in the other room.

"Not very," I reply, tucking the paper with the man's name and description into my pocket. I go back to my investigation of her house.

"That's too bad," she says. "What is it with him, anyway? Does he talk about me to you at all?"

Please make it stop….

I sigh deeply and stop at the mouth of the hallway, looking right at her. "If you have questions for or about Fredrik, please do me a favor and direct them at him."

Amelia tosses her hair back in a pride-filled fashion and with the rolling of her eyes. "Whatever. Just find out from Fredrik how long I'm supposed to babysit, will ya'?"

She pushes her way past me and into the kitchen with Sarai and Mrs. Gregory while I use the opportunity to inspect the rest of the house.

Speaking of Fredrik, I get a call from him just as I'm heading toward the spare bedroom.

"I have information on the New Orleans job," he says on the other end of the phone. I hear traffic in the background. "The contact believes the target is back in town."

"What makes her believe that?"

"She thought she saw him outside a bar near Bourbon Street. Of course, she could be seeing things, too, but I think we should look into it. Just in case. If we wait and he goes back to Brazil, or wherever it is he's been hiding, it might be another month or two before we get another shot at him."

"I agree." I close myself off inside the spare bedroom. "I'm with Sarai at Amelia's right now, but I'll wrap this up sooner than I planned. Go on to New Orleans ahead of me and I'll meet you there by early evening tomorrow. But don't do anything."

"Don't *do* anything?" he asks suspiciously. "If I find him, I can at least detain him and start the interrogation."

"No, wait for us," I say. "I want Sarai to do this one."

Silence ensues on the phone.

"You can't be serious, Victor. She isn't ready. She could ruin the whole mission. Or get herself killed."

"She won't do either," I say calmly with every bit of confidence. "And don't worry, you can still do the interrogation. I only want her to do the detaining."

I know there's a dark smile on his face without having to see it or hear his voice. Giving Fredrik the interrogation job is very much like giving a heroin addict a fix.

"I'll see you in New Orleans then," he says.

I hang up and slide the phone in the back pocket of my black pants and then finish the sweep of the house before joining the women all sitting in the living room with plates of food on their laps.

CHAPTER FOURTEEN

Sarai

"You really should get a plate," I say to Victor as he emerges from the hallway. "Dina is the best cook. Even better than Marta. But don't tell Marta I said that." I shovel a big spoonful of green bean casserole into my mouth.

Dina, sitting beside me on the couch, points to Victor. "She's biased. But if you're hungry you better eat while it's there."

"We need to talk," Victor announces standing in the center of the room, now blocking our view of the television.

I don't like the vibe he's putting off.

"OK," I say and lean away from the back of the couch, setting my plate on the coffee table. "What about?"

Victor glances at Amelia. She sits in the chair on the other side of me breaking apart a piece of cornbread with her fingers. I get the feeling he doesn't want her here during this conversation.

"Amelia," Victor says, reaching into his back pocket and retrieving his leather wallet. "I need you to go out for a while." He fingers the money in his wallet and pulls out a small stack of one hundred dollar bills. He lays them on the table into her view. "If you don't mind."

She looks down at the money, setting her fork on her plate and then she counts it.

"Sure thing," she says with a pleased smile. She gets up, taking her plate and soda can with her and disappears into the kitchen.

I hear the fork scraping the leftover food from the plate into the garbage and then the ceramic clanking softly against the bottom of the sink. Amelia walks past and begins to head down the hall.

"But I need you to leave now," Victor calls out. "There's no time for you to change clothes or to freshen up."

"Can I at least put on some damn shoes?" she snaps.

"Of course," he answers with a nod. "But please make it quick."

Amelia moves the rest of the way down the hall, mumbling words of irritation as she goes. Minutes later she finally leaves the house and her car pulls out of the driveway.

Victor looks down at us.

"We can't stay as long as expected," he says.

Dina sets her plate down now, too, and sighs miserably.

"Why not?" I ask.

"Something has come up."

I look down at my plate, the silver shine from the fork blurring into focus as I begin to contemplate heavily. I thought I had time to search for the right opening to begin to tell Dina everything that I planned to tell her. Now, I'm left scrambling to figure out how to even begin the sentence.

"Dina," I say and take a deep breath. I turn to the side to face her fully, sitting to my left. "I killed a man months ago." Dina's face appears to stiffen. "It was self-defense. I uh…," I glance up at Victor. He nods subtly, urging me to continue, letting me know that it's OK, even though I know he doesn't fully agree with me doing this. "…In fact, I killed a man in Los Angeles the night Dahlia and Eric were found dead."

Dina's weathered hand comes up and her bony fingers linger on her top lip. "Oh, Sarai…you…what are you—"

"Dahlia and Eric were murdered because of me," I cut in because clearly she couldn't figure out what to say. "Not only do I have the LAPD looking for me for questioning since I was with them, but the men who murdered them are looking for me, too. And that's why you're here."

"Oh, good Lord." She shakes her head over and over, her fingers finally falling away from her mouth, her eyes outlined by crow's feet, shrinking underneath her distressed features.

I take a hold of her hand, it's cold and smooth underneath my touch. "There's a lot you don't know. Where I really was that nine years my mom and me went missing. What really happened to me. And to my mom. And I wasn't shot by an ex-boyfriend when Victor brought you to the hospital in Los Angeles. I was shot by…," I glance up at Victor again, but I take it upon myself to keep this information from her. She doesn't need to know about Niklas, or anything about what he and Victor are involved in. "I was shot by someone else," I say. "It's really a very long story that I will tell you someday, but right now I just want you to know the truth about me." I brush my fingers softly across the top of her hand. "You're the only mother I've ever truly had. You've done so much for me and you've always been there for me and I owe you the truth."

Dina encloses my hand with both of hers. "What happened to you, baby girl?" she asks with such pain and worry in her voice that it chokes me up inside.

I begin to tell her everything, as much as I can without giving any information about Victor and Niklas away. I tell her about Mexico and the things that I saw and experienced there. I tell her about Lydia and how I tried so hard but couldn't save her. I leave out mostly the sexual relationship that I had with my captor, Javier Ruiz, a Mexican duglord, weapons and slave dealer, and just tell her that I was there against my will and made to do things that I never wanted to do. She breaks down in tears and holds me close to her, rocking me pressed against her chest as if I were the one crying and who needs the shoulder. But for once I'm not crying. I just feel terrible having to tell her any of this because I knew it would hurt her immensely.

Minutes later, after I've said all that I can say, Dina sits there on the edge of the cushion in a mild display of shock. But she's more worried than anything.

She looks up at Victor.

"How long do I have to stay here?" she asks him. "I would really like to go home. And I want to take Sarai home."

"That's not a good idea," Victor says. "And as far as Sarai, she is going to have to stay with me. Indefinitely."

I swallow hard at his words, knowing that Dina won't take them well.

"Then…but then what does that mean?" she asks nervously and turns her attention on me only. "Sarai, are you never coming home?"

I shake my head carefully, regretfully. "No, Dina, I can't. I need to stay with Victor. I'm safest with him. And you're safest without me."

She shakes her head solemnly. "Will you visit me?"

"Of course I will." I squeeze her hand gently. "I would never leave you permanently."

"I understand," she says, forcing herself to accept it.

She turns her attention back to Victor. "But I can't stay in this woman's house," she argues. "If you only brought me here to protect *me*, then I'd rather just go home. I'm not afraid of these men." She stands up and looks at me. "Sarai, honey, I would never tell the police anything. I hope you believe that."

I stand up, too.

"No, Dina, I know you wouldn't. Trusting you has nothing to do with why you're here. You're here because I want you to be safe. If something were ever to happen to you, especially because of me, I would never forgive myself. You're all that I have left. You and Victor. You're my family and I can't lose you."

"But I can't stay here, honey. I've been here long enough. Amelia is kind to me, but this isn't my home and I don't want to be here any longer than *she* wants me to be here. I feel like a burden. I miss my plants and my favorite coffee mug."

"Mrs. Gregory," Victor says, getting impatient but remaining respectful of her feelings. She looks over, but he pauses as if contemplating an idea. "Sarai cannot be safe if she's worrying about *your* safety. I'm telling you right now that if you go back to your home they will *find* you and they will either *kill* you the second they see you, or worse, they will take you hostage and *torture* you and put you in front of a video camera that they will use you to get to Sarai. Do you understand what I'm telling you?"

Dina's stiff, resolved expression falls under a veil of suffering and submission. She turns to me, pain twisting her features. Maybe she's looking to me for validity of his words, hoping I can soften the blow, tell her that he was only being dramatic. But I can't. What he told her, although harsh and to the point, was exactly what she needed to hear.

"He's right. Listen, we're going to take care of these men very soon, OK? I just need you to stay put for a while longer until we can."

"Though I agree with you, Mrs. Gregory," Victor speaks up, "I don't think you should stay here any longer, either."

Dina and I both look over at the same time.

Victor goes on, "Stay put too long in the same place when you're hiding, you're certain to be found."

"Then where is she supposed to go?" I ask, my head spinning with possible scenarios, none of which seem plausible. "Surely you don't mean to take her with us. As much as I'd love that—"

"No, she cannot go with us," Victor says, "but I can set her up in a place of her own. It's not like I haven't done it before."

Victor did, after all, get the house in Lake Havasu City for Dina and me.

"But I thought you said something came up, that we need to leave sooner than expected. There's no time to find her another place. That would take days."

"I have a house," Victor says. "Though it's far from Arizona, I think it will be best that you were out of Arizona for the time being, anyway. Fredrik's contact, the same man who brought you here, will take you to that location. Are you willing to relocate?"

Dina sits back down on the couch, pressing her palms flat against each other and wedging her hands between her legs covered by a pair of tan slacks.

I sit down beside her.

"Please do this," I say. "I will feel so much better knowing you're safe."

It takes her a long moment, but Dina finally nods. "I'm too old for this kind of excitement, but all right, I'll go. But I'm only doing this for you, Sarai."

I lean over and hug her. "I know and I love you for it."

~~~

"Where is the house?" I ask after we leave Dina at Amelia's place and get back on the road. He didn't want to say it out loud in Amelia's house, probably because he didn't trust our surroundings.

"Tulsa," he says. "It's one of a few that I keep. Nothing fancy like the house in Santa Fe, but it's livable and cozy and only we know about it."

"Who is this contact of Fredrik's, anyway?"

"He's not part of the Order, if that's what you're wondering. He's just someone that Fredrik knows, somewhat like Amelia."

"If they're not part of the Order, then who are they?"

Victor glances over at me from the driver's seat. "Amelia is just an old girlfriend of sorts, of Fredrik's. A lot like the safe-houses run by the Order, Amelia's house serves the same purpose. Though there's much less to worry about with someone like her since she doesn't even know what the Order is. All she knows is that she has an unhealthy obsession with Fredrik, and she'll do just about whatever he asks her to do."

"Ah, I see," I say, though I'm not so sure that I do. "She sounds clingy."

"I guess you can say that."

"What about the guy? The one taking Dina to Tulsa?"

Victor watches the road, one hand resting casually on the bottom of the steering wheel.

"He's one of our employees, per se. One of about twenty contacts we have recruited since I left the Order. None of them know more than they need to know. Fredrik or I will give them an order and like any job, they fulfill it. Of course, working for us is far from being like any job, but you get the picture."

"They don't know the danger they're in being involved with you and Fredrik? And how do you get them to do whatever you want? What do they do exactly, besides driving Dina around to some random location on a whim?"

"You are full of questions." Victor smiles over at me. A semi rushes past in the opposite direction, nearly blinding us with its headlights. "They're aware of the dangers to an extent. They know they're working for a private organization and that they are forbidden to speak of it, but none of our recruits are strangers to secrecy and discipline. Some are ex-military, and each of them are hand-picked by me. After I've done extensive background checks on them, of course." He pauses and adds, "And they do whatever we ask them to do, but to keep their noses clean and our outfit protected, we usually only pay them to do simple things. Surveillance. Purchasing real estate, vehicles. And driving Mrs. Gregory around to random places on a whim." He smiles over at me again. "How do we get them to do whatever we ask? Money is a formidable means of influence. They are paid well."

I rest my head against the seat and try to stretch my legs out onto the floorboard, already dreading the long drive.

"One of our men was at Hamburg's restaurant the night I found you."

Just as quickly as I had laid my head down, I raise it back up again and look over, needing him to elaborate.

"Mrs. Gregory didn't call me until after you had left for Los Angeles," he begins to explain. "I was in Brazil on a job, still searching for my target after two weeks. I left the second I got the call from Mrs. Gregory, but I knew I likely wouldn't find you in time so I got in touch with two of our contacts who were in Los Angeles, gave them your description and alerted them about watching the restaurant and Hamburg's mansion. I knew you'd go to one or the other."

I recall the man behind the restaurant after I killed the guard. The man who mysteriously let me go.

"I saw him," I say glancing over once. "I ran out the back exit and he was there. I thought he was one of Hamburg's men."

"He is," Victor says.

I blink back the stun.

"He and the other man were two of my first recruits," he goes on. "Los Angeles was my priority when all of this began."

"You knew I'd go there," I say, and although I don't want to jump to conclusions and make myself look like a delusional girl, I know it to be true. My heart begins to beat like a warm fist inside my chest. Knowing the truth, knowing that I was on Victor's mind all that time more than I ever could have imagined, it makes me feel both content *and* guilty. Guilty because I accused him of abandoning me.

"I had hoped that you would leave it alone," he says, "but deep down I knew you'd go back there."

Silence ensues for a moment.

"Is he OK?" I ask about the man behind the restaurant.

Victor nods. "He's fine. He had been employed by Hamburg for months. He knew the layout of the restaurant and knew that the only other way out of Hamburg's room on the top floor was the back exit." He adds suddenly, "By the way, he wanted me to relay an apology."

"What on Earth for?" I say. "He helped me get away."

"The order I gave him was to make sure you never made it up to that room in the first place. It was the white wig. He knew you to have long auburn hair, not short platinum-blonde. By the time he realized it was you, you were already being escorted into the room by Stephens. He couldn't get inside because the room was being guarded, so he went around to the back of the restaurant, hoping that by some chance he could get in from there, but there were two other men stationed in the back. They stalled him with conversation until he finally got them to leave the post duty up to him. Shortly after, you came out the back door."

I inhale a deep breath and rest against the seat again. "Well, you tell him there's no need for an apology. But why didn't he just tell me who he was? Or take me to you?"

"He had to hold Stephens off to let you get away, and it helps that he's still on the inside. He doesn't know what Hamburg and Stephens have planned, or anything about their operations. He's just a guard, nothing more. But he's still on the inside and that's valuable to us."

I break apart my seatbelt buckle and climb between the front seats, very unladylike I admit, with my butt in the air, and crawl into the back. I catch Victor checking out the view as I squeeze my way past and it makes me blush.

"I just have one more question to add to that list," I say.

"And what might that be?" he asks with a playful edge in his voice.

"How long will we be forced to travel like this?" I stretch my legs across the seat and lay down. "I really do miss the private jets. These long car rides are going to be the death of me."

Victor laughs. I find it incredibly sexy.

"You're sleeping with an assassin, running for your life every single day from men who want to kill you and you're convinced you're going to die of discomfort." He laughs again and it makes me smile.

"Yeah, I guess so," I say, feeling only a little bit ridiculous. I can't deny the truth, after all, no matter how nonsensical it may be.

"Not too much longer," he answers. "We have to lay low until I'm completely free of Vonnegut. He has his hands in many things, and easy, covert, expensive forms of travel are at the top of his list of priorities for obvious reasons. I'd be more off the radar taking an Amtrak than boarding a private jet."

Satisfied with his answer, I don't say anything else about it and I stare up at the dark roof of the car.

"For the record," I change the subject, "I'm not just *sleeping* with an assassin. I've grown *very* attached to one."

"Is that so?" he says cleverly and I know that he's grinning.

"Yes, I'm afraid it's true," I jest as if it were an unfortunate thing. "And it's a very unhealthy attachment."

"Really? Why do you think that is?"

I sigh dramatically. "Oh, I don't know. Perhaps because he'll never be able to get rid of me."

"Clingy. Like Amelia," he says, trying to get a rise out of me.

And he gets it. I raise up halfway and gently smack him on the shoulder. He recoils subtly, feigning pain all the while with a grin on his face. "Hardly," I say and lay back down. "He's got no chance in hell that I'd do whatever he wanted, like Amelia."

He laughs gently. "Well, I suppose he's stuck with you forever then."

"Yes, and forever is a very long time."

He pauses and then says, "Well, for the record, something tells me he wouldn't have it any other way."

I fall asleep in the backseat a long time later, with a smile on my face that seemed to stick there the rest of the night.

CHAPTER FIFTEEN

Victor

The streets of New Orleans are packed with people when we arrive the next day. Thousands of participants are dressed in white clothes and donning bright red scarves and bandannas and hats and belts, partaking in the annual San Fermin en Nueva Orleans, otherwise known as the Running of the Bulls. We weave our way through the farther side of town where the streets haven't been closed to traffic, detouring many of the distinctive balconies festooned with intricate European ironwork and courtyards in search of the warehouse where Fredrik awaits us, far away from the festivities.

Sarai had been asleep for the past three hours, in the front seat this time with her head pressed against the passenger's side window. She now sits wide awake, taking in her surroundings and massaging the back of her neck with her fingers.

I told her some about why we were heading to New Orleans last night on the drive, but other things I left out as I'm waiting to meet with Fredrik first to see what information he has gathered on our target, Andre Costa, also known as Turtle, a half American, half Brazilian whipping boy to a notorious gang leader out of Venezuela. I've been looking for Costa for weeks, mostly in Rio de Janeiro, where he was last spotted. But he moves too fast from place to place, despite his nickname, and for the first time in a long time I've had my work cut out for me trying to keep up.

We pull onto the grounds of the abandoned warehouse and slowly around to the side where Fredrik is waiting. When the car comes into view, a tall metal bay door raises and I drive beneath it, parking the car in the semi-darkness of the dusty building. It must have been an old garage of sorts, judging by the inspection pit in the concrete floor and the car lift and other heavy pieces of automobile equipment that had been left behind. One entire wall is stacked to the tall ceiling by shelves where a few old tires sit abandoned. Large windows are set along the top of the wall on the back side of the building, covered by a thick layer of dust, but allowing enough sunlight to spill into the area making it appear overcast.

The car doors echo through the wide, empty space when Sarai and I close them behind us.

"Geez, what's with the doom and gloom?" Sarai asks, craning her neck, looking up at the ceiling.

"It's good to see you, too," Fredrik says stepping up. He's dressed in his usual Armani suit and shiny black dress shoes, very unfitting of this place.

Sarai smirks and continues to look around, crossing her arms over her stomach and drawing her shoulders up around her neck as if the place is giving her the heebie-jeebies.

Fredrik flips a switch inside a breaker box and surprisingly a very small section of fluorescent lights hum to life near the back wall where it is darkest, I'm sure resuscitated by a generator somewhere. Fredrik has used this warehouse before. Two months ago during another interrogation. And I'm fairly certain he has also taken advantage of it for personal use as well.

"What is this place?" Sarai asks.

The light reveals an old dentist chair situated in the far corner with added touches such as arm and leg restraints, and thick leather straps to hold down a person's head and torso.

"It's my interrogation room," Fredrik says with the slight wave of his hand as if he were showcasing it. "Well, for now it is."

He bends over behind the dentist chair and retrieves a flat black suitcase, sets it down on the nearby metal table stained with paint and then flips open the silver latches on both ends simultaneously.

"I'm almost afraid to ask what you do during an interrogation," Sarai says, unfolding her arms and looking around the place until finally her eyes fall back on the suitcase.

Fredrik glances at me. "You sure she can handle this job, Faust?"

"Hey," Sarai cuts in, "I said *almost* afraid to ask. I can handle it." The intensity in her face speaks volumes.

Fredrik smiles and pulls a wheeled stainless steel utility tray over next to the chair and begins unloading various tools into a neat row on top of it. Three different sized knives. A pair of pliers. Syringes filled with drugs. And then he retrieves six small vials of liquid and places them next to the tools.

"She worries me a little," Fredrik says, glancing at me once.

He goes back to setting up his tools, a smile subtle in his face.

"Not as much as you worry me," Sarai says in a half-teasing manner. Her eyes sweep the tools. "Sadistic much?"

Fredrik looks at me. "You haven't told her yet, have you?"

"It is not my place to tell."

"Tell me what?" She looks back and forth between us. Fredrik places the last syringe on the table and moves toward her. She stands her ground despite the darkly seductive look in his eyes as he approaches her. It makes me uncomfortable when Fredrik reaches out and slides his index finger through the length of her loose auburn hair.

But this is also a test—to see if she can handle the truth about Fredrik—and I'm confident that she'll pass.

Sarai

Fredrik's magnetic blue eyes send a perplexing chill through me. His finger falls away from my hair and he gently cocks his head to one side, his gaze passing over every inch of my face as if he's contemplating which part he wants to savor first. I swallow hard and take a step back. Not because he frightens me, but because it frightens me that I'm not as afraid of him as my gut tells me I should be.

I glance over at Victor, moving only my eyes. His expression is calm and blank. Surely I have nothing to worry about if Victor doesn't seem worried. But what if he's testing me? What if he's looking for that misplaced trust I've always had in Victor, that trust he told me a long time ago *not* to have because in the end I should only ever trust myself?

No...that's not it. It's something else he's looking for and I can't quite place it.

I cock my head to one side and chew on the inside of my mouth, narrowing my eyes at Fredrik.

"Why don't you just tell me and skip the dramatics," I say to him.

An incredibly sexy grin appears and Fredrik casually steps away from me. The flooding light near the dentist chair casts a strangely fitting aura around his body making him look like a madman in the Devil's suit, standing against a grisly backdrop.

"We're all killers here," Fredrik says casually with that ever-present Swedish accent. He gestures, palm-up toward Victor. "The assassin," he indicates. "And you, of course. I think you've successfully joined the club, though you kill for vengeance, unlike Faust here who kills for money."

With a nervous knot sitting heavily in the pit of my stomach, I look over at Victor once more, but his solid expression is unchanging.

"And you?" I ask, turning to Fredrik. "Why do you kill?"

Fredrik laughs lightly and I feel that the dark atmosphere in the room has suddenly brightened. He doesn't seem so intimidating anymore. I look between Fredrik and Victor again, searching their faces for some kind of quiet communication and sure enough I find it. Fredrik was only messing with my head.

I'm thoroughly confused.

"I kill, but only when I have to," Fredrik says and I'm surprised by it. "I'm what Faust here calls a Specialist. Interrogation and torture are my areas of expertise." He waves a hand at the equipment behind him. "That was already obvious I suppose. And occasionally I've been given the opportunity to play Dr. Kevorkian."

I laugh it off and say, "I thought you were going to tell me you were a serial killer or something."

Victor and Fredrik's eyes meet again, though only briefly. I detect the clandestine nature of the mood they share immediately.

"No doll," Fredrik says and turns his back to me, pretending to be straightening his gruesome interrogation tools again. "I do not get pleasure from killing...."

Silence embraces the room.

Fredrik looks uncomfortable now, using the tools on the table as a distraction, his long fingers brushing over the polished metal with a careful grace. I want to be wary of Fredrik, to find his enigmatic personality annoying and his résumé repulsive, but for some reason that I cannot understand, I suddenly feel...sorry for him.

"We should get prepared," Victor says, cutting the awkward silence in the room.

Fredrik, as if his emotions are dictated by a light switch, smacks his hands together with a bright and eerily sadistic smile. "Absolutely!" he says. "Quite frankly, I'm tired of waiting on this piece of shit. Not that it is in any way your fault, Faust."

"Perhaps it is somewhat my fault," Victor admits and I get the feeling that he being to blame has something to do with me. "But some things are more important."

I look downward at the filthy concrete floor, hiding the faint blush in my face.

"Are you sure you're ready for this?" Victor asks.

"Ready is an understatement," Fredrik replies and then begins filling us in on the specifics.

"Andre Costa is in town for two more days," he says. "He's staying with a woman, an aunt I believe, across the river somewhere in Algiers. My contact overheard him talking in Lafitte's last night. Unless Costa was just lying to the women for conversation's sake, apparently he knows this city inside and out and it's like a second home. If we don't get him tonight, I'm sure we'll have another shot at him soon."

Fredrik's eyes skirt me.

"I'll get him," I say, only slightly offended by his lack of confidence in me, but at the same time I know I'd probably be just as concerned about the outcome if I were him.

He goes on, "Costa has been at this bar, Lafitte's, every night he's been here, so I'm confident he'll be there tonight as well."

Victor reaches around to his back pocket and pulls out a small envelope, putting it into my hand. I take out the photo inside and look down into the smiling face of Andre Costa, a rather young-looking guy with smooth, light caramel-colored skin and no evidence of ever having had to shave. A little mole sits just above the right side of his mouth. His hair is short and black with wispy curls around his forehead and down around the outline of his ears, almost giving him the appearance of a young Roman Caesar, minus the laurel wreath. He's wearing a black t-shirt with some kind of white writing on it and he appears to be sitting in a bar with his back turned against the bar-top, a mixed drink in a glass in his left hand. He has the stereotypical look of the party-goer with a huge, pearly-white smile lit by a whiskey buzz and a glossy film over his eyes, only partly due to the flash from the camera.

"He's...skinny," I point out.

"One hundred fifty-five pounds," Victor says. "Five-foot-nine. Twenty-four years old. But don't underestimate him. If he gets you alone and knows you're onto him—"

"I can handle it," I say. "Why is he the target?"

Victor starts to shake his head and I know it is to refuse me the information, but I stop him again. "You're not part of the Order anymore," I say. "You don't have to play by their rules. Just tell me what he's done."

Victor sighs and I watch as his shoulders relax. He gives in and says, "First of all, he's not the target and I've no intention in killing him. We need Costa to *find* the target, Edgar Velazco, a Venezuelan gang leader responsible for the murders of sixteen American, British and Canadian citizens in the last year. They were abducted in Rio de Janeiro and several other major tourist cities in South America. He has a three-million-dollar price tag on his head, but he's nearly impossible to find."

"Would be easy to find," Fredrik chimes in, "if he ever left the slums of Venezuela. Reminds me of Bin Laden when he was hiding out in the mountains with a large group of terrorists and a family of goats for company. People like us, clearly not natives of the country, are too easy to spot."

"Velazco is in some ways like Javier Ruiz was," Victor adds.

I look up from the photo of Andre Costa upon hearing Javier's name. I hadn't realized I was even looking at the photo all that time.

"Sounds like Velazco is a step higher on the criminal scale than Javier ever was," I say.

"Yes, he is," Victor confirms. "Javier's operations were small compared to Velazco. His are spread out over six countries and he's responsible for the murders of one hundred sixty-nine tourists to-date, including women and children."

"And that's just the number recorded," Fredrik says. "There's no telling how high that number really goes."

"So who's the client?" I ask, though I really don't expect either of them to give up that kind of information so easily.

"Anderson Winehardt, a wealthy man out of Boston," Victor says. "His son was one of those murdered tourists."

Still struck by shock that he gave up the name of the client so freely, it takes me a moment to get my questions back in order.

I hop up and sit down on a nearby wooden crate, letting my legs dangle over the side.

"Why did you tell me his name?" I ask.

"If you're in this with us," Victor says, "you're in it all the way."

"Thanks," I say, still unsure about it. I'm wondering if at any moment he's going to say that he was just messing with my head like Fredrik had done earlier.

But then I think of the Order and how old and intricate it is and I find myself with more questions than answers.

"I don't understand," I say. "How can you do hits at all anymore, especially ones like *this*, when you've got the Order looking for you? Wouldn't Vonnegut, hell even *Niklas*, know about a hit on someone bigger than Javier was?"

"It's possible they know about it," Victor says. "But that doesn't point me out as being the one commissioned to carry it out. There are twenty-two private organizations like the Order in the United States alone, in addition to the unknown number of private contractors like me. Neither Vonnegut nor Niklas would ever suspect I'd continue to work like this after leaving the Order and knowing there's a bounty on my head."

"You're hiding in plain sight," I say.

"I suppose you can say that," Victor says.

"But how do you get clients?" I ask. "I mean…didn't Vonnegut take care of all that when you worked for the Order?"

"He did," Victor says with a nod. "But I have been doing this all my life. I know people. I've met clients that not even Vonnegut has ever met face-to-face, the upside to being the one in the field. I have just as many, if not more connections than Vonnegut himself has."

I let out a troubled breath and shake my head. "Well, I think having so many connections, all made through the Order in some way, can be an equally dangerous thing. Aren't you worried someone might tip Vonnegut or Niklas off?"

"I think about that every day," he answers. "It is why I must choose my clients wisely, why I must be very careful, testing anyone and everyone who crosses my path. Sarai, you never know who might betray you until it's too late."

I leave it at that and let them both continue to brief me on the mission.

~~~

It's after ten p.m. and I'm dressed like a slutty, rich socialite, donning a short, thin ivory and pink dress with frilly layers that lay loosely four inches above my knees. Six-inch pink platform heels make me as tall as Victor. My long hair lays freely over both shoulders, moved away from my breasts which are pushed up by a cute pink, lacy bra that shows through the fabric of the dress. After the thirty-minute makeup session, I topped everything off with a few expensive rings and bracelets and two pumps of perfume, one in the hollow of my neck, the other rubbed between my wrists. Fredrik told me that I stink, just before Victor and I left the warehouse to go into the city. I can't say that I disagree with him. I've never liked perfume, but tonight I feel like the situation calls for it.

Victor pulls the car into a small parking lot of a red-brick school across the street from CC's Community Coffee House.

"Corner of Bourbon and St. Philip," he says pointing down the street so that I could get a good look at our surroundings. "I'll be waiting here. Remember, the bar is small, dark and often packed. It might be difficult to spot him, but you don't want to appear as though you're searching for someone and risk—"

"I can pull this off," I interrupt before he goes into another spiel about what I should and shouldn't do and how careful I should be. I lean across the seat and kiss him lightly on the mouth. "Have a little faith in me."

He smiles weakly. For a moment as he gazes into my eyes, I feel the urge to straddle his lap in the driver's seat and kiss him ravenously. But I snap out of it, knowing I have a job to do.

I open the car door and step out into the darkness, shutting it behind me and leaning over into the window.

"I'll be fine," I say and adjust the tiny wire I'm wearing, positioned strategically within the cloth of my bra right between my breasts. "Just promise me," I go on, "that you won't interfere unless I directly ask for your help."

He nods, but I'm not satisfied with that.

"Victor?" I say in a demanding tone.

He puts up both hands. "All right. I promise. I won't interfere."

"I'm not doing this to prove anything to you. I'm doing it because I want to and because I know I can. If I prove something to you along the way, then I guess it's just an added bonus. But that's *not* why I'm doing it." I need him to understand this, to understand that I'm not only doing this to be with him, but because it's truly what I want for my life.

He nods again. "I know."

I leave him in the car and go toward the sidewalk, allowing the dim lights from the surrounding buildings to guide my way down the dark street. Despite the late hour, I'm never alone as there are dozens of people walking past on both sides of the street. I slip through a group of people on the sidewalk in front of the school fanning themselves with cardboard cutouts of a skull, all listening to a guide talk about the building. Finally, I cross the street and head into the tiny, tightly-packed bar on the corner and instantly shed the façade of the girl I used to be.

CHAPTER SIXTEEN

Sarai

The moment I enter the building, I'm consumed by darkness. The space is lit only by candles spread throughout in random places: on tables and set along the walls and on the rock fireplace in the center of the room. The bar is so full that most people are shoulder to shoulder as they make their way to and from, and there's not a single empty seat anywhere as far as I can see. I pass up a full table accompanied by a group of chatty people and make my way through the crowd slowly. I'm overdressed, despite wearing so little. I'm likely one of few girls in the whole place who isn't dressed in more laid back clothes and trying to walk on tall heels through the dark in a place I've clearly never been before. I look exactly like a tourist here for a weekend of partying. Precisely how I intended to look. Andre Costa likes a party. And he likes the girls. But apparently he hones right in on the ones who are new in town and who act like they just rolled out of the Stupid Truck.

I walk straight to the bar and order a Dos Equis, presenting the hot young bartender with my fake I.D. and a glossy-eyed smile.

The bartender looks back and forth between me and the driver's license. "I suppose you're old enough." He smiles at me and places the card back into my fingers. I slip it down into my little black purse.

"How long are you in New Orleans?" he asks as he removes the cap from my beer and sets the bottle down in front of me. He's sexy, with short dark hair, tousled in the front, and dark blue eyes that peer at me amid a rounded baby-face.

I blush and lower my eyes, taking a quick sip.

"Am I that obvious?" I ask, letting my eyelashes sweep my cheeks momentarily.

His smile broadens and I notice his gaze move from my face downward toward my breasts. But he doesn't let his eyes linger so long that it's a turn-off.

Knowing I'm only a tourist was pretty obvious to both of us, so he doesn't bother to answer my question.

I hold out a ten to pay for the drink, but he brushes the gesture away.

"This one's on me," he says. "Enjoy your stay."

"Thanks." I take my drink from the bar just as two girls, probably on their fifth beer of the night, push their way through the room nearly knocking me over in the process.

I just barely hold onto my beer, the liquid sloshing out over the rim as I attempt to steady it.

"Damn, watch it," I say, but neither of the drunks hear me with the place being so noisy.

As I'm turning my back to them and the bar, I start scanning the area again, sipping on my beer and gently moving my hips as I walk as if I'm only enjoying the music and not looking for anyone. I walk around the rock fireplace and toward the back where the area splits off into two directions. There's another bar to my right with a couple more tables and a dead end. Left appears to lead back outside to a patio of sorts. I start to head left when I spot Andre Costa sitting at a table in a dark corner of the dead-end area, flanked by girls on either side of him and two other men, all enjoying drinks and conversation.

Those two girls with him are gorgeous, much prettier than me. At first I'm worried about my ability to draw his attention, but then I remember what Izel, Javier Ruiz's vile sister, taught me a long time ago:

"You're hopeless. A hopeless American puta," Izel said that day, dragging a comb harshly through my knotted hair, pulling it just to hear me whimper. "I don't know why Javier keeps you around. You're like a stupid virgin, except you're a whore."

She pulled on the comb harder, yanking my neck back so forcefully that I cried out in pain. But I didn't say anything. I was afraid of her then, afraid of what she'd do to me for talking back to her. It was bad enough the things she did to me just for hating me, when she and I were alone and I didn't have Javier's protection.

"You have to look good next to my brother," she said. "You have to make the men want to dream of touching you. You have to get their attention over every other girl in the room." She yanked on my hair again. I bit down on my lip as tears streamed down my cheeks. "I don't know why I'm helping you. I should just let you fuck it all up so Javier will get rid of you. Feed you to the dogs."

"Why do you hate me so much?" I finally spoke.

I felt a white-hot sting to the side of my face and heard the thick, cool plastic of the comb slap against my cheekbone.

"Shut up! Stupid puta! I hate you because I can! Now listen to me. When you go in there tonight on my brother's arm, you better do everything I've ever told you. Six months I've suffered having to teach you how to seduce a man! Six fucking months of my life wasted. You better get it right. If you fuck up and Javier punishes me, I'll slit your throat in your sleep and blame it on one of the girls. Comprendes?!"

I nodded nervously.

"Now what did I tell you is key?" She shook my shoulders from behind. "Answer me!"

"Eye contact," I said.

"And what's the right way?"

"The skirting of the eye," I answered more quickly. "Shy and not desperate."

"Sí. You want the men to feel as though you're fresh meat, that you haven't already been passed around to a hundred men. You want to appear coy and inexperienced, not as though you're a seasoned whore looking for a good time. Only old women do that. And how long do you give him your attention?"

"Two seconds," I said.

Izel turned me around to face her, my shoulders gripped tightly beneath her hands, her long red fingernails pinching my skin. "Sí, Sarai. Two seconds and look away. The longer you look, the more desperate you appear. Make him come to you."

As much as I hated Izel, I have to admit that I learned a lot from her. But back then I was being trained to seduce rich men only to make them want me. Javier would never sell me or allow another man to touch me. I was his arm trophy, the girl who represented all of the girls sold under Javier. I was the one the men saw first, the most beautiful and the most enigmatic. I was the poster child, the one used to show off Javier's business. And it worked. The men couldn't have me, but after spending ten minutes in a room with me while I put all of Izel's lessons to use, the men wanted the next best thing. And buying from the same 'batch' of girls that I had been 'bred' from was, in their minds, the only way to get it.

But tonight, with Andre Costa, only half of Izel's teachings will come into play. Costa isn't here looking for a submissive girl to take home and put a collar on. Costa is just a young, horny criminal, so the part of her lessons I'll be using tonight go only as far as the eye contact.

I position my purse underneath my arm and stand against the wall in Costa's line of sight. I let five full minutes pass while I drink my beer and pretend to enjoy the music funneling from a piano before I decide to make eye contact. I know he has looked over at me at least twice in the five minutes I've been standing here. I could feel his eyes on me. But the black-haired girl sitting on his left has done well to keep most of his attention.

One. I smile softly across at him. Two. I look away and take another small sip from my beer. And I wait.

A few minutes later, Andre Costa is standing in front of me and introducing himself.

"I'm Andre. And you are…," he looks around me to my left and right, "…alone, I take it?"

I blush stupidly and take another sip.

"Yeah," I say and let my beer hand drop, hooking my wrist with the other hand below my stomach. "Yeah, I'm alone."

"Is that your name? Alone?"

I figuratively roll my eyes at his attempt to be clever, but I never let the fake smile drop from my face.

"No," I say, almost giggling and drawing my shoulders up near my cheeks. "My name's Izabel."

Andre grins and looks at me in a sidelong glance.

He reaches out his hand. "Well, you should join us, Izabel. There's plenty of room at my table."

My eyes begin to wander nervously. "I-I don't know," I say feigning reluctance. "I don't know you."

"Of course you don't," he says, taking my hand anyway. "But I'm cool. I promise. Come on. You're in NOLA.

Should have a good time while you're here. No one will mess with you."

He pulls me gently along beside him and I follow willingly to the table where I'm greeted by both guys and only one of the girls. The other one, with jet black hair and a scowl on her face, doesn't seem so hospitable.

"Scootch the hell over, man," Andre says to the blond guy at his right. "Let the lady sit down."

The guy gets up and pulls out the chair for me. Andre motions toward it with a big smile plastered on his lightly-tanned boyish face, and I sit down. He sits after me.

"Get us drinks," Andre orders the blond guy, but he looks at me quickly and asks, "What'll you have? Another Dos Equis?"

"Sure, thanks."

The blond guy walks off, disappearing within the crowd.

"Yeah, thanks for asking *me*," the black-haired girl scoffs.

Andre laughs it off. "Baby-girl, you haven't even finished the one you got. Chill the fuck out. It'll be all right." He reaches over and pats her on the knee and even I find it condescending.

I smirk at her privately, letting her know that this one is mine. Instantly, I see the shift in her eyes from territorial to outright rage. She glares across the table at me, while her tipsy friend continues to fondle the tattoo inked around the other guy's wrist sitting next to her. That one couldn't care less that I'm here. The guy she's interested in seems only attuned to her.

"Do you live here?" Andre asks me.

I smile and twirl the ends of my hair around my finger. "No, I'm from Texas. Just here on vacation."

The black-haired girl laughs under her breath and says, "That explains the backwoods accent."

I hadn't even noticed I was speaking with an accent at all, but now that she's pointed it out I don't know whether to be proud of myself for falling so easily into the role, or scared of myself for how easily I'm pulling it off without realizing.

I smirk at her again. "And you must be from the Projects with an obnoxious attitude like that."

"Now, come on, ladies," Andre says, putting his hands out on either side of him as though he were physically breaking up an impending fight.

The blond guy comes back with four beers wedged between his fingers. He sets them down in front of us.

"Well, you're in good hands tonight," Andre says, swigging his beer and then setting it on the table. "And I'd be happy to show you around later if you want."

A burst of air discharges from the black-haired girl's lips. With narrowed eyes, she looks right at Andre. "Wait a minute, I thought we were—"

"Damn, calm down," Andre says, shaking his head. "I meant all of us, Ashley, not just me and her." He glances at me and says, "You don't mind, do you?"

I'm not sure exactly what he's asking but I couldn't care less; the sooner I get rid of this girl, the better.

"No, I'm good. I'd love to come along."

Ashley gets up quickly, pushing her chair against the wall behind her and grabs her purse from the table.

"We need to get home," she says to her light-haired friend. "Let's go."

Well, that was too easy. A part of me wants to continue our internal war. I was having too much fun.

The light-haired girl's upper-body sways a little as she stands from the table and takes Ashley's arm.

"I'm not ready to go back yet," she whines, holding onto the tattooed guy's hand. "Let's hang out for a while."

"No, I'm outta here," Ashley says while dragging her friend away.

"Oh, come on, babe!" Andre says, standing from the table with his hands out, palms-up. "Don't be like that."

"Screw you, Turtle!" She sneers and glances at me briefly. "I'm sick of your shit. You do this every time you come back here. Lose my fucking number."

Andre's mouth falls open, but he hardly looks hurt, trying his damnedest to suppress a smile. He reaches up and runs his hand through the back of his curly, dark hair. I notice a tattoo on the underside of his arm, close to his armpit.

Ashley and her friend argue all the way away from the table, leaving me alone with Andre and his other male associates. Suddenly, I feel exposed, being the only girl at the table.

"I hope that wasn't my fault," I say timidly.

Andre rolls his eyes and sits back down, resting his back against the chair with his legs splayed beneath the table.

"Nah," he says. "She's just that way. I'm just glad she's not my girlfriend." He raises a hand and moves his index finger around his head in a circular motion. "If ya' know what I mean."

I laugh and take another drink from my beer. "Yeah, she does seem a little out there." Really, I think he's a pig. Ashley may have been a bitch, but something tells me she has every right to be. They've obviously known each other for a while and it's apparent he screws her over every time he sees her, in some way, shape or form. The only thing I see she's truly guilty of is putting up with his shit.

"So you're here on vacation," Andre says, leaning over with his elbows on the table now. "Who did you come with?"

I smile timidly and fold both hands around my purse on my lap.

"Seriously," he urges me, leaning in closer. "I'm still trying to figure out why you're out partying by yourself."

I pretend to try hiding the blush in my face. "Well, I came with my friend, Dahlia. But she was feelin' like shit and didn't wanna' go out. She stayed back at the hotel."

"Ah." He nods. "Where are you staying?"

"The Sheraton. Over on Canal," I answer.

He has to think I'm naïve and giving up such personal information so freely, I'm confident it'll help with his assessment of me.

"That's a bit of a walk," he says. "All the way from Canal."

"Nah, it's not too far," I say. "But I admit, I cheated. I walked some of the way and then hitched a ride on one of those bike chariot thingies."

Andre tosses his head back lightly and laughs.

"Bike chariot thingie. That's cute." He points at me and looks at the guy with the tattoo on his wrist. "She's cute."

The guy acknowledges me with a short nod and peers back down into his phone, moving his fingers along the text screen.

"That's David," Andre says about the tattooed guy. "He has an unhealthy relationship with technology. I think his phone gets more sex than he does."

I stifle a small laugh.

"Shut up, Turtle," David says calmly and without looking up.

Andre smiles at me.

He points at the blond guy who brought the beers.

"That's Joseph," he says. "I don't know him well enough yet to embarrass him. But give me a day or two and I'll think of something."

"What kind of name is Turtle?" I laugh.

Andre's face falls just slightly. "It's just a nickname. Dear ol' Dad gave it to me when I was six."

"Oh…."

He smiles. "Don't worry about it. He's still alive and kickin'. Just an asshole."

David, the one with the tattoo, looks up from his cell phone briefly. I get the strangest feeling from it, like he doesn't approve of Andre calling his own father an asshole.

Andre ignores him.

Don't spend too much time chatting him up, I think to myself, knowing that Victor is waiting for me outside not far away. He can hear everything being said—hopefully over the music and chorus of voices—but I can't hear him grumbling about how much time I'm wasting. I'm just pretty sure that's what he's doing.

"Hey, uh, do you want to get out of here for a while and go for a walk?" I ask. It's a risk to show him that I've already put enough trust in him to walk outside alone with him, in such a short time. But I have to move this along and there's no telling how long we'll be in here, hanging out and drinking, before Andre feels confident enough that I'll leave with him, and makes the first move.

He looks slightly surprised, but easily accepts my sudden change of personality. He stands from the table, straightening his black wife-beater tank down over the waist of his jeans.

"Hell yeah," he says, taking up his beer in one hand and holding out the other to me. "Let's go."

He puts the bottle to his lips and drinks down the rest of it in one long gulp, afterwards setting the empty bottle down on the table. As Andre waves the other two guys goodbye, I suddenly feel his free hand rest against my lower back. And before we even make it out the side door and onto the patio, I realize how quickly his personality has changed, too. Like night and day, from fairly respectable gentleman to touchy-feely prick who has it in his head that he's getting laid tonight and I'm the girl who's going to be spreading her legs for him.

"Damn you are smokin' hot," he says and I inwardly cringe. "Are you sure you're not here with a boyfriend. I don't feel like getting my head beat in tonight."

I look over at him on my side, walking so close to me that his hip is pressed against mine, and I turn on the seduction, letting a suggestive smile tug the corners of my lips.

"No boyfriend. I promise."

I feel his fingers grasp my waist as he slides his hand away from my back and pulls me closer.

"Hey," I say as I gently push his hand away, "slow down some. I'm not that kind of girl."

He doesn't take my refusal seriously and just pulls me closer, but I wasn't exactly being serious, either.

"All right, all right," he says with an air of surrender and his big smile still in-tact. "I'll be good."

We start to head in the opposite direction of where Victor is parked at the school and I stop on the sidewalk, looking both ways, pretending to be in some kind of contemplation about which way I would rather go.

"Come on, I'll show you around," Andre says, trying to pull me along with him.

"Let's go this way," I say, pointing in the direction of the school. "I haven't been down that street yet."

"We'll make a loop around." He secures his hand on my lower back again. I hate that he's touching me like that. Or at all. "More stuff going on down this way."

I swallow hard and then give in to him, worried that if I continue to push him about going in the direction that I want to go, he might become suspicious of me.

Giving him my sweetest coy smile, I head with him in the opposite direction.

We walk along the flagstone sidewalk, passing many tourists coming and going in every direction. I hear the sound of hooves trotting against the street out ahead and when we round the corner, a mule-drawn carriage slowly moves by. I look up at the street name just as we're crossing and I say aloud, "Bourbon Street has just about everything." I stop in front of a building. "Maison Bourbon. I've never heard an actual jazz band. Let's check it out."

Andre takes my hand and gently pulls me along and away from the building. "Sorry, but jazz isn't my thing," he says.

It's not mine, either, but I wanted Victor to know where I was.

Minutes later, after two turns down considerably darker streets, the foot traffic is beginning to thin out. I continue to call out the street names or the name of a building, making casual comments about where we are and urging Andre to elaborate as I lay my clueless tourist act on thick. I don't know where he's taking me, but I have a pretty good idea of his intentions.

"Where are we going?" I ask.

"Not much farther." He points ahead. "There's another bar this way. Some friends there I need to meet up with real quick."

OK, there's no time for this...

Even if he's telling the truth, I need to take control of this situation now, while we're alone, before we're right back in a crowded atmosphere which will make it harder for me to lure him where I want him.

I whirl around in front of Andre, stopping us both in the middle of the sidewalk; a broad smile on my lips, coyness in my eyes. "Wait," I say, taking him by the wrist. I look to the side bashfully. "Why don't we...," I glance at the alley behind him, letting this new idea come to me as I go. I step up to him, coiling my fingers around the top of his belt which sits low on his waist. "Why don't we go down there for a few minutes?" I grin suggestively, sliding my index and middle fingers behind his belt.

Andre's eyes widen and his lips lengthen, surprised by my eagerness, but then the smile turns into a horny grin. He fits his hands on my hips and leans toward my neck, inhaling my scent, a low growl rumbling through his chest.

"What did you have in mind?" he asks, kissing the spot just below my earlobe.

I move to the side to make it seem as though I want him to follow, but really it was more to get his mouth away from my body. I smile back at him and say, "You'll see," and then gesture for him to follow me into the alley. I walk a quarter of the way into the darkness, passing up a small row of garbage cans and stop just beyond them. Andre is next to me a second later, his right hand propped against the stone building above my head.

I waste no time and start to undo his belt, fumbling the silver buckle with my clumsy fingers.

Fuck. I hope Victor heard me through the mic, dropping hints of my whereabouts.

"Damn, girl," Andre peers in at me with a feisty grin. "You want to fuck right here in the alley? Never expected that, but hey, I'm not complainin'."

I move away from the rock wall and push him around, shoving his back against it.

"All right, all right," he says with mild laughter, "you're the boss. Do with me what you will."

I push myself toward him, closing six inches of space between us. "That I will," I whisper to him and then jab my knee into his family jewels.

Andre yelps and doubles over. I spear my fingers through his hair and pull, forcing him forward. My knee collides with his face three times before he falls backwards against the wall, disoriented and bleeding from the nose.

"You bitch!" he spits out the words.

My fist soars at his face, hitting him so hard that his head springs back and snaps against the rock wall, knocking him out.

His unconscious body falls against the flagstones, knocking a nearby garbage can against the one next to it. The reverberating noise echoes through the thin alleyway, bouncing off the walls of the buildings on both sides of me.

"Victor!" I hiss into the mic between my breasts. "I hope you can hear me. Andre is out cold, but I don't know for how long. Hurry!" I speak details of my surroundings into the mic.

Three minutes that feel like thirty pass when Victor's car stops at the mouth of the alley, the brakes squealing to a halt on the street. He gets out leaving the door open and rushes toward us in an angry, rapt walk that sends a nervous shiver through my stomach.

"I've got it under control," I say and I look down at Andre next to my feet.

Andre is already beginning to stir awake when Victor grabs him by the backs of his arms and pulls him to his feet.

"You were supposed to lead him to the parking lot," Victor snaps.

Andre begins to struggle as Victor drags him toward the car.

"I said I had it under control," I snap back. "You see I'm not the one that ended up on the ground."

"What the fuck's going on?" Andre calls out, trying to fight his way out of Victor's arms.

Victor shoves him in the backseat, face-down, and plants his knee in his back as he secures his hands behind him with a plastic zip tie.

"Get in," Victor demands.

I do as he says, rushing around to the passenger's side and shutting the door.

"Who the fuck are you?! What's going on? Talk to me!"

Andre's voice is vociferous behind me, filling the small space in the car.

Victor turns around against the seat, leans over it at the stomach and punches Andre so hard he knocks him out cold.

"Thanks," I say as Victor sits back down and puts the car in Drive. "I was about to go deaf."

"I didn't hit him for shouting," Victor says without looking at me.

I glance over at him as he carefully weaves the car down the thin streets lined with tightly packed cars on either side.

"I hit him because he put his hands on you," he says.

I turn my face toward the side window, hiding my smile from him.

CHAPTER SEVENTEEN

Victor

Fredrik is waiting for us at the garage entrance when we return to the warehouse. I drive into the building and shut off the engine as Fredrik is closing the bay door behind us.

I pull Costa's unconscious body out of the backseat and drag his dead weight across the concrete floor with the back of his shirt wound tightly in my fist.

Sarai follows.

"I take it you ran into a problem?" Fredrik says likely detecting the quarrel between Sarai and me, as I help him hoist the body onto the dentist chair. He begins to strap Andre down, starting with his torso.

"No, there wasn't a problem," Sarai says with a trace of anger in her tone, coming up from behind me. "It just didn't play out the way it was planned."

I look right at her. "In and out. It should've been that simple, Sarai. You could've changed his mind and had him follow you toward the school."

She's getting angrier. It's highlighted on her face as she glares at me from the side. But I don't care. She needs to learn how to follow my instructions.

I grab her by the wrist, taking her by surprise, and I pull her harshly toward me. "Do you have any idea what this piece of shit could have done to you?" I wrench her closer, putting pressure on her wrist. Her eyes grow wide at first, but then narrow harshly at me, and tiny wrinkles of bitterness deepen along the bridge of her nose.

"You have no confidence in me at all, Victor," she says icily, pushing the words through her gritted teeth. She tries to jerk her hand away from mine, but I just clamp down tighter.

"It has nothing to do with confidence," I snap. "But everything to do with you following my orders, learning to take instruction. It has everything to do with *discipline*, Sarai." I let go of her wrist as if I were throwing it down. I inhale a deep breath, trying to compose myself. I can't recall the last time I had ever been this angry. "I know that you want to do things on your own. I know that you're capable, but the more you fight me on this—"

"The more like your brother I will become," she cuts in accusingly. "Right?"

Fredrik tightens the last strap around Costa's ankles. "Maybe the two of you should take it into the other room," he suggests, nodding toward a wooden door set in the far wall underneath a tarnished metal sign that reads OFFICE. "I can take it from here."

Sarai and I just stare at each other seemingly with nothing left to say, but then she drops her arms and walks toward the office. I follow immediately, shutting us off inside the decent-sized room. An LED lantern glows on a wooden table situated against the wall. A single metal fold-up chair sits beside it, pulled out as if Fredrik had already been sitting here before we arrived. The room is dusty and smells of water damage and something chemical that I can't place. A single window is set in the wall at the farthest end of the room, covered by dust and a tall metal cabinet that had been pushed against it.

"Why do you keep comparing me to Niklas?" she asks, leaving the anger out of her voice. She appears more hurt now than angry. She crosses her arms loosely, her delicate fingers arched over her biceps.

"Sarai, I...," I sigh and sit down in the chair by the desk, my legs bent at the knees. I throw my head back gently and then look back at her standing in the center of the room.

I start to finish what I was going to say, but she walks toward me and speaks up before I can.

"I'm sorry," she says almost in a whisper. "I'm not trying to resist you, Victor. I don't have some kind of secret plan to do things my own way just to show you that I can. I'm sorry. I was playing it by ear, doing what I felt was right in the moment. That's all."

She stops in arms reach before me. I look up at her, the way her long auburn hair drapes her soft, bare shoulders. Her tall height in those heels. The slim curvature of her little body that I can't seem to get out of my head. She tilts her head to one side. Unable to resist, I reach out and pull her onto my lap, propping her on one leg. I position my left hand on the back of her waist, the other rests on her bare thigh. She looks down at me from the side and then reaches in and brushes the backs of her fingers down the side of my face.

"Victor," she says in a gentle voice, "I'm not Niklas. I never will be. Look what he did to you. I could *never* betray you."

"It's not about that," I say, moving the palm of my hand across her lower back. "I don't mean to compare you and my brother, but the similarities, your recklessness, your temper, your inability to follow my orders—"

"Your *orders*?" she asks, her brows drawing inward. She shakes her head faintly and then turns on my leg to better face me. Her features are soft, the look in her eyes not at all offended, but at the same time I feel like I'm about to be corrected. "We need to get something straight before we go any further."

I cock my head to the side, gazing up into her dark eyes. I've never been so absolutely captivated by a woman before. Not ever. Not in any way like this. I'm used to always getting my way, to being the one in charge. I've never been able to look a woman in the eye and utterly give in to what she wants from me. I couldn't with Samantha, who I know at one time loved me very much. I left her. I couldn't give her what she wanted. But when I look at Sarai, the way she gazes upon me with that soft yet very much unyielding look in her beautiful green eyes, I know that no matter what she says to me next, or how much she defies me, I won't be able to walk away from her.

"I'm not one of your soldiers, Victor. One of your informants, or contacts, or liaisons. Yes, I want you to teach me things. I want to do whatever it takes to stay with you and be a part of your life. But you can't change who I am. And you can't treat me like you would one of your men." She tilts her head to the other side. "I mean sure you *can*, if you want, but I'm not going to change. Do you understand that?"

What in the hell is wrong with me? Instead of turning me off and dropping her from my lap, her defiance only makes me want her more.

I sigh.

"I don't want you to change who you are, but you're going to have to learn to listen to me in these types of situations."

"It was just one guy," she argues. "You know as well as I do that I could take him down. I *did* take him down. He barely weighs more than me."

I shake my head. "No, Sarai, you don't get it. You wouldn't believe how many people, mainly tourists, women, teenagers, that Andre Costa has had a hand in abducting in South America."

"But we're not in South America," she says.

"You don't have to be. People are abducted every single day in the United States and transported overseas, made as slaves, murdered. The list is endless. You of all people should know how easy it is to be forced into a life of slavery and how difficult it is to be set free from it. Most never are."

"But I knew you could hear me on the mic," she says and I sense that she's beginning to lose her confidence in herself. "I was smart enough to tell you every street that I was on."

"I know," I say softly, rubbing my palm across her thigh. "But *what if* I didn't hear the hints you were dropping? *What if* Costa had led you to a car or a building—much like this one—and the men who were with him in the bar were there waiting to restrain you?"

"We can't live by the what if's, Victor."

"We *absolutely* live by the what if's," I come back. "We don't live a life in fear of them, but yes, we must always take them into account."

Her chin drops and her eyes stray from mine.

"You wanted me to help you, to train you," I say, raising her chin again with the edge of my finger. "You said you'd do anything. I'm asking you to trust my lifelong experience and do not defy me anymore."

She nods. "OK, but I don't want you to get pissed at me if I fall off the wagon."

A smile warms my eyes.

I know that I'll never be able to change her, but that's what I like about her. I don't *want* her to change. I just want her to realize that I'm the one that knows what I'm doing. I won't say it to her, but I would never send her on any kind of mission that I knew she couldn't handle. Luring Costa to the car was a simple task. I knew she could pull it off. I knew she could handle Costa if they were alone, or else I never would've sent her there in the first place. Allowing her to do this wasn't my way of seeing if she could pull it off, or letting her 'practice on the easy people', it was my way of seeing how well she could follow orders.

But Sarai has a mind of her own. And as much as it infuriates me that she doesn't listen as much as I'd like her to, at the same time it makes me mad for her.

I feel her lips touch mine. The smell of her skin sends me into a brief high. I suck a breath deep into my lungs and reach up, cupping her face firmly in my hands as she turns around on my lap, straddling me. "You're going to be the death of me," I whisper onto her lips before slipping my tongue into her mouth.

Costa's blood-curdling scream echoes through the warehouse.

Sarai pulls her lips from mine and her body shoots upright on my lap.

"What the hell is he doing to him?"

I fit my hands on the sides of her waist. "You don't want to know."

She nods steadily and climbs off my lap. "Yeah, actually I do."

CHAPTER EIGHTEEN

Sarai

"Mother*fucker*! I don't know anything! *AHHH!*"

Andre's screams fill the space around me when I open the office door. His hands are clenched into fists, restrained against the arms of the chair by two leather straps pulled so tight against his skin that they're turning colors as he struggles against them. Dark blood glistens on his lips, pouring down over his chin and down his throat.

Fredrik holds a pair of bloody pliers in his hand which is covered by a white latex glove.

"You fucking whore," Andre growls at me as I step into the dull gray light. His enraged eyes dart back and forth between the three of us. Victor stands behind me now. "My brother will find you before you leave this city. And he'll fucking *kill* you!"

Fredrik drops something from the end of the pliers into a silver tray on top of the table next to him. It clinks into the bottom. He is so calm, so refined, and I find it eerie as he stands over a bleeding man who is precisely the opposite, how their stark differences can exist in the same room without one canceling the other out.

"Who is your brother?" Fredrik asks in a relaxed manner.

"Go fuck yourself!" Andre spits out the words and a spray of blood spatters from his lips.

Fredrik very calmly grabs a hold of Andre from underneath his chin, his fingers fitted firmly against his cheeks, the white latex quickly becoming red. Andre struggles in his grasp, trying to thrash from side to side but can barely move his head two inches with the leather strap bound tightly around his forehead.

"I won't tell you shit!" Andre screams and gurgles as the blood drains into the back of his throat. "Go ahead! Pull them all out! Nothing an implant can't fix!" he taunts Fredrik, but his struggling body and the way his fingers dig aggressively into his palms tells a much different story.

Fredrik brings the pliers into view and clamps them around one of Andre's front teeth. Andre gurgles and spits some more, which I realize is him trying to speak, but actual words are indecipherable now. He screams through moans and grunts, his eyes open and shut from pain and mental exhaustion.

"Where is Edgar Velazco?" Fredrik asks, holding the pliers still around Andre's tooth.

Andre gurgles something inaudible, but what sounds very much like, "Fuck you!" and the bones in Fredrik's hand harden as he begins to pull. Andre cries out in pain, his fists shaking against his restraints, his whole body stiffening and jerking against the chair. The tooth comes out after a few stomach-turning shifts of the pliers back and forth, the grinding of the bone makes me want to cover my ears until it's over.

I'm disgusted by the act, but indifferent to its purpose.

A second later I hear another *clink* as the second tooth is dropped into the bottom of the tray.

Andre still manages to say, "Fuck you," over and over, but it comes out through tears of anger and undertones of revenge.

"His brother's name is David," I announce, stepping up farther into view. "And I know what he looks like."

Fredrik looks across at me, the bloody pliers still clamped in his hand.

"How do you know this?" Victor says from beside me.

Andre has fallen silent, an unintended testament to the truth of my words. It was just a hunch, after seeing the way David looked at Andre when Andre called his father an asshole back at the bar. I wasn't so sure of myself until now.

"He was with Andre at the bar," I say.

Victor walks past me and moves across the room toward the car. The sound of the car door shutting echoes throughout the space and then he comes back with his briefcase clutched in his hand.

Fredrik lowers the pliers at his side while Andre finally tries to lead us away from the truth, though he knows it's too late for that.

"My brother isn't even *in* New Orleans!" he shouts, now speaking with less control over the formation of his words. It sounds as though he's having a time trying to keep his tongue from slipping through the empty space where his two front teeth once were. "He's not even in this country!" He attempts to laugh, but more blood drains into the back of his throat, causing him to choke instead.

"Oh, but you just said, moments ago," Fredrik begins, "that your brother will find and kill us before we leave this city. How would that be possible if he wasn't here?" I hear the devilish grin in Fredrik's voice, but he does well to keep it hidden from his face.

Andre's bloody lips snap shut.

Victor opens his briefcase on a nearby crate and pulls out a series of photographs. I join him and he hands them to me.

Already knowing what he wants me to do, I begin sifting through them, while he moves over to stand on the opposite of Andre from Fredrik.

He clasps his hands together behind his back and peers down into Andre's tormented face.

"Your brother, David, will be next," Victor says as calmly as Fredrik might. "And everything that happens to you here tonight will also happen to him. Now tell us, where is Edgar Velazco?"

Andre adverts his eyes and glares up at the tall metal ceiling. He refuses to speak.

Victor takes a subtle step back so as to prevent being sprayed by Andre's blood just as Fredrik places the pliers into Andre's mouth again. Andre screams in agony, his voice booming through the wide space.

Clink.

"This is him." I point into a photograph and then hold it up to show them. "He was there. Same tattoo around the wrist. This is definitely him."

A pathetic sob rolls through Andre's body, but I get the feeling it has nothing to do with his brother suffering the same fate. He's clearly in tremendous pain. I also get the feeling that Fredrik is just getting started, that removing every one of Andre's teeth is just the beginning of a very long night of torture.

~~~

Sixteen minutes have passed. I've subconsciously kept track of time, letting the glowing green numbers from the battery-powered clock Fredrik set on the table keep my attention. It has been better than watching Fredrik remove Andre's teeth. But Andre still hasn't broken. Tears and sweat stream down his face, mixing with the blood. His body appears limp restrained in the chair, only able to tense up when Fredrik is inflicting more pain, but the second Fredrik stops, Andre's body just gives up and melts into the leather. His head falls exhaustively to one side, his clenched fists loosen, allowing his fingers to fall away from the palms of his hands.

"W-What is that?" Andre says fearfully through his tattered gums.

Fredrik pulls out a small round plastic case and twists it with his thumb and index finger. A shiny silver needle pops out of one end and he takes it carefully into his fingers, setting the plastic case down on the table.

"Where is Edgar Velazco?" Fredrik asks again, still with no emotion in his voice.

He takes a hold of Andre's left hand, uncurling his fingers forcibly and flattening his hand against the chair arm. Andre's eyes grow wider. He tries desperately to pull his hand away, to curl his fingers back toward his palms, but with the restraints and the weight Fredrik is putting on the tops of his knuckles, his efforts are wasted.

With his free hand, Fredrik brings the needle down to the tip of Andre's pinky finger and holds the sharp point against the skin.

I'm starting to feel lightheaded. I've no clue as to how I could stomach the pulling of Andre's teeth, but the thought of Fredrik pushing needles underneath his fingernails is just too much to bear.

Victor glances over at me, and I realize I'm not hiding my uneasiness as much as I'd like.

"I'll ask you once more," Fredrik says. "Where is Edgar Velazco?"

Andre's body begins to shake, his nostrils flare, and the whites of his eyes are more visible than they were just moments ago. His jaw is clamped, his cheeks moving as if he's biting down on the insides of his mouth, hoping to filter some of the pain to other parts of his body. But he still doesn't answer. I wish that he would. I just want him to give in to save himself. I couldn't care less what happens to him, but I can't stomach the torture. I'd rather Fredrik just put him out of his misery.

A bloodcurdling scream of agony rolls out of Andre's lungs as Fredrik pushes the needle underneath his fingernail. Finally, my hands come up quickly over my ears and I clench my eyes shut tight, arching my back. I feel a hand on my shoulder and I turn, using the opportunity to look in any direction other than at Andre.

"Why don't you go wait in the office," Victor suggests, carefully fitting his hand around my elbow, ready to walk me there.

"He's my father!" I hear Andre scream out. "Don't ask me to sell out my father! Please!"

Victor and I turn around at the same time.

"Take her out of here," Fredrik says to Victor and I've never seen him look so brooding and persistent. Before, he appeared to be enjoying what he was doing, he appeared to enjoy letting me glimpse this dark side of him. But now, he is all business. And he no longer wants an audience.

Having no argument, I follow Victor back into the office. The moment the door closes, Andre's cries begin to fill the warehouse again and I may not be watching anymore, but the visual is still there as vividly as if I was. I can't erase the pictures from my head and with every scream they etch themselves deeper into my memory just like the needles being pushed underneath Andre's fingernails.

In under five minutes, after Andre has endured all that he can endure, I hear him sell his father out. He spills everything. A location in Venezuela so precise that not only does he freely give Fredrik key details of the surrounding area and how to get there, but he gives him an address. He also sells out his brother, David, and provides Fredrik with David's New Orleans locations and all of his contacts.

Thirty minutes pass and I'm still in the office. Fredrik came in here once and spoke with Victor about them checking out the validity of David's locations in New Orleans.

"What now?" I had asked just before Fredrik left the office.

"We wait," he said just before he walked out the door.

"Wait for what?" I asked Victor.

"To make sure our contact calls back with the go-ahead," he said. "We have to be sure Costa was telling the truth about where to find his brother before we proceed."

"Proceed?"

Victor nodded but didn't answer. He didn't have to. I knew what was going to happen next.

Minutes later, everything goes eerily silent. Not even the sound of Andre's whimpers or the squeaking of the leather chair as he'd struggle under the restraints trying to free himself can be heard.

My eyes fall on Victor, a questioning and worried look on my face.

"Are you OK?" he asks in a calm, standard voice.

I nod, but I'm not as OK as I'd like to be. My skin is still crawling and the beds of my nails tingle and ache uncomfortably. "I'm fine." I swallow and start walking toward the door.

Victor reaches out and places his hand on the tarnished silver knob before I have a chance to.

"Perhaps you should wait until Fredrik has cleaned up."

"Cleaned up...what exactly?" I already know what he's referring to, but in a small way I want to hear him say it, but I don't give him the chance.

"I said I'm fine," I repeat softly, assuring him that even when I walk out that door, that no matter what I see, I'll *still* be fine.

And I know I will be.

His hand slides away from the knob and mine replaces it.

As I walk out of the office and approach the dull gray light that bathes the area where Fredrik stands, I see Andre's lifeless body still sitting on the chair. Heavy rivulets of blood drip from the leather seat onto the floor into a dark pool, staining the filthy concrete below. My eyes trail upward from the blood to Andre's hands that are now fully splayed, his dead fingers hanging over the ends of the armrests having no more muscle function to allow them to curl.

The eyes. It's always the eyes...

Andre's are open, appearing to look across the room and right at me, but they are empty. Completely empty. A deep gash sits across the front of his throat, cut from ear to ear.

Fredrik begins to unfasten the restraints as I approach.

"I thought you kill only when you have to," I say, looking only at the body and not at all traumatized by it. The torturing of the living body was what I could not stomach.

Fredrik slides the silver prong out of the last leather strap.

He straightens his back and turns to face me.

"I did have to kill him," he says.

Somewhat perplexed by his limitations, which I thought before meant that he would only kill in self-defense, I just stare at him desperate for the answers. He turns away from me and goes back to 'cleaning up his mess'.

"But he told you what you wanted to know," I point out.

"We could not let Costa live," Victor says as he steps up and stands beside me. "He would have alerted Velazco and his brother. Velazco would relocate before we could get to Venezuela. And his brother, he would leave New Orleans before we had a chance to apprehend him."

"You're going after him, too?" I ask, still confused by how this played out.

Victor nods.

"If Costa and his brother's information match then we'll know that the location we were given is correct," Victor explains. "We'll keep the brother alive long enough to find Velazco and then he will be eliminated with the rest of his family."

He walks over to his briefcase sitting on the crate.

"We go after the brother tonight," he says, flipping the latches and it opens.

Fredrik reaches into a large duffle bag sitting on the floor in the nearest corner, out of the light, and unrolls a black body bag onto the floor, away from any blood spill. He unzips it straight down the center.

"Where is the recorder?" Victor asks Fredrik.

Fredrik reaches into the pocket of his black slacks and tosses the small electronic device the short way across the room. Victor catches it in mid-air. He listens to the horrific screams of Andre Costa and the information that Andre gave before closing the device safely away inside the briefcase.

Victor then pushes his hands down into a pair of white latex gloves and walks over to the body in the chair, positioning his hands underneath the armpits. With Fredrik at the feet, they lift the body from the chair and place it in the body bag on the floor, Fredrik zipping it up afterwards.

"What are you going to do with it?" I ask, overly curious.

I hear the sound of rubber snapping as Victor removes his gloves. Fredrik leaves his on and begins to clean the area, spraying the chair and the table down with some kind of clear solution from a plastic bottle with a long red nozzle. It smells strongly of bleach.

"Someone will be here to retrieve it within the hour," Victor answers. "We should get going."

"But…where are they going to take it?" I ask.

"To the swamps," Fredrik answers evenly as he begins to scrub the blood from the chair with a white shop rag. And then he glances up at me and adds with that small, devilish grin behind his eyes that I'm so used to seeing, "Alligators love turtles."

I roll my eyes and laugh.

Before I make my way back to the car with Victor, I turn and look back at Fredrik.

"Is there anyone you were never able to break?" I ask.

Instantly, the grin disappears from his face and the mood shifts in the room. I regret the question without knowing the answer.

I notice Fredrik's throat move as he swallows. The hardening of his jaw. The darkening of his eyes as if the memory is torturing him worse than the torture he inflicted on Andre Costa minutes ago.

"My wife," he answers.

I suck in a sharp, quiet breath and swallow the lump lodged in my throat. But instead of being sickened by the truth, instead of feeling only revulsion and blame toward him, my heart begins to ache for him instead. I don't know why, but all I can feel is pain.

CHAPTER NINETEEN

Sarai

On the way to a hotel where I'll be staying while Victor and Fredrik find David, Victor tells me about Fredrik.

"My God…Victor, why would he torture his *wife*?" I ask from the passenger's seat. "I just…can't imagine why he—"

"He had no choice," Victor answers. "Years ago, Fredrik was just a contact. He never interrogated or killed anyone. He ran a safe-house in Stockholm. And that's how he met Seraphina."

"She was an operative?"

Victor nods.

"She worked under Vonnegut, just as I did," he goes on, making a turn onto Canal Street. "A couple of years with Seraphina visiting him, they fell in love. But being in the Order, as you know, they couldn't allow anyone to know how strongly they felt for one another. They married in secret—not legally, of course—and then after two years together, Fredrik began to suspect that Seraphina was deceiving Vonnegut."

"But if he loved her why would he tell Vonnegut?" I cut in, assuming that was what he had been about to say next.

"He didn't," Victor says. "Fredrik confronted Seraphina. He wanted first to stop her, to save her from being eliminated by the Order. She admitted to him that she was employed by another organization and working against Vonnegut. When Fredrik couldn't change her mind, instead of turning her in because he loved her so deeply, he fell for her lies and began working *with* her."

My heart falls into the pit of my stomach, knowing where this story is going. The pieces of the puzzle that is Fredrik Gustavsson are finally starting to fall into place.

"She betrayed him," I say, this time knowing I'm right.

"Yes," Victor says. "Seraphina began using Fredrik to relay false information about her missions back to Vonnegut. Then, from what I understand, Seraphina began visiting Fredrik less. Long story short, it took him six months to find out where she had been going. He found her in another safe-house. With another man. You can paint the rest of the picture."

I shake my head absently, trying to understand this hole in my heart that I'm feeling for Fredrik.

We drive to the end of Poydras Street and park near a riverside hotel. Victor turns off the engine and we sit in partial darkness for a moment.

"Blinded by rage and pain for Seraphina's betrayal, Fredrik…," he looks out through the windshield, lost in deep thought of that day, "…It was as if a switch had been flipped inside Fredrik's brain." He glances over at me, washing enough of the memory out of his mind so that he can continue in the same consistent manner as before. "He interrogated and tortured them both. He killed the man in front of her, hoping it would be enough to break her because he didn't want to kill *her*. But she never broke. She was more loyal to her employer than she was to Fredrik, a man whom she claimed to love. She destroyed him. He has not been the same since. It was a very long time ago."

I look down into my lap, still seeing only Fredrik's face in my mind and I shake my head some more, not wanting to believe any of it.

"Is that why he is the way he is?" I look back over at Victor as he pulls his keys from the ignition.

"I think it played a large part in how he turned out," Victor says. "She was his first interrogation and the first—and only—person that he could never break. After that day, after he told Vonnegut about her betrayal and further securing himself within the Order, Fredrik requested to be placed in the field instead of just being a safe-house contact. Vonnegut agreed, and a few years later, Fredrik was officially an interrogator."

"I didn't realize that interrogators had such a morbid list of trades," I say with a hint of disbelief in the form of laughter. "He mentioned he occasionally assists in suicides, too. Kevorkian? That's morbid."

Victor laughs lightly.

"Fredrik is full of morbid surprises," he says and then opens the car door. He gets out, carrying his briefcase in one hand and walks around to my side. "I need you to stay in the room until I get back. Though it will likely be sometime tomorrow before I do."

I get out of the car and he closes the door behind me.

"You're not going to let me lure David?"

"No. He's already seen you, knows that you left with Costa. By now you're probably the one person in this city who he *wants* to find."

Before we make it into the lobby, I stop Victor in front of the tall glass doors.

"What happened to Seraphina?"

Victor looks behind me briefly in thought for a moment.

"I don't know," he answers. "He refused to talk about it, which led me to believe that ultimately, he killed her."

~~~

Victor didn't come back to the hotel until almost noon the following day. I did exactly as he had instructed and I never left the room, not even to get a drink from the machine we passed in the hallway on the way up. I ordered room service and requested it be left on the floor outside the door. I watched television and showered and peered out the window of the fifteenth floor at the bustling city of New Orleans below, all the while wondering what Victor was doing. If he and Fredrik found David and if David was suffering the same fate as his brother.

When Victor returned, he was as clean as he was when he left; not a drop of blood on his suit anywhere. Of course, I knew that didn't mean anything.

He and Fredrik got the information they needed out of David and it happened to match the information that Andre Costa had given. Apparently, David was easier to break. Victor told me that Fredrik didn't even have to resort to the needles. A part of me was glad for that. I just didn't want to think about it.

Fredrik stayed behind with David, and Victor drove me back to Albuquerque.

"I thought we'd already established this, Victor. Why are you leaving me here?"

"Because you're not ready for me to take you with me on missions." He's carefully packing a few items of clothes into a brown suitcase on the foot of the bed. "Certainly not all the way to Venezuela. It becomes much more difficult to stay in hiding when crossing international borders."

I sit down on the side of the bed and then lay across it, letting my legs hang off the sides at the knees. I gaze up at the tall, vaulted ceiling.

"How long will you be gone?"

"Until the job is done," he answers and I hear the latches on the suitcase clicking closed.

"What am I supposed to do while you're gone?"

"Whatever you want. Just stay out of trouble." His crooked smile gives him instant forgiveness.

"Well, can't I stay with Dina in Oklahoma? Or she could come here and stay with me. I'll go stir crazy here by myself."

"You'll be fine," he says. "It's too soon to risk visiting Mrs. Gregory either way. Once Fredrik is free, he will stay with you here in the house."

I raise my back from the bed and hold myself up with my elbows propped against the mattress.

I narrow my eyes at him.

"Fredrik. You're going to leave me with *Fredrik*?" I know that he trusts him, but he doesn't trust him fully.

I don't understand his reasoning.

Victor grins faintly. "Are you afraid he's going to stick needles under your fingernails?"

I blink a few times. Was it that obvious?

"Like I said, you'll be fine." Victor leaves the foot of the bed and comes around to my side where he crouches down in front of me. I raise up the rest of the way and look down at him.

His expression has changed, the grin has gone leaving only a soft look of wonder and concern in his face. The shift in mood makes me eager and uncomfortable.

"Sarai," he says, placing his hands upon my bare knees, "remember everything that I've told you about trust. Just remember *everything* that I've ever told you."

"Why are you saying this?" I cock my head to one side and lines of confusion and worry deepen around my eyes. "I don't like the way that sounds."

He stands up. "Always trust your instincts." He picks up his suitcase from beside me and heads toward the bedroom door.

"Wait," I call out, following him.

He stops and turns to look at me.

"Why are my instincts telling me right now that you're keeping something important from me?"

He sets the suitcase back down and steps up to me, enclosing me within the circle of his arms. His mouth brushes mine, the warmth of his tongue gently parting my lips. He kisses me hungrily, winding his hands within my hair, and as much as I want to bask in the passion of the moment, I can't help but wonder if this is a kiss goodbye.

He pulls away from me reluctantly and touches the bottom of my chin with the side of his index finger.

"Because they're right," he finally answers and I blink back the stun of his confession. "Let's just hope they never let you down."

Without another word, Victor walks out of the house and heads to a commercial airport to catch a plane to Venezuela.

CHAPTER TWENTY

Sarai

Two days have come and gone uneventfully and I'm growing more restless alone inside this big southwestern-style house, the tall yellow-painted walls and terra cotta flooring my only company. I can't stand television much, though after being imprisoned in Mexico for most of my young life with only Spanish soap operas for entertainment, one might think American television would be a welcomed luxury. But I grew quickly out of it very early on after I started my temporary life with Dina in Arizona eight months ago. Rarely do I ever listen to the radio even. But I did start playing the piano more. I'll always love the piano. I kind of wish that Victor had one here for me to play.

I pace the big house in my bare feet, double-checking all of the doors and windows, making sure they're locked. But it's the last time I check as I refuse to become paranoid, not even for Victor's sake and his sometimes peculiar, but always incessant concern for me. But I can't deny that I like that about him.

I think a lot about what he said to me before he left. I want more than anything right now to know the meaning behind his cryptic words. I feel like he's testing me again. That's what my instincts are screaming at me. But what worries me more than anything is that deep down I know this test has a lot to do with Fredrik. I'm beginning to wonder just how far Victor will go to train me.

And I'm beginning to wonder just how much he really trusts me...

Hours into the late afternoon, just when I've decided to give in to suffering through a round of television, I hear a vehicle pulling into the driveway in front of the house, little pieces of loose rock popping underneath the tires. I race to the window to make out who it is.

My heart leaps inside my chest when I watch the lever-style knob on the front door turn halfway as it is being unlocked from the outside. All I can think about is why Victor gave Fredrik a key.

"There you are, doll," Fredrik says as he steps into the room, his dark, tousled hair always styled as though he literally just left the salon.

"What are you doing here?" I ask, pretending not to know and failing to conceal the nervousness in my voice.

I glance quickly toward the sofa where I've hidden a 9mm under a cushion and then near the hallway where a cherry-wood console table hides a .380 in its small drawer. They are among several guns that are placed throughout the house. Every one of them loaded. In this life there's no such thing as a safety lock.

"Victor didn't tell you?" he asks, breaking apart the buttons at the wrists of his dress shirt and rolling up his sleeves to his elbows. "I'm to stay with you until he gets back. You keep it incredibly warm in here." He slides his index finger behind his collar pulling the fabric away from his throat with a look of discomfort.

"Sorry," I say. "I get cold easily."

Fredrik smiles and walks past me and into the living room. I follow him, keeping my eyes on his every move. I feel like I'm not supposed to trust him, but the truth is that I *do* trust him. I'm baffled by my own insecurities.

"You could at least open a few windows," he suggests.

Fredrik walks around the tawny leather sofa and flips the latches on the tall window behind it. A light breeze filters inside, blowing the long, see-through tan curtain covering it. He does the same to the window next to it.

He's dressed in a pair of casual dark-brown slacks and a white button-up shirt where I can see the outline of his chest and arm muscles through the thin fabric. A pair of brown leather loafers dress his bare feet. A gun grip peeks from the back of his pants, held firmly in place by his belt.

Maybe that's what this test is about, if in fact it is a test; more and more I'm unsure of everything, it seems. But it seems out of character for Victor to go out of his way to see if I'll sleep with another man. Though if that's the case, what man better than Fredrik, a gorgeous and darkly intriguing specimen of the male form, to tempt me with? But I'm not a sick and demented girl. I find Fredrik's casual ability to torture and murder not-so-innocent people, rather disgusting and barbaric...OK, so maybe what he did to Andre Costa didn't disgust me as much as it should have. Maybe I should still be traumatized by what I saw considering it's only been a few days. Maybe I should be so uneasy around him right this very minute that I feel like I have rocks in my stomach and my hands should be shaking. But I'm perfectly at ease and...OK, perhaps I *am* a sick and demented girl. Victor must see it. Why else would be choose to tempt me with Fredrik of all people?

"I know what Victor's doing." I warn, crossing my arms and manipulating the inside of my cheek with my teeth. I sit down on the sofa, drawing my bare legs up and onto the cushion that hides the gun. I bend them at the knees and get comfortable, making sure that my short cotton shorts aren't riding up too far and revealing more of my legs than necessary. "Don't even waste your time," I add.

Fredrik tilts his head curiously to one side and walks the rest of the way around the sofa and toward the nearby matching leather chair.

"Waste my time doing what?" He really does appear to have no idea what I'm talking about.

He sits down, propping his right ankle on the top of his left knee, his long arms stretched across the chair arms where the tips of his fingers touch the little golden buttons embedded deeply in the leather.

"I don't care how attractive you are," I say, "there's no way in hell you can seduce me."

Fredrik laughs lightly, shaking his smiling head. A deep breath expels from his lungs as his shoulders relax.

"I didn't come here for that, doll." His smile accentuated by his bright blue eyes framed by almost-black tousled hair. "Victor simply asked that I keep an eye on you."

"But I don't need an eye on me," I say with a soft, yet stubborn tone. "I'm perfectly capable of taking care of myself."

Fredrik never loses his smile, though now it shows more in his eyes than on his mouth.

"Of that I have no doubt," he says, "but just the same, Victor asked that I be here. And I apologize, but his requests come before yours."

I narrow my eyes at him, but I'm hardly offended. I know he's right, but I'm not giving in that easily.

"What is it with you and Victor, anyway?" he asks.

"What do you mean?"

"Oh, come on." He shakes his head, grinning across at me. "You've bewitched him. And very easily, I must say.

You're more dangerous than I could ever be. To Victor, anyway." He flashes a grin.

I feel my eyebrows crinkling in my forehead.

Fredrik laughs softly and gently slaps the palms of his hands down once on the tops of his legs, smoothing them across the fabric of his pants afterwards. He moves them back to the chair arms.

"If you're implying that I'm trying to seduce him with some kind of false intent, then you're wrong." I *am* offended this time and it shows in my voice.

"I wasn't implying that at all." He takes another casual breath and relaxes his back against the seat, slouching a little. "I've known Victor for many years, Sarai, and I can tell you—though I probably shouldn't—that I've never seen him the way he has been since he's met you."

My stomach flutters for a moment. I push it away. I'm not really the stomach-fluttering type. Or, at least I try not to be, as if it might somehow make me weak. But I can't deny, either, that when it comes to Victor I find myself 'pushing it away', often. I swallow and raise my chin.

And then I change the subject.

"Forgive me if this seems blunt—"

"I like blunt," he cuts in and flashes me another smile. "Blunt cuts out all of the bullshit."

I nod.

"Well, do you get off on torturing people?" I ask, as though it's exactly what I think. "Or murdering people, for that matter."

Fredrik reaches over to adjust his thick silver watch around his right wrist. He places his hands back down on the chair arms.

"Coming from someone who can't wait to slit a man's throat," he says, grin still in-tact, "that's a strong accusation. Borderline hypocritical."

"I thought you liked blunt," I point out, referring to his dodging of my question.

He catches on fast.

"If you mean 'get off on it' in a sexual manner, then no, I do not. But yes, in a retributive manner, I *very much* get off on it."

"Retributive?"

"Absolutely," he says. "People like Andre Costa and his brother, David, deserve what they get. And I'm happy to oblige." He laughs gently and adds, "Of course, I'm no saint. And when the time comes that the roles are reversed and I'm the one in the chair, then I can live with that. But no one will *ever* break me…not again."

I can only wonder what that last part meant. And I get the sense that it had been a comment not meant for me.

Flashes of the needles and cruel images of them being pushed underneath Andre's fingernails sear through my mind momentarily. I shudder and my skin crawls. The back of my neck dampens and my hands feel clammy.

Squeamishly, I look over the coffee table at him.

"But the…things you do," I try to shake the image out of my mind. Another shiver rolls up my back. "Why *needles*?"

A faint smile appears at the corners of his mouth, which I recognize right away as an attempt to soften my image of him and not to gloat inwardly about my discomfort of it.

"The method is very effective, as you saw."

"Yeah, but…," I search for the words, "how can you stomach it?"

Fredrik's smile fades, replaced with a blank expression as he stares out beyond me.

"I really don't know," he answers, and I get the feeling that the answer troubles him somehow.

Just as quickly, his smile returns and he's folding his hands over his stomach, and interlacing his long, manicured fingers.

"How long do you think Victor will be gone?" I ask.

Fredrik shakes his head. "Until the job is done."

I knew he'd give me the same answer that Victor gave, but it was worth the shot. What I really want to know is more about Seraphina, but I'm too afraid ask. I feel like Victor told me what he did about Fredrik and Seraphina, in confidence. And I don't want to let Fredrik know about our conversation.

But it's killing me.

I unfold my legs from the sofa and let my feet drop on the floor. I stand up and cross my arms, looking across at Fredrik who watches me with mild curiosity. I pace once down the length of the coffee table and then stop.

"How did you…well, what made you the way you are?" I ask, carefully tiptoeing around the things I already know and hoping he'll tell me himself.

He looks at me from the side, cocking his head thoughtfully.

"What you really want to know," he says, "is how Seraphina made me the way I am. Or, did Victor not get around to telling you about her yet?" He grins, knowing.

For a moment, I can't look him in the eye. I run my hands up and down the softness of my arms a couple of times and then sit down on the edge of the coffee table, directly in front of him. I bury my hands in the loose fabric of the bottom of my gray t-shirt.

"He told you?" I ask.

Fredrik nods. "He asked me if I minded that he tell you. He respects me enough to ask first. It's a very delicate conversation."

"She must've hurt you pretty bad," I say carefully.

"Despite what Victor thinks," he says, raising his back from the chair and draping his loosely-folded hands in-between his knees, "Seraphina was only part of the reason I turned out like I did. A small part. She was, as my shrink appointed by the Order said, the trigger. The spark in a room full of gas. But I was ruined long before I met her." He laughs lightly, but I find no humor in it. Something tells me that he really doesn't, either.

Suddenly, Fredrik gets up and walks toward the opened window behind the couch. I stand up, too, allowing my eyes to follow him to keep him in my sights, but I remain standing by the table. I can't be sure because his back is to me now and I can no longer see his face, but I sense the mood in the room has darkened significantly. He stands with his arms down at his sides, the light breeze from the window brushing through the top of his dark hair.

But he divulges nothing and I'm left only wondering what terrible images are torturing him, what unbearable memory is haunting him in this moment. And all I can do is stand here and let it run its course.

Fredrik

Twenty-five years ago...

The man with the wiry red hair, whose name I was unworthy of knowing, slapped me across the face so hard that a flash of white covered my vision. I fell against the cobblestone slab, my bare legs so bony and malnourished collapsing beneath me. Blood sprang up in my mouth the moment the tip of his boot connected underneath my chin.

"Foolish boy!" he hissed through spit and hate. "You cost me more than you're worth! Insolent boy!"

I cried out and doubled over when the pain seared through my ribs.

"What are you doing?" I heard Olaf say sternly from somewhere behind me.

I couldn't move, other than holding my emaciated arms over my ribs, hoping to guard them from any more blows and trying to stifle the pain. I could hardly breathe. Bile churned in my stomach and I tried so hard to keep from vomiting because I knew, just like before, that it would only make my ribs hurt more intensely.

"You'll never sell him if you damage him," Olaf said.

I hated Olaf as much as I hated all of the men who kept me in this place, but I was always glad when he came. He would stop the other men from beating me. From raping me. Olaf also had his way with me, but he was gentle and never hurt me. I hated him and I wanted him dead, just like the rest of them, but he was my only comfort in the hell that was my life.

The man with the wiry red hair spit on the floor beside me, so close that I felt a trickle on my cheek as it lay pressed against the cool stone.

"Then you deal with it," he barked. "I wash my hands of this one. He is a stupid boy! Not so much defiant as he is stupid. Four months and he has learned nothing!"

I refused to open my eyes. I wanted only to remain on the floor, curled in the fetal position and left alone to die there. I could smell feces and urine and vomit coming from the lavatory down the hall. I could feel the humid breeze from the broken window nearby, filtering against the stones and onto my face. I thought about my mother, though she wasn't truly my mother. She was a horrible beast of a woman who ran the orphanage that took care of me. The orphanage that sold me to these men three months previous, two days after I apparently turned seven. Like Olaf, I hated Mother. The way she would beat me across the buttocks with the switch until I bled. I hated how she sent me to bed without food three, sometimes four nights in a row. But I would give anything to be back in her care than to be with these men.

"Perhaps it is the teacher," Olaf accused in a calm voice. "You are too rough on him. He is more fragile than the others. The runt of the litter, as Eskill calls him."

"He will not eat!" the red-haired man shouted.

I could picture him throwing his hands up in the air around him, his large nostrils flaring with anger, aggravating the scar on the left side of his nose. I could picture the bright red flushing of his cheeks that always looked like a splotchy rash when he'd get angry.

"He cannot hold food down," Olaf said. "Dr. Hammans looked the boy over yesterday before you got back. He said the boy is emotionally stressed."

"Stressed?" The red-haired man cackled loudly.

"Yes," Olaf said, retaining his calm demeanor. "I think it is best that I take over from here on out."

My eyelids broke apart a crack, just enough to see the look on the red-haired man's face hovering over me. He was smiling, but it frightened me. I shut my eyes again quickly when I noticed his looking my way.

"You just said you no longer wanted to deal with the boy," Olaf said. "Is there a problem?"

A few seconds of silence ensued.

"No," the red-haired man said. "Take him with you. Perhaps you can succeed where I have failed."

No more words were spoken between them.

Olaf carried me to his car and laid me down carefully across the backseat.

"I will take care of you," Olaf said softly from the front.

I shook uncontrollably from the pain of my ribs and my head. Tears and snot and blood seeped into my mouth.

"I will be kind to you, boy," Olaf said as the car pulled away from the building, "until you give me no choice."

He drove me to someplace I had never been before. And I remained there in his care, learning to overcome my fear of him and the other men and of the life that I was forced to live. Until I poisoned him in his sleep five years later and escaped.

Sarai

"Fredrik?" I ask, concerned by his long bout of eerie silence.

He turns away from the window and smiles softly.

"Are you all right?" I ask as I walk closer.

He nods and that devilish grin I'll always associate with him spreads over his face.

"Are you worried about me, doll?" he playfully taunts and I feel myself blushing.

I shrug. "Maybe a little. But don't let that head of yours get too inflated."

He smiles and I feel nothing but sincerity and reverence in it.

I head toward the kitchen, stopping just before I make it around the corner and out of his sight.

"Are you hungry?" I call out.

"Can you cook?" he asks in return, still poking fun at me.

"Not like that maid of yours," I admit. "But I make a mean peanut butter and jelly sandwich."

"Sounds good to me," he says and I smile at him before I disappear into the kitchen.

CHAPTER TWENTY-ONE

Sarai

I leave early in the morning, taking the car Victor left in the garage in case I needed it for an emergency. Driving to Santa Fe to Spencer and Jacquelyn's Krav Maga studio isn't exactly an emergency, but it's important to me, nonetheless. And I can't sit around the house like this anymore when I could be training.

I've been sparring with Spencer for thirty minutes. I hate how easy he goes on me, but I guess at the same time I'd regret thinking that way if he decided to hit me with his tree trunk fist.

"Move with your shoulders," Spencer says, moving in a circle with me, both of us bent partway at our waists, our arms out in front of us defensively. "Punch. One. Two. Left. Right." He demonstrates as he speaks, jutting each of his massive fists at the air in front of him.

I do exactly as he instructs, over and over, to perfect my technique. And then I jab at him hard, but he blocks and defends himself easily from all of my attempts.

He comes at me and instinctively I duck and move around him, long wisps of my hair that had fallen from my ponytail get trapped between my lips and stick across the bridge of my nose. Sweat pours from my hairline and down the center of my back, making the thin fabric of my black t-shirt stick grossly to my skin.

Spencer comes at me again and I use something I've already learned, hitting him in center of his throat, a vulnerable spot that instantly takes him off balance. I reach out quickly before he has a chance to redeem himself and grab him around the back of his head, shoving him over forward where I drive my knee into his face, once, twice, three times in fast succession.

He stumbles backward, pressing his hand over his nose. If Spencer didn't want to refrain from really hurting me, he never would've stopped. He would've pushed through the stun and the pain and kept coming after me until I was dead.

"Damn, girl," he says, injecting laughter in his deep voice muffled behind his hand. "I think you broke my nose."

I shake my head at him, disappointed that he stopped, though I learned to accept that he always will, weeks ago.

"Nah, I think it was already crooked," I say in jest.

He laughs again, and removes his hand from his face to point at me warningly, his right eye narrower than his left.

I walk over to the edge of the black mat where my towel is lying on the floor and I use it to wipe the sweat from my face. Pulling my t-shirt rapidly in and out at the collar, I attempt to air myself out, glad that the tight black spandex pants I'm wearing were made to reduce sweating.

Fredrik walks through the tall glass door at the front of the studio. He doesn't look pleased.

He walks across the mat in a pair of dark jeans, a muscle-hugging gray t-shirt and a pair of bright white Converse shoes with red shoestrings. I can't decide what's more imperative: explaining myself to him, or asking him if he woke up this morning and thought he was someone else.

"How'd you find me?" I drop the sweaty towel back on the mat beside my black running shoes.

"Why'd you leave?" he asks in return.

I roll my eyes and shake my head subtly, glancing over at Spencer standing not far away looking between Fredrik and me curiously, his huge arms crossed stiffly over his thick chest. His wife, Jacquelyn, enters the building through the same door Fredrik just walked through.

I turn to Fredrik.

"What are you, twenty?" I ask, scanning his attire.

He looks good in it, I admit, but I doubt I'll ever get used to seeing him in anything other than his suit. I just can't adequately picture him torturing a man to death in a pair of Converse. I shake the odd image out of my mind.

"Answering questions with questions," he points out with slight annoyance. "I found you after calling Victor. He told me you might be here."

"Is he pissed?" I feel my face fall. I hope he's not pissed.

Fredrik shakes his head. "No," he says as though he's disappointed by the truth. "He said you coming here today would be no different than any other day." He looks at me authoritatively. "But you should've at least told me instead of sneaking out. What are *you*? Fifteen?"

I smirk at him.

"Is everything all right?" Spencer asks stepping up, eyeing Fredrik coldly from the side. Jacquelyn disappears inside the office on the other side of the room.

"Yeah, everything's fine," I say. "Spencer, this is Fredrik. Fredrik, Spencer, my trainer."

Spencer's dark brown eyes move in his motionless head to see me and then fall back on Fredrik. "Is this someone Victor knows? He specifically told me not to allow anyone but him in here to see you." He narrows his eyes on Fredrik and looks like he's ready to take him down any second.

Fredrik, on the other hand, is smiling faintly, standing with his hands folded in front of him, his posture refined. Fredrik may not be able to win against Spencer in hand-to-hand combat, but I truly am more worried about Spencer because I know what Fredrik is capable of.

I step into the space between them.

"Victor knows Fredrik," I say. "He just never expected that Fredrik would have to come here."

The two size each other up quietly and then Spencer nods and says to me, "OK, but if you need anything...."

"I know. Thanks." I smile.

Spencer leaves Fredrik and me standing alone. He disappears inside the office with Jacquelyn just a few students enter the building and drop their bags on the floor by the far wall.

"Victor's coming back tonight," Fredrik says, lowering his voice and afterwards looking over his shoulder.

I walk with him farther way from the people getting prepared to train.

"I'm surprised you got through to him," I say. "I tried calling him once last night but I couldn't get through."

Fredrik nods. "No signal where he was for the majority of the time."

I look over my shoulder now. "So then he...finished the job?" I ask in a whisper.

"Yes. Velazco has been taken care of. I'll be dealing with the other son tonight."

"You're going to kill him?" I whisper even lower, constantly looking at my surroundings to make certain no one is in earshot of our very criminal conversation.

Fredrik's eyes widen just a little around the edges to indicate that he'd rather I not say anything else incriminating inside this place. He takes me by the arm, carefully fitting his fingers around my elbow, and walks me toward the front door. Not until we're standing outside on the sidewalk does he feel it's safe enough to speak.

"He deserves to die," Fredrik assures me and I get the feeling he thought I might have a problem with it.

Maybe I do, in a way. Only now am I realizing it.

"Well, what…," I pause and take a deep breath, "…what exactly has David done to deserve to die? What did Andre Costa do? I know that their father, Velazco, has done a lot of bad to a lot of people, but I just…I don't know, I feel like you're punishing them just as brutally as Velazco for the things that only Velazco has done."

Fredrik shakes his head glumly at me. "No. Velazco's sons and the men who work for him are the ones who get their hands dirty. They are the ones who do the kidnapping, who carry out most of the kills, the rapes. Every single one of them deserves what they get."

"But how do you know that Andre Costa and David have directly kidnapped, raped or killed someone?"

"I have my sources," he says. "That's all you need to know."

"I thought I was part of this," I say with slight offense.

"You're not the one killing them." He buries his hands deep in the pockets of his jeans. "If it ever comes down to that, you being expected to kill someone, then you can ask all the questions that you want."

I don't like his answer, but I accept it and leave it alone. I sigh heavily and walk over to stand with my back pressed against the brick wall, crossing my arms over my stomach and propping a foot on the wall behind me to hold my balance.

"Speaking of me killing people," I say. "I feel like Hamburg and Stephens are drifting farther away from me every day. I'm tired of waiting. I want to kill them. I want this done and over with."

Fredrik stands next to me, with his back against the wall, too.

We both look out into the street, watching cars pass through the green light.

"What are you going to do when they're dead?" he asks. "Is that going to be it? You finish them off, get your revenge, and then go about your life?"

"No," I say without looking over at him, my voice distant because my mind is faraway thinking about it all. "No, they won't be the last."

I realize that this is something that I haven't even said to Victor yet. Not because I was keeping it from him, but because I'm only now understanding it myself. Surprised by my own answer, I become lost in the moment, staring at the intersection as the cars blur in and out of focus.

"You're not so different from me. You know that, right?" Fredrik asks.

Finally, my head falls to the right and I look at him. I look at his tall brooding form, his calm demeanor that I know is only a disguise which perfectly hides away the dangerous man who truly lives in there, not so far from the surface. I see a man who although I haven't the slightest clue as to why or how he turned out the way he did, other than what Seraphina did to him, I know that he went through something much worse than she could ever inflict. I feel it. I sense it. And disturbingly enough, I feel like I can somehow relate to it.

"Maybe so," I say and look away. "Though, when it comes to how we…deal with people…you and I are nothing alike."

"Oh, I'm not so sure that's true," he says with a smile in his voice.

Perhaps the fact that I don't argue with him about it right away is proof that he might be right.

Thankfully, Fredrik changes the subject. "Have you had breakfast?" he asks.

"I'm not really hungry."

He leans away from the wall, dropping his hands to his sides and then steps around in front of me. Jerking his head back once he says, "Come on, I'm starving. There's a bakery down the street. I haven't had a decent pastry in a long time."

I start to decline the invitation, but then decide to join him anyway. I poke my head inside the studio, standing halfway outside at the front door and yell across the room to Spencer and Jacquelyn, telling them where I'm going and that I'll be back later. Spencer, with that untrusting look in his eye, argues with me for a second, saying I shouldn't skip out on anymore training. He's right about that, but I know really what he's worried about is me leaving the studio with Fredrik.

Moments later, I hop in Fredrik's car and we're driving toward the bakery a few miles from the studio.

"Fredrik, why do you think Niklas would betray Victor the way he has?"

Fredrik merges onto the freeway.

"I don't know," he says. "Jealous, I suppose. Niklas always did live in Victor's shadow in the Order. For as long as I've known them."

"Yeah but...," I sigh and glance over and then keep my eyes trained out ahead, "...I just don't understand why he'd do that, I mean...," I look right at him now, finally figuring out what I had wanted to say. "Niklas tried to kill me to protect Victor. He *shot* me. I guess I'm just having a hard time understanding what could make him do what he's done after everything he did before to protect his brother. How *any* person can change like that."

We turn right onto Paseo De Peralta and before long I see the big red oval sign on the bakery building out ahead as we get closer.

"I've worked with both of them for many years," Fredrik says watching the traffic. "Niklas was always on the unhinged side. He would do anything for his brother, but I just felt like he was a disaster waiting to happen." He glances over at me, and our eyes meet for a brief moment. "Honestly, I think you had a lot to do with why Niklas betrayed Victor."

I swallow hard and look down into my lap momentarily, coiling my nervous fingers around one another. I have often wondered about this, a part of me almost convinced that this was all my fault, but not only did I not want to believe it, I also felt stupid thinking that I could cause such a rift between two people. I'm not that important of a person. I don't have that much power, not even over Victor.

Surely not...

"Why do you think that?" I ask, hoping that whatever answer he gives me, isn't believable. Ridiculous, even.

"Because in a sense, Victor chose you over his brother."

All of my hopes and dreams of the moment come crashing down around me. His answer isn't ridiculous at all, it makes perfect sense. And I hate myself for it.

"Victor decided to leave the Order after he met you," Fredrik begins. "He may have had his qualms with Vonnegut before, but ultimately you were the turning of the key. And even before Victor went rogue, he was risking his position in the Order, and his life, by helping you. Niklas was trying to keep Victor from destroying himself. Killing you, he thought, was the only way to do that because reasoning with Victor regarding you didn't work. Victor even lied to Niklas about you." He looks over at me again. "In Niklas' eyes, Victor chose, *replaced*, him with you."

We come upon the parking lot of the bakery but instead of pulling in, I catch Fredrik staring toward the rearview mirror, his eyes focused on it and the road out ahead at the same time.

Getting the distinct feeling that he's looking at something behind us, I start to turn around.

"Don't," he says quickly. Everything in that word shakes me to my bitter core. But his expression, his demeanor and the way he continues to casually steer with both hands on the bottom of the wheel, is as if nothing is wrong.

"What is it?" I ask, unable to mask the concern in my voice as he could.

"We're being followed."

My chest hardens and I stop breathing for a moment. I want so desperately to look behind us, but I opt for peering through my side mirror instead, and making no obvious movements. There's a black SUV, looks like a Navigator, tailing us.

CHAPTER TWENTY-TWO

Sarai

My hands clench stiffly onto the corners of the red leather seats beneath me. I don't take my eyes off the side mirror, or my mind off the possibility that it could be who I think it is and what I know is about to happen. I can't see the passenger or the driver through the Navigator's tinted windows.

"Are you sure?" I ask.

Fredrik turns his blinker on and we turn left at the next street. He maintains the speed limit and doesn't appear to let those in the vehicle know that he's on to them. I just hope he's wrong.

"They've been following us since we pulled out of the studio," he says and my heart sinks. "They were watching us, parked in the lot across the street."

"So, they're why you decided to get breakfast," I assume.

Fredrik nods and turns right at the next stop light.

I'm kicking myself, feeling so goddamned small and inexperienced that I wasn't smart enough to notice these things. I wasn't observant enough of my surroundings to know that we were being watched the whole time. But this isn't the time or place to be frustrated with myself. I just hope there's time for that later.

"What are we going to do?" I ask nervously.

Fredrik presses on the gas pedal and suddenly we're doing fifty in a thirty-five, and heading straight for the on-ramp to the freeway. The Navigator is close behind, staying on our tail. I grab my seatbelt strap and pull it tighter and then I grip onto the seats again.

"We're going to lose them," Fredrik answers as we go from fifty to seventy in a couple short seconds as we get onto the freeway.

I'm holding on for dear life, my heart in my throat, as the car weaves recklessly in and out of traffic, cutting people off and even going around vehicles by way of the shoulder. But the Navigator stays right on us, weaving its way through the same path that we take. Horns honk noisily, angrily at us as we speed by.

"HOLD ON!" Fredrik shouts.

In that second, my shoulder is crushed against the side window as Fredrik makes a sharp turn from the center lane into the right, just mere inches from the front bumper of a little white car. I hear the squealing of the tires, ours and the white car's, and then I'm shoved to the other side of my seat when he abruptly steadies the vehicle.

I turn awkwardly at the waist in the front seat, the seatbelt still wrapped around my body, holding me in place, to see the Navigator coming at us from behind a blue car. The car swerves left, trying to get out of the way and clips the front of the white car we just passed. Both cars spin violently in the middle of the freeway, the white one squealing to a stop in the far left lane, narrowly missing the concrete wall barrier separating this freeway from the other side. Smoke billows from underneath the tires. The blue car rolls over onto its side, crashing. I gasp, my hand comes up over my mouth.

The freeway from the wreck backward comes to a halt, everyone except for us and the Navigator following closely behind. Out ahead, people aware of what's going on, already parting the way for us. We rocket past at ninety miles per hour, forcing a line of cars to pull over on the side of the freeway.

The farther we get from the wreck, the more numerous the cars ahead of us thicken and we're right back in the same situation as moments ago, weaving in and out, horns honking, my body hitting the door and the window with every other sharp turn.

Fredrik moves quickly over into the far left lane, the fast lane.

"We need to get off the freeway!"

"We have to lose them first!"

"How the hell are we going to do that?" I look back again. They are still behind us, their front bumper just feet from ours.

Fredrik doesn't answer. He's watching everything, keeping his eyes on the road in front, the vehicles on all sides of us, the Navigator in the back. After a few moments of this, I'm beginning to feel like he's putting together a plan in his head.

Suddenly, at the very last second, Fredrik races from the fast lane, across three lanes of traffic, and hits the exit at ninety, mere inches from the concrete wall and orange barrels separating the exit from the freeway. There wasn't enough time for the Navigator to figure out what Fredrik was doing and to make the exit with us. My head hits the side window. There's a stop light at the end of the road, but Fredrik is going too fast to stop and he zips right through it. Thankfully it appears to be a less-traveled road and no vehicles are there to meet us.

"What the hell was that?!" I scream at him from the side, my hand pressed against my chest, trying to steady my heartbeat.

He doesn't answer until we're far away from the exit and driving down a series of streets. Both of us keep looking around in all directions searching for the Navigator.

"If I had stayed in the right lane," he says, "he would've expected me to get off at any exit."

As much as it scared the shit out of me, I can't deny that his crazy plan worked.

"You could've killed us!"

"You act like that's something new to you," he says.

I laugh out loud.

Fredrik gets back on the freeway going in the opposite direction, back toward the Krav Maga studio. But before we get anywhere near the studio, he turns down an unfamiliar street and bypasses it altogether.

"Where are we going?"

"Back to Albuquerque," he answers. "The long way around. Just in case."

~~~

Six hours of vigilantly watching through the windows of the house and Victor finally pulls into the driveway. Fredrik and I are both on our feet the second we hear the tiny rocks popping and grinding underneath the tires.

Victor drops his keys on the kitchen counter first and comes into the living room, setting his briefcase on the coffee table.

"Any sign of them?" he asks Fredrik right then.

He looks at me now and I can't read his expression, which, I have learned, is usually because he's got too much on his mind and he's trying to stay focused.

Before Fredrik has a chance to answer, Victor asks me, "Are you all right? Are you hurt?"

"No, I'm not hurt." I look off toward the wall when I hear Fredrik speak up.

"I wasn't followed here," Fredrik says. "I made sure of that. Went an hour out of the way just to be sure. And there has been no sign of anyone here, just a few vehicles on the highway, but nothing suspicious."

Victor comes around the coffee table and sits on it, the same way that I often do, and he looks down into my eyes as I sit on the center cushion looking back at him. He appears concerned. And angry. Not at me, though, but I think at whoever was in that Navigator.

"Before you say anything—"

"Like I told Fredrik," he cuts in calmly, dropping his hands between his thighs, his elbows resting on the tops of his legs, "I didn't expect you to stay here, cooped up in this house the whole time I was gone. Don't apologize for leaving."

Surprised by his tolerance, I'm rendered quiet for a moment.

"I wouldn't have gone anywhere else," I finally say, still feeling like I screwed up again. "I figured since I've been staying here all this time and training with Spencer, that it wouldn't make any difference whether I chose to go today or to wait until you got back."

"And you're right," Victor says. He reaches out and places his hands on my knees. "This isn't about you leaving." He looks over at Fredrik as Fredrik takes the empty seat. "We have to figure out how they knew where to find you."

I see something in Victor's face that Fredrik can't see, something that puts me on edge. Victor has the look of a man who is suspicious of someone, who is suspicious of Fredrik. I look back and forth between the two of them, trying to understand Victor's mindset. Is this Samantha back in Texas all over again? Did Victor put too much of what little trust he possesses in the wrong person again? Was this the test all along, by leaving Fredrik with me, alone?

My hands collapse into fists beside my thighs on the couch, my fingernails jab into the skin of my palms. Did Victor use me to test Fredrik's loyalty?

"I've already been thinking about that," Fredrik speaks up. "And I hope I'm wrong, but I have a feeling I know how they found her."

It was something Fredrik and I already discussed before Victor got here. But now…now that I see the suspicion in Victor's eyes, I can't help but wonder if all this time while we waited for him to return, if Fredrik was only filling my head full of lies to deter us from the possibility that it was him.

I don't trust either one of them now. I feel like a captive all over again, stuck between dangerous men who I know I can't get away from.

And my heart hurts.

Victor's hands slide away from my knees and he gives Fredrik his attention. I remain calm and motionless, doing what I do best: faking it.

"I think we should get to Phoenix as soon as possible," Fredrik goes on. "I tried calling Amelia, figuring maybe she knew something, but she hasn't answered or returned any of my calls. It's not like her."

Victor moves from the coffee table and sits next to me, leaning forward to open his briefcase. He removes his laptop and slides his fingerprint across a sensor to unlock it.

"What are you doing?" I ask.

"Checking my feeds at Amelia's house," he says, opening something on the desktop. "I haven't bothered since we got Mrs. Gregory out of there."

Several minutes of sifting through various videos—one clearly in question as men enter Amelia's house and apprehend her—he shakes his head and closes the laptop.

"What is it?" Fredrik asks.

Victor packs the laptop back inside the briefcase. "They were there. The feed went dead shortly after. They must've found one of the devices I planted the night I took Sarai to see Mrs. Gregory."

I'm panicked by thought of what Stephens might've done to Amelia, or more-so what she might've told them.

"Fredrik's right," I say. "We should get to Phoenix."

"Then let's go." He reaches out for my hand.

Reluctantly, I take it and go to my feet with him. What I really want to do is slap him across the face.

"Victor?" I say just as he turns his back, intent on going toward the door.

He stops and turns back to look at me.

"This wouldn't be happening at all if Hamburg and Stephens were already dead."

Phoenix, Arizona – 1:00 a.m.

We fly to Phoenix on a commercial plane and take a cab to Amelia's house. A six-hour drive apparently wasn't going to cut it as Victor wants answers now and not a moment later. I fear that Amelia's dead, and that's why she isn't answering any of Fredrik's calls. I think Fredrik has the same idea. Back at the house in Albuquerque, each time he'd call her and she wouldn't answer, he became more frustrated. Worried, even. I found that strange coming from someone like Fredrik, who I get the feeling uses women for sex and does not have the ability to care about any of them. But now, I can't help but believe it was all for show, that he only pretended to worry about Amelia when in truth, he probably had her killed himself.

In any case, I'm just glad that we got Dina out of her house when we did.

The cab drops us off a block away from Amelia's house and we walk the rest of the way under the shroud of darkness. Her porch light is on illuminating the dirty white siding on the little house and the broken concrete steps leading up to the front door. Another small light glows from the den window where shadows move in a confined pattern giving the impression that the light is coming from a television. When we ascend the concrete steps and stand in front of the door, Victor reaches up and twists the hot bulb above the door frame, snuffing out the light.

Fredrik moves over to the window and peers inside.

Victor stands in front of me and tries to push me behind him protectively, covertly, but I shove his hand away. He turns at an angle and looks down into my angry face. I grind my jaw and shake my head, letting him know that I'm infuriated and that he better not touch me.

He looks away, keeping his attention on Fredrik.

"I don't see her," Fredrik whispers. "No sign of a struggle."

Victor pulls his 9MM from the back of his pants, places his hand on the door knob and tries to turn it. It's locked. I get nervous when Fredrik pulls his gun, too. Victor stands back and motions for Fredrik to get in front of him, making it appear that he wants Fredrik to be the one to knock on the door when I think it's more to keep Fredrik in his sights.

Fredrik knocks three times and we wait. Victor doesn't look at me anymore, but I wouldn't expect him to in a time like this. I find myself more interested in Fredrik's movements as well, waiting for him to turn on us any minute now.

There's movement inside. The curtain on the window near the door shifts and then the sound of a body pushing against the door itself as whoever is inside peers through the peephole. Victor forces me behind him this time and I don't argue, worried more about who's on the other side of that door than my bitterness towards Victor.

I hear the chain sliding away and then the clicking of a deadbolt, lastly the sound of the knob turning carefully. When the door breaks apart from the frame, it does so only inches and a pretty face peeps through the crack with long blonde hair disheveled around her puffy eyes.

"Fredrik?" Amelia says in a low, harsh voice. "You shouldn't *be* here." I see her eyes darting around nervously, looking beyond us toward the street.

Victor steps up beside Fredrik and pushes the door open with the palm of his hand. The smell of cinnamon potpourri and burnt coffee rises up into my nostrils. Amelia steps back quickly, burying her hands underneath her tightly crossed arms covered by a blue bath robe that stops just above her bare ankles. The left side of her face is heavily bruised and there is blood in the white of her eye. Her lip looks as though it has been slowly healing from being busted.

Victor pulls me inside the house with him and Fredrik follows, shutting and locking the door afterwards. And before anyone speaks, Victor and Fredrik rush through every room in the house, guns in their hands, making sure that no one is hiding in wait.

They come back into the den at the same time, sliding their guns back behind their pants.

"What happened to you?" Fredrik asks Amelia. "Why haven't you been answering your phone?"

She's shaking, her arms trembling inside her robe.

Victor looks at everything but her. He begins searching the room, while I know at the same time hanging onto every one of her words.

"I didn't answer because I knew it was you," she says to Fredrik. "And you didn't leave any voicemails. You never leave voicemails. They tapped my phone, Fredrik. I couldn't risk answering."

Fredrik takes Amelia carefully by the elbow and walks with her into the den area. He sits down next to her on the sofa.

"Tell me what happened," he persists.

I sit down on the edge of the recliner in the corner, my back arched, my hands folded together draped between my knees.

Amelia looks over at Victor as he's running his fingers along a bookshelf, searching for something.

"They found all of that stuff," she says to him. "When they came in here, three men ransacked my goddamn house, turned it upside-down, looking for whatever those devices were you hid everywhere."

He goes back to searching the house, though staying in sight of us. In sight of me.

Amelia turns back to Fredrik. She sits with her hands pressed together between her knees, her right leg constantly moving, her foot bouncing nervously against the rust-colored carpet.

"They came here three days after you left," she goes on. "Tied me to a kitchen chair. They beat me. They threatened me with my family—"

"What did you tell them?" Victor cuts in, standing in front of her now.

"I didn't have anything *to* tell," she says, fear rising up in her shaky voice. "They wanted to know where *she* was." She glances over at me. I notice how yellow the skin around her eye is now that we're in the room with the light from the television. "But I didn't know. I couldn't tell them what I didn't know. Shit! They wanted to know where Dina was, too. I didn't know that, either. They didn't believe me so they beat me some more!" She takes a deep breath and tries to compose herself, maybe to keep from crying. She looks as though she could burst into tears at any moment.

"But you had to have told them something," Fredrik says from beside her. His voice is urgent but not at all accusing. "*Think*, Amelia."

Amelia looks down at her shaking hands and then brings them both up and pushes her messy blonde hair back away from her face.

"I-I couldn't take it anymore," she says shamefully, unable to look Fredrik in the eyes. She stares down at the carpet. "I thought they were going to kill me, to beat me to death. I-I only told them that Dina had called her Sarai and she talked to me about her sometimes." She looks up at Fredrik now, worry all over her face, straining the corners of her reddened eyes. "But it wasn't anything I thought they could actually use."

"What did you tell them?" Victor asks sternly.

She looks up at him. "T-They asked about recent information, anything that Dina said to me about Sarai, or Izabel, or whatever her name is. They wanted something current. I thought really hard about the conversations that Dina and I had about her and the one that came to mind was when you guys were here. She talked about training. Maga or something like that."

My eyelashes sweep my face and I shake my head solemnly. I remember telling Dina that I was learning Krav Maga.

I shoot up from the recliner.

"I can't fucking do this!" I yell. "Victor, I'm sorry. I-I just screw everything up. You were right. This isn't the life for me. I wanted it to be so badly, but I can't do this. I'm going to get everybody killed!" I've momentarily forgotten that he apparently used me to test Fredrik's loyalty. Maybe not forgotten, but I've pushed it aside for now because my idiot actions are more unforgivable that what Victor has done.

Victor takes my hand and guides me to sit back down.

"Did you tell Dina Gregory where you were training?" Victor asks in a calm voice.

"No," I say, looking up at him. "I was careful not to give away detailed information. I didn't even tell her where I was living. The three of us were just talking in the kitchen. Dina wanted to know what I had been doing. It was just casual conversation."

Fredrik looks at Victor.

"Stephens has probably had men scoping out every Krav Maga studio from here to Florida since that day. It would explain why it took them nearly three weeks to find which one she was training in."

"Wait—," Amelia speaks up as if a horrible thought just came to mind. "Is Dina all right? Please tell me she's OK. I wanted my house back, but I really liked that woman. She was kind to me."

"Dina Gregory is fine," Victor answers and Amelia and I are both relieved.

Amelia lets out a thankful breath, but then just as quickly her body locks up again and she's looking at Fredrik with desperate eyes, craning her neck toward him. "B-But you can't stay here. You have to leave." She looks at us. "All of you."

"That was my next question," Victor says. "Why didn't they kill you?"

"They expected you to come back," she says. "Or to at least contact me by phone." Her eyes dart to Fredrik again. "I couldn't answer."

Fredrik nods, accepting her explanation and her apology, letting her know that he understands.

She looks back to Victor.

"After a while, I pretended to hate all of you," she goes on. "I complained about how I was pissed that Fredrik would dump that old bat on me like that. Then I talked shit about you," she adds, looking back at Fredrik. "By the time I was done filling their heads full of bullshit, they thought I could be used to find you, to lure you here. I was just a woman scorned, who wanted to get back at Fredrik. That's what I was shooting for, to gain their trust so they wouldn't kill me. I was *afraid*, Fredrik. I think they would've killed me if I didn't think to do that."

Fredrik nods again. I feel like he's about to place his hand on her knee to comfort her, but he can't bring himself to do it, that the gesture makes him feel awkward. Instead, he offers her more assurance by way of words.

"You did the right thing," he says kindly. "And you're right, they would've killed you."

He stands up and turns to Victor.

"The only unanswered question left," Fredrik says, "is how did they know to look *here*." He puts up both hands in a surrendering fashion. "I swear to you that it wasn't me."

My body stiffens. My eyes dart back and forth between them, trying to gauge their expressions. The tension in the room deepens, nearly drowning me in it, but I soon realize that the tension belongs only to me as I subconsciously prepare for some kind of showdown between them. But the more I watch, the more I feel that Fredrik is telling the truth and that Victor believes him.

"I know it wasn't you," Victor finally says.

I'm stunned. And confused. And a little stung by Victor's immediate trust.

"How the hell do you know that?" I ask sharply.

"Because if Fredrik was going to give you up, it wouldn't make sense that he tell them where Dina Gregory *once* was. Weeks ago."

I snarl and cross my arms.

"You used me to test Fredrik," I snap. "You left me alone with him to see if he'd betray you by telling Stephens where to find me." I glare at him accusingly, unforgivingly. This isn't the time or place to confront him about this, but I can't hold it back any longer.

Victor steps up closer and reaches out both hands, intent on placing them on my arms. I start to step away and refuse him, but the recliner blocks my path. His warm hands fall upon my skin, his long fingers curling around my biceps. He peers down into my eyes and I see sincerity and determination in them.

"That is not what I did," he insists. "You have to trust me on this. And you have to trust Fredrik. He's not the enemy."

"So easy to judge and trust," I say with an edge in my tone. "Then why did you leave me alone with him like that? What did you mean by the things you said about trusting my instincts before you left?"

Victor's hands fall away from mine.

"We have to get out of here," he says.

He turns to Fredrik now and I'm left feeling both livid by his lack of explanation and apprehensive about the current situation because of the urgency in his voice.

"Fredrik," Victor goes on, "it's your decision. Take her to a safe-house or leave her here to her fate."

Amelia's swollen, reddened eyes widen with alert and dread. She jumps up from the sofa, her blue bath robe coming undone around her waist, revealing a white nightgown underneath.

"What's that supposed to mean?" she asks fearfully, fumbling the tie around her waist to tighten the robe closed again. She looks right at Fredrik. "What does he mean, Fredrik?"

CHAPTER TWENTY-THREE

Victor

Sarai blames herself for a lot of things, and in some cases, she is right to do so. It was foolish to speak of her training with Spencer—although vaguely—with Dina and Amelia. But she was careful with the information that she chose to divulge. She was careful, but not careful enough. Sarai is young. Inexperienced. Yet, she is learning, and learning the hard way, when it comes down to it, is really the *only* way.

"You can't learn to swim by reading it in a book," I tell her on the drive back to Albuquerque. I thought it best we take a car back this time rather than risking the airports again so soon. "It is the best way, Sarai. To learn from your mistakes is to *make* them. Authentically. No amount of training, no rehearsed scenario is going to teach you better than the real thing."

Sarai sits quietly on the passenger's side staring out the side window. She won't look at me. She has hardly spoken since we pulled away from my liaison's location near Phoenix thirty minutes ago. The moon hangs low in the early morning sky, appearing enormous across the dark expanse of the desert landscape.

"It's no excuse," she finally speaks up, although distantly.

"It *is* an excuse," I correct her. "This isn't Hollywood, Sarai. You're not going to learn the things you want to learn in the time you wish you could. You've made mistakes. You'll make plenty more—"

She snaps around to face me.

"I *said* it's no excuse," she pushes the words through her teeth, her eyes are wide and unforgiving. Unforgiving of herself rather than me. "I'm the one that got myself into this," she says. "I chose this life. I told you it's what I wanted. I begged you to help me." She points her index finger harshly at herself, pauses and grits her teeth. "I *chose* this life. I'm not a child, Victor. You can't sit me down and tell me that what I did was OK, that I have a right to make mistakes. Because in this life mistakes get you killed."

I admire her more now than I did moments ago. Because she understands it. She refuses to take the easy way out by accepting the get-out-of-jail-free card that I offered her. She refuses to be allowed mistakes and though I know she will still make them because she is human, she will learn faster from them than someone who chooses to accept the excuses. Sarai is a defiant girl. She is hard and reckless and fearless to a fault. But she is determined and she is strong. Despite her problem with discipline, and how she still hasn't fully tapped into that criminal, killer mindset in which is key in helping to keep her alive, I know that she can succeed in this life.

"Do you regret it?" I ask. "Do you regret the life you chose?"

"No," she says flatly, honestly, her eyes trained out ahead watching as the black asphalt on the highway is swallowed up by the hood of the sedan. "I don't regret it. And I don't want out."

She raises her back from the seat and faces me again.

"I want to kill Hamburg and Stephens," she says with determination, "and then after that…," she pauses, but never moves her hardened eyes from mine. I only glance away long enough to check the road. "I have to tell you. It's something that I told Fredrik. After Hamburg and Stephens are dead, I don't want them to be the last."

I felt all along, from the moment she told me she wanted to kill them herself, that they would only be the first in a long line of future assassinations. I could see it in her eyes, the lust for revenge, the hunger for bloodshed. The death of Javier Ruiz by her hands is what sealed Sarai's fate. The first kill is always the trigger, the instant in one's life when everything changes, when a person's character takes on a new, darker form. I know she thought about killing Hamburg every single day from the night she met him. I know because I remember the face of *my* second kill, the way I hunted him for a week like a serial killer might hunt his next victim. All I saw was his face. All I wanted was to end his miserable life the way I ended the life of my first mark. Because it was what I was bred and trained to do. I longed to feel the praise that Vonnegut bestowed upon me after my first successful mission at the age of thirteen. To see him smile proudly as I had always wanted to see my father do. I longed to taste the admiration that the other boys in the Order had for me. So, from my first kill onward, I devoted my life to my job, giving up my resentment for being forced away from my mother. I killed to please Vonnegut for the majority of my life, until I began to see that Vonnegut took more from me than he ever gave.

Now, I kill because it's all that I know.

Sarai and I kill for different reasons, we are driven by very different needs, but in the end we are both killers and I know that will never change. We can't come back from that, and most who kill more than once, don't want to.

I look back out at the road.

"Does that bother you?" she asks about the truth she just revealed. "That I don't want them to be my last?"

"No," I say softly. "It doesn't bother me."

I sense her look away and silence fills the car, only the sound of the tires moving briskly over the highway filtering through the confined space.

"What's going to happen to Amelia?" she asks.

"Fredrik will either take her to a safe-house, or he'll kill her."

I expected her head to snap around again upon hearing that, but she doesn't even flinch. She nods, accepting it as casually as I would.

Already she is becoming harder. Already she is adamant about not letting her mistakes define her, betraying the only things she has left, to make certain that she doesn't make them again.

Her humanity.

Her conscience.

~~~

It's late afternoon when we make it home. I thought Sarai might sleep most of the way, but she didn't sleep at all. She's been awake for more than twenty-four hours and yet she is entirely conscious and shows no signs of lethargy. It's the adrenaline. I'm all too familiar with its effects on the mind. But right now, I'm so exhausted by the drive that if I don't get some sleep soon, I'll be useless.

I check the house thoroughly before I feel it's safe enough to relax, even though I checked the surveillance on my laptop before we arrived. I've no reason to believe Stephens and his men know the location of this house, but as always, I cannot let my guard down. It's still a mystery as to how Stephens found out about Amelia McKinney and Dina Gregory. No matter what it looks like, I know Fredrik had nothing to do with it. But as much as the breach concerns me, it's not important right now. Right now, I know I'm going to have to drop everything, my plans for training Sarai while hoping that I could drag this out for months or even years so that maybe she will change her mind. Or, until she decided to let me kill them for her. I know now that nothing will change her mind and no matter how hard I try to convince her, she'll never agree to let me do it.

Perhaps I should kill them anyway—

"Victor?"

I snap out of my deep contemplation.

She's standing at the sliding glass door looking out into the endless expanse of dehydrated landscape. The sun is setting on the horizon, illuminating the thick bands of ribbon-like clouds with a deep pinkish glow.

"There's something I need to say to you," she adds.

I walk toward her slowly, curious and impatient and even troubled by what she's about to say.

"What is it?" I ask, stepping up closer.

She doesn't turn around to look at me, but remains gazing through the tall, spotless glass. Her arms are crossed, her fingers resting atop her biceps.

"I've made a decision," she begins in a soft, apologetic voice. My insides are beginning to harden. "I just hope you'll understand."

She finally looks over at me, turning only her head. Her long, soft auburn hair cascades down the center of her back, pulled away from her bare shoulders. She changed into a thin white tank top while on the drive back. I love to see her in white. It makes her appear angelic to me. An angel who carries death in her pocket.

"Tell me," I urge her in a relaxed voice, though I am anything but relaxed right now and I've no idea why. "What decision?"

Her dark eyes stray from mine and I find that small, seemingly insignificant gesture a tragedy.

She moistens her lips with her tongue, leaving her plump bottom lip wedged delicately between her teeth for a brief moment.

"After Hamburg and Stephens are dead…I'm going to leave." She turns around fully to face me. My heart has stopped beating. "I'm going to take Dina with me somewhere and I'm going to do my own thing."

I can hardly get my thoughts together much less form a sophisticated sentence.

"…I don't understand."

Sarai tilts her head gently to one side and uncrosses her arms, letting them hang freely in all of their elegance. She steps right up to me. I want to take her into my arms and kiss her, but I can't.

Why the hell can't I?

"Victor," she goes on, "I know now that I can't live like this. At least not with you. And with Fredrik. The two of you are professionals and I can't keep this delusion up, thinking that someday I'll be able to keep up with either one of you, much less *both* of you." She puts up a hand as if I had been about to argue and although I wasn't prepared to speak, I realize she must see the growing argument in my face. "Look, this isn't a cry for attention. I'm not saying this to make you tell me that I'm wrong. I know that as much as I wanted to stay with you, it's just not possible. If I don't get myself killed,

I'll end up getting *you* killed. And I know I could never live with that."

"Well, I *do* think you're wrong," I manage to say, wishing that I could say more.

"No," she says, "I'm not. And you know it."

"But where would you go? What would you do?" My tone becomes urgent. "Sarai, you tried living a normal life already. You tried and look what happened."

Why am I saying these things? I should be rejoicing in the fact that she has finally come to her senses.

She sighs softly. I watch her delicate shoulders rise and fall.

"Don't do this," she says, shaking her head. "Don't pretend that this bothers you, or that you want me to change my mind. Just don't. You know this is the right thing as much I do now. If only I had listened to you long ago, if I had just dropped this stupid vendetta against Hamburg, went on with my life, I'd be at home in Arizona with Dina and Dahlia and even Eric—"

"But you didn't love him," I point out.

Why did I say that? Of all the things I could've said, all the topics I could've explored, why did it have to be that one?

"No, I didn't." She looks into my eyes thoughtfully. "But he was normal. He was what you wanted for me, but at the time, I was too selfish to understand that you were right. That kind of life was right."

I take a step back from her. "Wait," I say, putting up my hand momentarily and then running the edge of my finger across my mouth, my head hung low, "So you're saying you *want* a normal life now?"

"Not at all," she says, shaking her head. "I could never go back to that. I'm just saying that if I hadn't have gone through with my plan to kill Hamburg, things wouldn't be as bad as they are now."

I cock my head to one side, a confused look on my darkening face. "Then what exactly are you saying?" I ask. "What, you're going to just start killing people on your own?" That's almost laughable to me, but I certainly keep that contained. I know Sarai would try it. I know she would kill and maybe even get away with it a few times, but she couldn't get away with it forever. Not without the resources that I have.

"I haven't figured that out yet," she answers.

Sarai places her hand on the glass door's handle and slides it away from the frame, letting the mild, early evening air rush in from outside. She steps out onto the back patio.

I'm standing outside with her before my mind catches up to the hurried movement of my legs.

"You're not making any sense," I say.

The back motion-activated light floods the concrete patio when Sarai steps across the path of the sensor. She stands just on the edge of the bright beams, leaving only part of her face cast in a darkening shadow as the sun is nearly set.

"I have unfinished business in Mexico," she says, and I go numb. "Hamburg isn't the only person I've thought about killing the past eight months, Victor." She gazes out at the flat landscape again. I can't look at anything but her. "When you and Fredrik told me that Javier's brothers are running the compound now, it only fueled my hatred. They need to die. All of them. Every one of the bastards involved. All of the Andres' and the Davids'." She looks over at me. "There are still a lot of girls there. I know there were twenty-one when I escaped in the back of your car. Nineteen now, minus Lydia and Cordelia. What kind of person would I be if I went on with my life knowing that back in Mexico there's a compound where many girls whom I came to care about, are being held against their will? Being raped and beaten and killed?"

I start to reach out for her, but I stop at the last moment.

I don't know why this is so hard for me...why there is so much conflict inside of me...

Sarai steps away from the sensor path just as the light blinks off, bathing us in subdued darkness. A light breeze catches her hair, making it dance against her back softly.

"This is foolish, Sarai," I say, finally managing words I feel are suitable. "Even with my help, pulling something like that off would take a very long time. What makes you think you could do it by yourself? How would you even find the compound without me?"

"I *can* do it alone," she says calmly but with unshakable resolve. "I mean, I can at least *try* and that's better than doing nothing. And you don't give me enough credit, Victor. I can put two and two together as easily as you can. I can take what I've learned, pieces of information that has crossed me, and make my way from there. Cordelia shouldn't be hard to find. I know she lives in California. I know that she's Guzmán's daughter and that you were sent to that compound by Guzmán to find her and to kill Javier Ruiz for abducting her. Even without you, I can find out the location of the compound. I'll start with Cordelia and Guzmán."

My throat is dry. My stomach is a rock solid mass of knots.

She's right, I didn't give her enough credit. She's much smarter than I ever knew. I knew she was intelligent, but she quite simply, just blindsided me.

She doesn't smile or gloat, she just stands there looking at me with focus and strength and the kind of determination that scares the shit out of me. Sarai's vengeful bloodlust runs deeper than I knew, deeper than she let on to me.

How could I have missed this?

"And then there are the rich men who Javier toted me around to, showing me off to them to make them want to buy the other girls from him," she says, sneering. "I remember what you told me. John Gerald Lansen, you told me is the CEO of Balfour Enterprises." She nods, affirming the revelation on my face. "Yeah, I remember a lot of things. And I spent a great deal of time at Dina's before I left for Los Angeles to kill Hamburg, researching these men. Slowly remembering their names, their faces, putting that two and two together to find out who they are, where they live, how much they're worth. When I wasn't thinking about you, I was immersed in them, learning everything I could about them so that I could slowly kill them all off one by one." She steps right up to me and gazes into my eyes. "And that's what I intend to do."

"You can't do this without me," I say.

I'm getting angry. How can she say these things, make such a decision that doesn't involve me?

My hands are shaking.

I look away from her, knowing that if I look too long, I'll fall helplessly into the depths of her green eyes.

"Foolish," I say, ready to call it a night and be done with this ludicrous conversation. "I'm going to shower and get some sleep. You can join me if you want."

I want her to say yes.

I feel like she's not going to…

"I won't be joining you," she says. "I meant what I said. When this is over, when they're dead, I'm leaving."

I whirl around at her, my hands in half-fists at my sides, the cuffs of my white dress shirt somehow seeming tighter around my wrists. "You're not going anywhere. Not like that. I won't let you." I laugh dryly. "Jesus, Sarai, you really *do* have a lot to learn. I'm dumbfounded by how you don't see how *stupid* this is!"

"Stupid?" she scorns. "No…OK, maybe you're right, but what's more stupid than anything that I've just explained to you is thinking that I could ever have any kind of life with you. I hate myself for what I've put you through, for what I've put Dina through. And here I am, like an orphan dropped on your doorstep, expecting you to take care of me and feed me and teach me how to live an unconventional life and not get killed doing it. You didn't ask for this and I never should've thrown it on your lap the way I did."

My teeth are starting to taste like plastic as I grind my jaw so hard and for so long without realizing. My chest rises and falls with deep, angry and even fearful breaths. I feel like I haven't blinked in minutes, my eyes are beginning to dry out from the unrelenting breeze that pushes against the whites, widely exposed from my lids. It feels like my heart is trying to pound its way right out of my chest.

I've never felt this way before…not since I was a child. I've never been so furious and…scared.

"I'm sorry that I put you through this, Victor," she says softly and with sincerity. "I want to thank you for everything you've done to help me. I doubt that anything I could ever do or say to you will make up for your help. I know. But the least I can do is leave you alone and let you live your life the way you know how. You don't need me in it fucking it up all the time."

She turns her back to me and starts to walk away.

"Sarai!" I shout and she stops instantly. I try to calm my voice. "Just...just wait a minute."

She turns to face me.

I'm stumbling over every single word in my mind, trying to pick each one out of the disarray and put them all together properly so that they make sense. But it's hard. It's so damn hard!

"I...," I look down at my dress shoes, over at the wrought iron patio chair, up at the strands of her hair blowing against her soft, bare shoulders. Back at my shoes again. "...I don't want you to go."

"But I have to, Victor," she says with such kindness and understanding in her voice that it nearly breaks me in half. "You know I have to. It's the best thing for both of us."

"No," I say simply, sternly, rounding my chin and gathering my composure. I will not accept this. "You're staying with me. I can keep you safe. We won't talk about this anymore. Now let's go to bed."

I reach out my hand to her.

"No, Victor. I'm sorry."

I grab her hand and pull her to me. She doesn't stir or recoil or even look surprised for that matter. I grab her cheeks within my hands and I stare down into her beautiful face, her almost childlike eyes, though they are so illusory. A little wolf hides behind that doe. *My* little wolf.

"I-I want you to stay with me."

"Why?"

"Because it's what I want."

"But that's not a reason, Victor."

"It doesn't matter, Sarai, you need to stay with me."

"But I'm not going to."

I shake her, her cheeks still engulfed by my hands.

"YOU CAN'T LEAVE!" My soul is trembling. I cannot bear these emotions.

She still doesn't flinch, but I see a thin layer of moisture begin to coat her eyes.

She shakes her head in my hands, gently.

"I'm going to leave and there's nothing you can do to change that."

"NO, SARAI!" I roar. "I NEED YOU IN MY LIFE!"

I pull my hands away from her abruptly and look down at them, wide open in front of me, as if they have betrayed me somehow. My chest swirls chaotically inside as if emotions that have lain dormant all my life have finally awoken and don't know what to do with themselves anymore.

Wanting only to hide myself away in my room so that I can try to understand what just happened to me, I turn on my heels and head for the glass door.

"Victor," I hear her call out softly behind me.

I stop. I can't bring myself to turn around.

I feel her step up behind me, the warmth of her presence, the sweet scent of her skin.

"Look at me," she says with a voice as light as the wind.

Slowly, I turn around.

She steps up and places her hands against my cheeks, gentler than I had done to hers. She tilts her head to one side and then the other, gazing into my eyes with her tear-filled ones. She pushes up on her toes and kisses me lightly on the mouth.

"Don't hold any of it back," she says with soft urgency. "Say everything you're feeling right now. In this very moment. No matter how wrong or uncomfortable or foreign it seems, say it anyway. Please…"

I didn't notice when my hands came up and hooked around her wrists. I hold on to them gently, as her fingers touch my cheeks. And I search inside myself, trying to understand what she's doing to me. What she's *done* to me. I think about what she said and against my hard external identity, I want only to give her what she wants.

"I've...Sarai, I've never felt this way before." I can't look her in the eyes, but she forces my gaze anyway.

"Tell me everything," she urges. "I *need* to hear it."

The desperation in her voice is passionate and matches what I feel deep inside. I search her face. Her eyes. Her pouty mouth, lips parted ever so slightly that it makes her mouth look innocent and inviting. The curvature of her cheekbones. Her chin. The elegant slope of her neck.

But her eyes...

"Sarai, you are important to me," I say desperately through an urgent whisper. "You're more important to me than anything or any*one*. To have you here, with me, isn't a burden. I *want* to train you. For as long as it takes. I *want* to wake up every morning with you next to me. I *need* you in my life more than I have ever needed or wanted anything."

I pause and avert my eyes downward. And then I step away from her. Her hands fall away from my face.

I swallow hard. "I won't force you to stay with me," I compel myself to say, despite what I feel. "But just know this...if you leave, you *will* become a burden. If you think that by being here you're fucking up my life, you have no idea how true that will be if you set out on your own. Because I will spend every waking moment of my life trying to protect you!" My heart is racing. "I won't be able to sleep, knowing that you're out there, trying to fit into a life that's nothing but a death sentence when you've not had proper training! Sarai...IT WILL KILL ME! DON'T YOU SEE? YOU'LL KILL

ME IF YOU CHOOSE TO LEAVE!" I'm shaking all over, my entire body wracked by pain and fear and heartache.

Sarai is in front of me again so fast, standing mere inches from my chest, her fingers dancing upon my face again, just like before. She appears calm. But there's something else in her eyes now that wasn't there moments ago. Relief? Happiness? I can't quite decipher the emotion when all I want to do is pull her against me and hold her until we both die.

She reaches up and brushes the tip of her index finger underneath my eye. A tear.

A tear?

Consumed by confusion, I can't speak and I can't move. I look down at her hand first, where the remnants of the tear glistens on the edge of her finger. I look back into her soft green eyes, which are smiling back at me, not with arrogance, but with warmth.

Clever little wolf...

CHAPTER TWENTY-FOUR

Victor

"I'm sorry," she says with nothing but kindness. "But I needed to know how you really felt, Victor."

I sit down against the black wrought iron patio chair, extending my legs out before me. I prop my elbow on the arm and rest my head exhaustively upon my fingertips.

Sarai kneels down in front of me, between my splayed legs.

"To be with you," she says, "means more to me than to be part of your job. I needed to know that you want the same from me that I want from you. And…when we're together, I always feel like I'm more a part of your job than a part of your heart." She tries to catch my gaze, but I'm too focused on the concrete. I hear every word she's saying to me, but I'm still too perplexed by the emotions that she pulled out of me to look down into her eyes.

I feel like I can't face her. Not because I'm angry with her, but because I'm ashamed.

"You've been this impenetrable man since the day I met you," she goes on, her fingers coiling around those of my free hand. "The only time I've ever felt a real *emotional* connection with you is when we're sleeping together. I would get *so* frustrated. Because I knew, deep underneath your many layers, that *this*, this right *here*," she tightens her fingers against mine with the emphasis of those words, "what you showed me, it was there all along just wanting to be set free. I—Victor, please look at me."

Reluctantly, I raise my head from my fingertips and look down into her eyes.

"I don't want to be your job," she says. "I want to work alongside you. I want to learn from you. But I want to feel like I'm yours emotionally when business isn't getting in the way. Victor, I know it's not your fault. I know you can't help the way you are, how emotionally detached you are from the world. But I needed to try to help undo what Vonnegut and the Order did to you."

"You manipulated me," I say simply.

She lowers hers eyes.

"I'm sorry."

"Don't be." I raise my back from the chair, leaning over and fitting my hands underneath her arms. I lift her onto my lap. "Don't *ever* be sorry."

Reaching up with one hand, I turn her chin toward me so that she'll look at me.

"You did what you had to do," I say and I can only hope that she will remember that later. "I cannot fault you for that."

"You're not angry?" she asks.

I shake my head. "No. I think 'thankful' is a better term."

She smiles. I smile, too, and kiss her on the mouth.

"It seems we're helping each other," I say.

She tilts her head thoughtfully and listens.

"I'm helping you become what you want to be, to live the life you *choose* to live. Something you've never had—a choice—because it was taken from you. And you're helping me take back the kind of life that was taken from me, showing me what it's like to be something more than a killer, to *feel* something more than the need to kill. And for that, I could *never* be angry with you."

Still propped on my left leg, she leans over and kisses me softly on the corner of my mouth. I wrap both hands around her waist, interlocking my fingers. We sit quietly together for a few moments. The sun has fully set and the stars are awake in the dark expanse of sky that lingers over us in all of its breathtaking dominance.

"So, how much of it was true?" I ask her.

"All of it," she says, "except the part about me leaving you."

I nod absently, thinking heavily about all of the things she revealed to me tonight.

"You know there's no payday in going back to Mexico," I say. "It would all just be settling scores and cleaning up."

"I know." She nods. "But it's important to me. Those girls are important to me."

I slide my left hand up the length of her back and then rest it at the back of her head. Pulling her toward me, I press her head carefully against my shoulder and hold her there.

"Then it's important to *me*," I say. "It might take months, a year or two even, to gather all of the information we need, all of the resources, but we'll get it done. And we'll do it together. But you have to promise me that you'll be patient and that you'll—"

"I give you my word," she cuts in. "I don't care how long it takes. And I'll follow your lead and your instructions every step of the way. I'm not going to make the same mistakes again."

Soon after our conversation on the patio, I take Sarai into the bath and I wash her hair as she sits between my legs in the tub.

We talk for the longest time about life the way it was before. About her time growing up with her mother, before her mother found drugs and men. When she used to sit curled next to her watching Saturday morning cartoons. We talk about my life before I was taken by the Order. About how I used to play *Dosenfussball* ('tag') and *Verstecken* ('kick the can') with Niklas when I was six-years-old back in Germany.

We get so lost in the memories of when our lives were so much simpler, so innocent, that for a long time we both forget how things are now.

I also forget, just for a moment, that things between us are still not set in stone.

And that they might never be.

Sarai

Victor is gone when I wake up the next morning, his side of the bed empty and cold. I crush his pillow against my chest and hold it close to me. He had an eight o'clock appointment with a contact in Bernalillo. He wanted me to go along with him, but I'm quite exhausted by travel, especially when it doesn't involve a plane.

Since the Krav Maga studio location has been 'compromised', as Victor calls it, he feels it's best that we move from New Mexico as soon as possible. My goal for the day is to pack as much of the house as I can, though that shouldn't be too difficult since Victor's closets and such are devoid of the average person's daily living. He doesn't have a 'junk drawer' where he tosses miscellaneous items that will sit there unused for a lifetime. His closets are not cluttered with old shoe boxes and stacks of keep-just-in-case paperwork, or clothes that he hasn't worn in five years. The cabinets in his kitchen aren't stocked with expensive matching dishes that only get taken out of their neat little spot on holidays and special occasions. There are no family portraits hanging in a neat line on the walls down the hallway, or keepsake items sitting on a shelf given to him by important people which he can't bear to part with for sentimental reasons. A few boxes should do it. His suits. My growing collection of clothes and wigs and jewelry and makeup and plethora of shoes. Looks like I'm mostly packing my own stuff.

I press the Power button on the remote and the flat screen television in the living room hums to life. I leave it on one of the national news stations for background noise. The sun beams through the glass door which frames the New Mexico landscape behind the house. I stare out at it for only a moment, feeling like I need a change of scenery. After spending most of my life in Mexico, surrounded by sand and thin trees and dried grass and heat...well, I'm glad to be moving. Victor said the new house will either be in Washington or New York. Either is fine with me, both of them a stark difference from what I'm used to.

I'll know for sure tomorrow.

I make a small breakfast of a scrambled egg and a single slice of wheat toast and wash it down with a glass of milk. I do my morning workout and then take a quick shower, afterwards, slipping on a pair of black cotton shorts and a tight black cotton top. I pull my hair into a ponytail and slip my fingers between two halves, pulling it tight against my scalp. Standing in front of the enormous bathroom mirror, I start to put on makeup, but decide I'm too lazy to mess with it right now, and I go back to packing. As I'm taking Victor's suits down from the closet, one by one, and securing them in tall, zippered garment bags, I feel something underneath my hand as I'm patting a sleeve down neatly against the jacket breast. I move the sleeve away, setting it against the bed and then open the jacket. I slip my hand into the inside pocket and grasp a small envelope in my fingers. It feels somewhat thick, about half an inch.

Before I pull it from the pocket all the way, for a moment I start to put it back, my conscience telling me that it's none of my business. But I look anyway.

The envelope is old and worn, with thinly tattered edges and a yellow-brown discoloration. It's a small envelope, more square than rectangular, and probably held a birthday card or an invitation at some point. There are photographs inside. Old photographs. I pull the flap from inside the envelope and open it the rest of the way, taking the small stack into my hand. The photograph on top is of a man, with light hair and a strong jawline. He's wearing a white shirt with a maroon tie. He's sitting in a leather chair surrounded by walls covered in tacky tapestry wallpaper. A young brown-haired boy and an even younger girl with white-blonde hair stand on either side of him, smiling widely for the camera.

The next photograph is of the same young boy and girl, posing with a beautiful woman with long, blonde flowing hair, outside in what appears to be a park.

All of the photos are aged, with a brown-orange tint and cracks running along the edges where they had been bent over the years. I flip each one over and read the backs. Versailles 1977, Paris 1977, Versailles 1976, scribbled in the left-hand corners and almost unreadable as the ink has begun to fade. In the next few photos the boy is older, maybe seven or eight, and he's standing with his arm draped over the shoulder of another boy. München 1981, Berlin 1982. My heart sinks when I realize that all of these photos are of Victor and Niklas and who I believe to be their father and Victor's mother. The girl must be a sister.

It breaks my heart to know that he carries these around with him like this. It's further proof that Victor is not emotionless, that deep inside of him is a man who has been hidden from the world, who has been forced to carry around the only memories of his childhood inside a pocket.

It's proof that he's human, a lost, emotionally damaged human that I want so desperately to restore.

My head snaps around when I hear footsteps inside the house.

I drop the photos on the bed and grab the 9MM from the bedside table, releasing the magazine into my hand to check that it's full. I pop it back inside the gun and rush quietly across the room in my bare feet, pushing my back against the wall, and walk alongside it toward the door. I keep the gun fixed at head-level, gripped in both hands, and stop at the door to listen. Nothing. At least, I hear nothing but the damned television that I'm wishing I had never turned on.

I begin to think it could just be Fredrik, but I'm not taking any chances.

With my back still against the wall, I move around the doorframe and step into the hallway when I see that it's clear. A shadow moves against the terra cotta tile floor at the far end of the hall and I freeze in my steps. I feel my heart drumming in the tips of my fingers, itching to put all of my force on that trigger. I remain still, the back of my neck breaking out in beads of sweat, and I watch the floor for a long moment without allowing myself to blink for fear of missing anymore movement. When I hear the footsteps again, farther away this time, I move stealthily down the length of the hallway on the pads of my feet.

Approaching the end, I stop feet from the corner and take a deep breath into my lungs. I let it out slowly, quietly, and then listen again. The voices of the people on the news carrying on and on about 'Obamacare' grates on my nerves as it only helps to drown out any voices or footsteps I might be able to hear, and from which direction they might be coming from.

Finally, I *do* hear voices, whispering:

"Check the rooms," I hear a man say. "She's probably hiding underneath a bed or inside a closet."

No, asshole, I'm waiting for you to come walking down the hallway so I can put a bullet in your face.

A man in a black suit rounds the corner with a gun in his hand and I squeeze a shot off the second he appears at the end of the hall. The shot rings out, vociferous in my ears, and the man falls against the floor, blood spewing from the bullet wound in the side of his neck. He gasps and chokes, trying to cover the wound with both of his hands now covered in blood.

I step around his body, ignoring the unsettling gurgling sounds that he makes and round the corner firing off three more shots. I manage to hit one more man before a white-hot pain sears through the back of my head. As I'm going down, I see the second man that I shot going down with me out ahead. And I see Stephens, standing next to his dead body in all of his tall, brooding glory. My gun is no longer in my hands and I'm so disoriented by whatever just made contact with the back of my head that it takes me a moment to realize I'm lying on the cool floor with my cheek pressed against a crevice in the tile. I reach back to feel my head and there is blood on my fingers when I touch my hair.

Stephens crouches beside me, a menacing grin etching deep lines around his hard mouth. His salt and pepper hair appears darker, his height, taller, the chasm of a dimple in the center of his chin, deeper. He peers down at me, propping both elbows on the tops of his thighs, his big hands hanging freely between them, the right wrist dressed in a thick gold watch. He smells strongly of cologne and cigars.

"You're a hard girl to find," Stephens says.

"Go fuck yourself," I say as casually as if I were telling him how nice the weather is.

Stephens smiles a big, close-lipped smile and it's the last thing I see before everything goes black.

CHAPTER TWENTY-FIVE

Sarai

I slowly stir awake to the sound of something humming low and deep, high above me, accompanied by a fast and constant whooshing sound. My vision is blurred, allowing in only a limited amount of dull gray light which at first bends and distorts as it hits my eyes. The air feels incredibly humid, the back of my shirt and the area between my breasts and underneath my armpits, soaked to the point that when the strange breeze hits me, it chills me to the bone. My hands are tied behind my back, just like I tied Izel's hands behind hers when she came for me after I'd escaped in Victor's car. I think of her briefly, the way she looked at me that day, how her sweaty dark hair was streaked across her face. I imagine I must look like her now, except that my hair is still pulled into a ponytail.

My ankles, I realize quickly, are also bound.

I force my eyes open the rest of the way and try hard to focus my vision. I'm sitting in a chair in the center of an enormous dark and dusty room of what appears to be an old warehouse.

I laugh inwardly at myself as I now see Andre Costa's face in my mind, as it was inside that warehouse back in New Orleans.

What comes around goes around, I suppose. Retribution for every death I caused or have been a part of is coming sooner than I had hoped.

The strange air and the whooshing sound above me I see is coming from a large industrial fan jutting out from the wall near the high ceiling. The walls are made of concrete, the ceiling of metal beams that stretch from one end to the other, held up by tall concrete pillars. The place smells intensely of paint thinner and glue and other lung-damaging chemicals.

My throat is painfully dry. My first instinct is to ask for water, but just like with removing the rope around my wrists and ankles, I know that nothing I ask for will be given to me.

I look down when I feel the tops of my feet burning and I see the skin on my toes has broken, indicating that at some point I must've been dragged.

Loud footsteps, like hard, flat soles, echo through the enormous space as Stephens makes his way toward me.

I laugh under my breath at the ridiculousness of the situation.

"What, might I ask, is so funny?" Stephens says in his deep voice, tinged with amusement of his own.

I smile brazenly up at him as he stands over me with his hands folded behind his back.

"I thought you and that sick fuck you work for wanted me dead?" I laugh. "This is a little overkill, don't you think?" I smirk up at him.

Stephens smiles chillingly and I immediately compare it to the look I saw on Fredrik's face after he strapped Andre Costa to that dentist chair. Instead of answering, he looks to his right as another man walks over with a chair. The legs hitting the concrete briefly as the chair is placed on the floor echoes through the small space separating us. Stephens sits down, casually straightening his fine black suit, tugging gently at the lapel and then brushing away invisible dust from his leg.

"Seriously?" I say, shaking my head. "Let me guess, Hamburg still wants to get his peep-show. Didn't get it with me and Victor in his room at the mansion. Didn't get it with his guard in his office at the restaurant—I'm glad that piece of shit is dead by the way. Was he a friend of yours?" I smirk more evidently.

Stephens' eyes smile. He crosses one leg over the other and places his hands gently on his lap. It's incredibly unnerving at how relaxed and unaffected by my words he appears. But I don't let him know that it bothers me in any case.

"Trust me, Izabel, Sarai, whatever you're called, if it were up to me, I'd have killed you in that house instead of bringing you here."

"Of course," I taunt, "you're just the lackey, sitting at Hamburg's feet waiting for his next blowjob."

The ceiling appears in my vision in an instant as my hair is pulled from behind, my neck forced back so far it cuts off my airflow. Another man is standing behind me, looking down into my widened eyes. I try to swallow, but I can't. I start to choke and gasp instead.

"Release her," I hear Stephens say.

My head is forced forward as the man lets go; the weight of my body causes the chair to shake and wobble briefly and then it steadies itself. I'm relieved I can breathe again. I raise my head and glare at Stephens sitting just two feet in front of me. I begin to gaze about the room, looking for a way out, searching for a plan that I know will likely never materialize. Even if I could get out of this room, I don't know how I'd pull off getting myself out of these bonds. The one around my wrists is so tight that it feels like the blood circulation is being cut from my hands. The ones around my ankles are almost as tight, but I feel like I can move them just a little more, my ankles grinding against the wood of the chair legs. But I'm not going anywhere. Except maybe to Hell very soon.

I'm not afraid of Stephens. I'm not afraid of what he'll do to me. I'm not afraid of being tortured. I'm just afraid of how long it will last.

"Why don't you just get this over with?" I lash out at him, hatred and vengeance evident in my voice. "I don't care what you do to me, or what Hamburg does to me, so just do it."

"Oh, but you're not here because of Hamburg." Stephens flashes a chilling smile. "And no, I don't want to get it over with." He leans forward in the chair, pushing his square-shaped jaw farther into my view. I can smell his aftershave. "I hope that you don't talk for at least a few days because I very much look forward to spending this time with you."

I swallow down my fear of knowing what his words mean, that he's going to torture me and for a very long time. I try to play it off, hoping he doesn't detect the slightest bit of worry in my face.

"What could I *possibly* know that you'd need to get me to talk at all?" I laugh smugly. "And what kind of aftershave is that? It smells like you've been dumpster diving between a crack-head's thighs."

Stephens' eyes dart behind me, narrowing thinly in a way that tells me he just stopped the man from pulling my neck back again, or maybe from hitting me across the face. He ignores my insult.

Stephens pulls away and rests his back against the chair again. And he says nothing. I hate that. I'd rather him talk a cheesy monologue of circles around me than to say nothing at all. And I think he knows how much it bothers me. That smug expression in his eyes tells me so.

"OK, so then if I'm not here because of Hamburg, then why am I here?"

Another pair of footsteps moves through the room behind me. I try to look back, but can only stretch my neck around so far.

Finally, the figure steps around and into my view.

"You're here because of me," Niklas says, dropping a cigarette butt onto the floor and snuffing it out with his black leather boot.

I gasp quietly. My entire body freezes solidly against the chair. I hear my mind searching for my breath, desperately trying to regain its control over my body again, but for the longest moment I'm nothing but an unmoving shell.

"Niklas...," I finally say, but it's all that I can get out.

Rage churns inside of me, my need to kill Stephens suddenly overshadowed by my need to tell Niklas everything I've been wanting to say to him.

Unlike Stephens, Niklas doesn't smile or grin or feel the need to taunt me with threats. I sense something else within him, something much darker than Stephens, something more threatening than words could convey. Looking up at his tall height and tousled light brown hair, his fierce blue eyes framed by a perfectly round, yet sculpted face, I see someone more attuned to vengeance than I could ever be.

And finally, I'm terrified.

Niklas steps forward to stand directly in front of me, completely undaunted by the short distance. Stephens had kept away from me a couple feet at least, as if worried I might manage to spit on him, or break free and grab him. But not Niklas. I feel like he's daring me to move. He *wants* me to make a move.

I swallow hard and raise my chin arrogantly at him and try to remain strong in the face of my fate.

"You know what I want," Niklas says evenly, the German accent just as I remember it, still evident in his voice. "Or, do we need to discuss it in detail?" He cocks his head to one side.

He looks *so* much like Victor. I wonder how on the inside he can be so very different.

"You're gonna have to explain it," I say. "Is it Victor?" I glance briefly at Stephens. "This piece of shit was just at his house. You already know where to find Victor. And not that it surprises me much, but what are you doing with *them*?"

I catch Stephens look over at Niklas, but Niklas doesn't take his eyes off me. He crouches down in front of me, between my opened legs, and looks upon me with a face so calm and dark that it sends a shiver up the back of my neck. I can smell the leather from his slim black jacket and a faint layer of cigarette smoke lingering on his dark gray shirt underneath.

"I've been looking for Victor for months," Niklas begins and I listen closely, keeping my eyes trained on his. "I'm sure he's told you that he left Order, betrayed Vonnegut and betrayed me—"

My eyes grow wider and my mouth falls open with a quick breath. "Betrayed *you*?" I cut in with disbelief. "You can't be serious. *You* betrayed *Victor*! You were the one—"

I choke and gasp as his strong hand shoots out and fastens firmly around my throat. I thrash about within the chair, unable to bring my hands up and try to pry his away. My eyes roll into the back of my head as his grip tightens.

He releases me.

I wheeze and pant trying to catch my breath, the corners of my eyes wet with tears of exhaustion and pain. I'm terrified of him, but not enough to cry or beg for my life. I'll die before I beg for anything.

"My brother betrayed me long before he left the Order," he says with a little more emotion in his voice than before—resentment. "He betrayed me when he went against everything we stood for to help you. He betrayed me when he *lied* to me about helping you. He lied, Sarai, because he knew it was wrong." He pushes up on his toes and is mere inches from my face. "He almost *killed* me because of you. And he would have if you hadn't have stopped him. *He* betrayed *me!*"

My hands begin to tremble against the arms of the chair. My heart is in my stomach, swirling around inside, lost and frightened. I can't deny that what Niklas said is the truth.

I can't deny it…

He pulls away a few inches to where I can no longer smell his toothpaste, but he's still too close. A mile would be too close.

"Niklas," I say in a slightly desperate voice, just enough to try to make him listen to me. "Victor was going to kill you only because it was wrong to kill *me*. Don't you understand, he would've done that for anyone. Not just me."

A small grin appears on one corner of his mouth and I'm both intrigued and worried by it. He rises to his feet and turns his back to me as he approaches Stephens. And then he turns around again.

"You don't know my brother as well as you think," he says. "No, he would not have done that for anyone else. Seems my brother is human after all, with all the falling for you and whatnot."

I shake my head and my gaze strays from his.

"Why am I here, Niklas? Just get to the reason you brought me here. I'm not going to grace you with my conversation."

Stephens stands up from his chair, looking like a giant next to Niklas. He is a very tall man, with broad shoulders and a large square-shaped head. "I hate to say it," he says, "but I agree with the bitch. Let's get on with this." He looks down at me coldly. "You're alive because he needs you first, but when he's done with you I'll be putting a bullet in that pretty little head of yours, per my contract with Arthur Hamburg."

I look to Niklas. "You need me for *what*?" There is poison in my voice.

"You're going to tell me everything you know about my brother and his new…organization. I want to know the names of his associates, where any of his safe-houses are located and who runs them." I notice his jaw grind behind his cheeks. "And I want to know how deeply Fredrik Gustavsson is involved in Victor's affairs."

I shake my head. "Well, first of all, who the hell is Fredrik Gustavsson? Secondly, I don't know anything about Victor's *organization*, whatever that's supposed to mean. He told me he left the Order, yes. And he told me that you betrayed him by staying in the Order and taking the assignment from Vonnegut to kill him. But he hasn't told me anything else. He said it's better that I don't know."

Niklas' eyes warm with a faint smile. Without moving his head, he glances at the man behind me and suddenly I feel like I'm falling as the chair is pulled backward, the front legs rising off the floor. Instinctively, I heave my body forward as far as I can to keep my head from hitting the concrete behind me. I'm dragged across the room in the chair, to where, I don't think I want to know.

Everything stops. The front legs of the chair come back down hard against the floor and then three more men, in addition to the one who dragged me, are holding my arms and legs. They begin to untie me, but just as quickly as the ropes come undone, I'm in their firm grasps, both hands and both legs, and no matter how hard I struggle to get away, I can't move. "LET GO OF ME!" I thrash and twist my body, trying to kick my legs out at them, to pull my arms from their hands. "NIKLAS! LET ME GO!"

He doesn't respond. He stands there in the grayish-blue hue of the dusty building next to Stephens, as my arms are forced above my head and bound again at the wrists by leather straps hanging from a lower ceiling. The same is done to my ankles. I hear a squealing noise and the sound of the contraption binding me, popping into place before my hands are stretched higher above me and my bare feet are lifted from the floor.

"GODDAMMIT! I'M GOING TO KILL YOU! LET ME GO!" I grind my teeth together so harshly that a shot of pain sears through my lower-jaw.

Niklas is standing in front of me again. I never even saw him move, I was too busy trying to get at the man closest to my left.

"Why are you working with them?" I shout into his face. "Make me understand that! I thought you were working for Vonnegut!"

Niklas folds his hands together on his backside.

"If you really want to know," he says, "Sure. I'll tell you."

He paces back and forth in front of me once before stopping in the same spot. But I can't help but notice Stephens standing in the background, the glint of a silver blade flashes within his hand. He remains in position, gripping a knife down near his pelvic bone, a look in his face that is eager to get at me.

"When I found out about what you did in Los Angeles," Niklas says, "I knew that if you were still alive, Hamburg would want to make sure that it wouldn't be for long. You had gotten away. There was no sign of you at the restaurant, or among the bodies that were found at the hotel." A flash of Eric and Dahlia's faces moves painfully through my mind "You had gotten away and I knew it had to be because Victor helped you. Suddenly, Hamburg and Stephens and myself had something in common. I wanted to find my brother. They wanted to find you. I knew you would be together, so therein lies the common ground."

My wrists are already hurting being held up by the straps, the weight of my body putting so much pressure on them. I feel my face straining as he talks.

"Why couldn't you find Victor yourself?" I lash out, trying to hide my discomfort. "Or why couldn't they find me themselves?"

"They had information on you that I did not have," Niklas says. "They had been keeping tabs on you for months, since the night you and Victor left the mansion."

I laugh out loud, throwing my head back. "Bullshit. If that was true why didn't they just kill me a long time ago?"

Stephens steps up closer from behind Niklas.

"Because Victor Faust threatened Arthur Hamburg that night," Stephens says. "He wasn't going to do anything to bring Victor Faust down on him again. I kept tabs on you just in case. I knew where you lived—easy to find and follow one leaving a Los Angeles hospital after being shot—I knew where you worked. Who you associated with. The places you frequented. I checked into Dina Gregory's background and learned everything there was to know about her family. She wasn't hard to track down later, either."

The corner of my nose and mouth harden into a snarl.

"That still doesn't explain why you teamed up to find us," I say icily, thinking more about what he was saying regarding Dina. And the truth is that I don't care much about why they are working together. I'm just trying to buy myself some time by keeping any conversation going for as long as I can.

Stephens and Niklas trade places and now Stephens is the one looming closely near me. He slides the blade between his fingers into my view, making certain that I see it and am intimidated by it.

He looks at me in a narrow, sidelong glance. "Surely you remember what Victor Faust did to Arthur Hamburg's wife. Surely you didn't think that he was going to just forget about it." He leans in close to my face, the smell of his breath, like old cheap wine and cigars, makes me lightheaded with disgust. "My employer has wanted Faust dead since the night he killed his wife. We knew where you were at all times, but we had no idea where Faust was and had no reason to believe that you did, either. And we certainly didn't know that he gave a shit about you. I suppose he didn't really, or he would never have left you alone like that." A taunting grin sneaks up on his face.

Just as he starts to pull away, I throw my head forward at him, hoping to get at him with my teeth, but he's out of reach too soon. I coil my fingers around the leather straps above me and lift my body up for a moment to relieve some of the pressure on my wrists. I fall back down harshly, shaking the contraption.

Niklas smiles.

I spit at him, but it doesn't come close to hitting him.

"They can't find Victor without me," Niklas says. "And I can't find him without you." He gets in my face again and though I know I could spit on him this time and not miss, I don't. That look in his dark blue eyes scares me into submission. "So we made an arrangement. They help me find you and I kill my brother for them."

"FUCK YOU!" I rear my head back and butt him in the forehead with mine. Pain shoots through my temples and down into my jaw and my vision blurs for a moment.

Niklas steps away from me, clearly stunned by the contact, but he doesn't retaliate. He turns to Stephens and Stephens does the honors. I start thrashing again as he comes at me with the knife.

"Willem," Niklas calls out in a strangely casual tone from behind.

Stephens doesn't turn around to look at him, but he stops.

"I need her alive," Niklas says. "Remember that. Remember our agreement. I find out what I need to know and then you can do whatever you want with her."

I shake my head and laugh low under my breath at them both.

"I'm not telling you anything," I snap. "You can't fucking break me. You think you can. But you are *so* wrong. You have no idea." My voice is surprisingly calm.

"Well, we'll have to see about that," Niklas says.

He turns on his heels and walks away, the sound of his shoes tapping against the concrete echoes throughout the warehouse until it fades as he disappears on the other side of a metal door.

Stephens' smile has gotten bigger now that Niklas is gone.

And I just became more afraid of him.

CHAPTER TWENTY-SIX

Victor

Two days later...

Staring at the laptop screen, the frozen image of Sarai's sweaty and bleeding face stares back at me. I've watched the video over and over again, as Stephens beats her, and my brother, as he tries fruitlessly to get her to talk. It kills me to see Sarai this way, to watch as this man who will be dead sooner than later hurts her. And it kills me that I can do nothing about it.
Not yet.
"She's not going to talk," Fredrik says from behind, a deep concern for Sarai's well-being in his words.
He stands in the doorway of the office in my Albuquerque house, free of dead bodies now that Fredrik and I have gotten rid of them. I refuse to leave this house. If Stephens wants me he is more than welcome to send men here for me. But my brother, on the other hand, wants information first and they all know he will not get it out of *me*.
"Victor," Fredrik speaks up again with urgency and even a bit of pleading, "you have to do something. We can't just sit here. They're going to kill her."

"There is nothing we can do," I repeat as I have explained this to him already. And as much as it pains me to do so, I explain it to him all over again. "I have no clue where she is, Fredrik. Niklas isn't going to reveal her location until he gets from her the information that he wants. I *know* my brother. He is smart. He will not risk facing me. Not like this. Vonnegut wants more than my head, he wants information. Niklas will get what he needs from Sarai and then send me another message telling me where to find her. I'll go after her and he knows this. And then he'll have me. He'll have me and everything about you and our outfit and our contacts."

"So what!"

I push myself out of the desk chair, causing it to roll across the floor and smash against the nearby wall.

"DO YOU THINK I'M *ENJOYING* THIS?" I point my finger at him and then at the floor.

I calm myself, steadying my breath, and I look down at my vague reflection in my shiny black shoes.

"Victor, I don't understand. Why don't *you* just give them what they want?"

It intrigues me that Fredrik, the master of interrogators, wants so desperately for Sarai to talk, that his concern for her is showing me another side to him.

It also concerns me.

"It's not that simple." I look up at him. "Even if I told Niklas what he wanted to know, Sarai is still dead. In fact, she'll be dead a lot sooner if I give in, if I gave you up and everyone involved in our operation. The longer she holds out, and the longer I hold out, the longer she lives. Until I figure out what to do."

Fredrik leans against the doorframe, crossing his arms. He sighs deeply.

"But it's been two days," he says. "She can't hold out much longer."

"She will hold out," I say with confidence.

I turn back around and look down at the video paused on the screen, the tips of my fingers braced against the edge of the desk.

"Then how are we going to find her?" he asks.

I stare at her face for a long, tense moment and then close the lid on the laptop.

"I will find her."

Sarai

The stench of my urine on the floor in the corner of this dark room I've been locked in for two days is becoming unbearable. I lie against the cold, filthy concrete, my cheek pressed against the rough, grain-like texture. My back stings, burns as though the open wounds inflicted by the whip Stephens used to beat me with are becoming infected. It happened last night when Niklas left me alone in this room. By the time Niklas came back, Stephens had already beat me so badly that I passed out briefly from the pain and woke up in a pool of my own vomit. I heard Niklas and Stephens arguing just outside the room, on the other side of the tall metal door. Niklas didn't approve of how Stephens handled me and he made it known.

"I NEED HER ALIVE, GODAMMIT!" Niklas had yelled at Stephens. "YOU'LL KILL HER BEATING HER LIKE THAT!"

I hate Niklas for what he's done. To me. To Victor. For what he's doing right now by keeping me in this place. But a small part of me is grateful that he is intolerant to Stephens' brutality. It doesn't matter to me that he's only intolerant because he wants me alive for information. I'll take what I can get.

I hear the lock slide away from the metal door to my prison and then the door breaks apart with a small grating echo.

Niklas steps inside. He's carrying a plate of food and a plastic bottle of water. Another man closes the door and locks it behind him.

"Don't even bother," I say from my spot on the floor as he approaches me. "If you won't kill me, or let Stephens kill me, maybe I'll die faster of dehydration."

Niklas sets the food on the floor beside me. I raise my body from the concrete and slap it away. Backing myself against the wall, I sit upright, trying not to touch the wall with my back because of the wounds. My ribs hurt, too. And my left wrist. My bottom lip feels swollen. I taste blood in my mouth. Metallic. Disgusting.

"Why don't you just talk," Niklas suggests with an air of surrender. He too is tired of all of this, how long it's taking. "You can end this right now if you just tell me what I want to know."

I say nothing.

Niklas sits down on the floor in front of me. He knows I'm too weak to fight him. I tried that already and only made the pain in my ribs and my back, more unbearable.

"I should look at your back," he says.

"Why the fuck do you even care?" I snap. "Oh, I forgot, because you need what I know." I push my head toward him, my eyes filled with unwavering hatred. "The truth is, I know *everything*. I know who Victor is involved with, who's helping him, where six of his safe-houses are located. I know *everything*, Niklas, and I'm not going to tell you *any* of it!"

I wince and cover my ribs with my arms as the pain shoots through my body.

"Very well." He rises into a stand.

He walks over to the food, placing it all back on the plate — a destroyed sandwich, a pickle and a handful of potato chips — and then picks the bottle of water up from the floor. He walks over and sets it beside my feet.

Then he crouches in front of me.

"He's not coming for you, Sarai," he says calmly.

I start to reach out with what little strength I have, to grab him, but I stop cold, wanting to hear what he has to say. It doesn't matter that I won't believe him. I still want to hear it.

He softens his blue-eyed gaze.

"I've sent my brother two videos of you," he says. "I've given him this location, telling him where you are, giving him a chance to give himself up. To give the information up. But he hasn't responded." He opens his hand, palm-up, and motions it about the room while balancing his arms on his legs. "And you see that he's not here. Two days and nothing." He drops his hand. "He's not coming for you. And do you want to know why? I'll tell you why. Because his job is and always will be first in his life. He will never make the same mistakes that Fredrik Gustavsson made because of a woman."

I round my chin. "Oh, but that's not true," I say disdainfully. "He betrayed you because of me, remember? You said so yourself. He left the Order because of me. He almost killed you because of me. Remember, Niklas?" I rub it in, glaring into his churning eyes while trying to bite back the physical pain.

Niklas smiles slimly. "Yes, he did those things. But I saw in my brother the desire to be free of Vonnegut long before you came into his life. But he's not with the Order now. He is free from it all, and yes, you were a huge part of it, of why he left. You gave him that boost he needed, I suppose." He seizes my gaze, a stern look in his eyes. "But don't you see what hasn't changed? Think about it, Sarai. Instead of freeing himself from a life of killing, like anyone in their right mind, anyone with a conscience would do, he creates his own Order. He is still all about his job. All about killing for a living.

Because it's all that he knows and it's all that he will ever know." He shakes his head at me as if he feels sorry for me, for how ignorant I have been, because I don't see the things that he sees.

I look away.

A part of me, a shameful, guilty part, can't help but believe him, after all.

He rises back into a full stand again.

"Believe what you want, Sarai," he says softly from above, "but you know as well I do that if he was going to come for you, he would've been here already."

He walks to the metal door, knocks twice, and the man on the other side opens it. Niklas walks out and I'm left in darkness again, surrounded by dark walls and a dark ceiling and dark thoughts that are breaking my heart into a thousand tiny pieces.

It doesn't matter.

If the things Niklas said to me are true and Victor never comes for me, I will still die without telling Niklas anything.

I will die in here.

CHAPTER TWENTY-SEVEN

Sarai

Day Three

I have refused food and water for nearly sixty-three hours. I only know this because Niklas keeps reminding me. I am weak, physically and mentally exhausted. Stephens hasn't beat me since Niklas stopped him before. It's only because of Niklas that I'm still alive. After all, I haven't given him any information yet. Only that he's a traitorous bastard who doesn't deserve the air that he breathes. I've told him over and over that I'll die before I give Victor up. I believe he knows that it's true, that I cannot be broken.

Except…maybe by my thoughts.

My thoughts are all that I have in this dark, dank prison of a room which shuts out all light, night or day, having no windows and only a single metal door that doesn't allow even a slither of light beneath it. That voice inside my head, the one that you never listen to until you have nothing left with which to shut it out, has been very cruel to me. *Niklas is right, and you know it*, the voice tells me. *It's been three days, and if what Niklas said about Victor knowing where to find you is true, then why hasn't Victor come? Why, Sarai, hasn't Victor given himself up for you and told Niklas what he wants to know, in order to save your life?*

I scream at the top of my lungs into the empty, confined space, gripping my head in my hands. Tears of anger stream from the corners of my eyes. My hair is drenched with sweat. My shorts and tight black top feel glued to my skin. My bare knees are bruised, my legs covered in filth. My back burns whenever I position myself the wrong way and the scabs forming over my wounds break apart and start bleeding all over again. I stay lying on the floor either on my side or my stomach.

I hear the grating echo of the metal door open behind me, but I don't care to roll over to see who it is.

"If you won't drink," I hear Niklas say standing over me, "then I'll force water into you."

I'm hoisted off the filthy concrete floor into his arms and carried out of the room. I don't fight against him. I don't look up at him as he walks with me down the hallway, but the fluorescent light running along the ceiling above me is so bright I wince and quickly shut my eyes. Quietly, I bask in the comfort of the new air as it hits my skin. I feel my legs draped over Niklas' arms, his left arm fitted underneath the back of my neck. We turn left and then right and then descend a set of metal stairs.

In moments, my head is being forced underneath water and held there.

My instincts betray me and I open my mouth to scream, taking even more water into my lungs. My body thrashes violently, my arms flailing wildly, trying to press against the thick plastic rim of the container I'm being held in. But I'm too weak to push myself out of the water, Niklas easily holding me under. Water burns my throat and my lungs even after I manage to close my mouth and hold my breath. And just when I think I'm about to drown, that finally I'm going to die and be at peace, Niklas pulls my head from the water and holds me above it.

Betraying me yet again, my first instinct is to gasp desperately for air and to cough up the water in my lungs. I'd really rather just die and get it over with, but my body has a mind of its own, another one that I can't seem to control. My heart beats so powerfully that I can feel my chest rocking against the plastic rim of what I recognize as a fifty-five gallon barrel. Droplets of water constantly fall from the ends of my hair and the tip of my nose and my chin and my eyelashes into the water just inches beneath my face. *Plop. Plop. Plop-plop.* It's eerie how it's the only thing that I hear.

"Who is working with my brother?" Niklas' voice is composed.

I say nothing.

His hand tightens a little within the back of my hair.

"You were seen with Fredrik Gustavsson in Santa Fe," he goes on. "What is his and my brother's relationship? Are they plotting against my Order?"

No answer.

A gush of water hits my face as he shoves my head back into the barrel. My nostrils and my esophagus burn like hell as the water is forced into me. I flail again, both arms grasping for anything, finally finding the circular plastic rim, but still not strong enough to push myself against Niklas' hands and out of the water.

I choke and gasp for air when he pulls me out again.

"Give me something, Sarai. *Anything.*"

I'm too weak and exhausted even to taunt him anymore, and still, I say nothing even as much as I want to tell him to go fuck himself.

Niklas only gets one thing from me before he carries me out of the room many minutes later; he manages to get that water into me he spoke of before.

Day Four

Thin, dust-filled beams of sunlight stream from the windows near the ceiling of the warehouse, casting pools of ivory light on the floor out ahead of me. I'm back in the chair in the larger space, surrounded by concrete pillars and that annoying industrial fan running incessantly high above me. Neither my wrists nor my ankles have been bound this time, but it's unnecessary as I can hardly will myself to stand on my own anymore. I'm not entirely physically weak. I could walk if I tried. I could throw this chair across the room, although only a few feet maybe, if I wanted to. I just don't care.

I just don't care anymore.

Stephens sits in that same chair in front of me as he did so four days ago. One leg crossed over the other, his large hands rest on the top of his knee. A foreboding look in his deep, dark eyes; one that says he's tired of waiting. That *this* is the day. That no matter what I say or don't say, no matter what arrangement he and Niklas have, that he's going to kill me.

Niklas enters the warehouse through a side door, briefly letting in the bright early morning sunlight. He had gone outside with the other four men that apparently work for Stephens. I heard them talking, something about watching the building for any signs of 'unwanted guests'. In my heart

I'm hopeful it has to do with Niklas having reason to believe that Victor is coming. But that cruel voice in my head shoots my heart down.

We are alone in the vast space. Just the three of us. Me, the Devil and one of the Devil's henchmen, though truly I don't know which one of them is which.

I raise my head.

I smile weakly up at them, fixating my attention mostly on Niklas.

"This is your last opportunity," Niklas announces standing next to Stephens with a gun in his right hand, held down at his side. "I won't bother with sending my brother another video of you being interrogated. It's apparent that seeing you in such pain isn't enough to stir him out of hiding."

"Kill me," I say, still with a smile. "It's what you're gonna have to do."

Niklas' chest rises and falls, but his eyes never leave mine. I gaze into them, searching for whatever I can find left in him that might still be like his brother, the man…I think I'm falling in love with.

The man that I thought, for a brief moment in time, might have felt the same way.

Time seems to stop. There is no sound or movement or air on my face, just an infinite silence suspended in the last moment of my life.

And as I feel my eyes begin to close, in the same frame of motion, Niklas raises the gun out beside him and pulls the trigger. The shot rings out and blood spatters from the other side of Stephens' head. The chair beneath him falls over onto its side as the weight of his massive body slumps against it.

Stephens falls to the floor. Dead.

I feel the softness of my lashes finally sweep my face as my eyes close and my own body, overwhelmed by relief and exhausted by everything, begins to fall over, too.

Niklas fits his arms underneath mine, catching me before I hit the floor.

"I've got you," I hear him say. "I've got you." His voice seems farther away now, though I can feel myself pressed against his chest and the wind on my face as I'm being carried through the warehouse.

"Give her to me," I hear Victor say from outside, and it's the last thing I hear.

Victor

The Plot – Three weeks ago...

Niklas sits across from me at the elongated table covered in scattered paperwork and coffee stains and photographs of future hits. His brown hair is disheveled, and the edges of his eyes are red as he had far too much to drink last night. He moves his hands across the stack of various photos of Edgar Velazco, a notorious Venezuelan gang leader who we've been commissioned to kill.

He shakes his head with aggravation and leans his back against the chair, bringing up both hands and running them over the entirety of his face.

"We can't put this on hold," Niklas says, looking across the table at me. "We have a location on Andre Costa. We need to deal with it now."

I don't look up from scanning the text in front of me.

"Things have changed," I say evenly. I move a sheet of paper on top of another. "Sarai is my priority. It was unexpected, I know, but I can't change what she did." I look directly at him, hoping that he will understand and not argue with me on this. "Niklas, I won't abandon or compromise what we're achieving here. The contract on Edgar Velazco will be fulfilled. Before the deadline."

He sighs again and lowers his eyes for a brief moment. Then he reaches out and removes a cigarette from the pack lying on the table in front of him. Putting it between his lips, he sets the end aflame with a flick of his lighter.

He knows I dislike it when he smokes inside, but I suppose I need to cut my brother some slack, seeing as how he has done so much for me, and for Sarai, in the past several months.

"No disrespect, brother," Niklas says as smoke streams from his lips, "but what are you going to do about her? You can't juggle both lives, and you know it. And we can't use our resources forever for babysitting, not when it's someone like her who isn't so easy to keep up with. She's as reckless as I was at twenty-three."

I nod. "Yes, you're right about that," I say. "She is more like you than I care to admit."

Niklas grins and flicks his ashes in the little plastic ashtray.

"Oh come on, brother, I'm not so bad, am I?"

I don't need to answer that question and he knows it.

He takes another short pull from the cigarette and sets it down on the edge of the ashtray.

"So then what are you going to do?" he asks.

He leans his back against the chair again and interlocks his fingers fitted behind his head.

"Are you sure you want to know the answer to that?" I ask.

That seems to have piqued his curiosity.

"Hell yes, I want to know." His hands come away from the back of his head and he leans over forward, resting the length of his arms across the tabletop. He looks worried. "What have you done?"

I pause and answer, "While at Fredrik's house, after a lot of pleading, and Sarai threatening me with her safety, I agreed to help train her."

"*What?*"

"Yes," I confirm it for him because he seems to need the confirmation. "She's adamant about killing Hamburg and Stephens herself. I could do it but—"

"You *should* do it, Victor."

"No," I say, shaking my head, "I gave her my word—"

"So fucking what," Niklas argues. "Victor, it's suicide. What the hell were you thinking?" He seizes the cigarette back into his fingers and takes a longer pull as if needing the nicotine to calm his nerves. Craning his neck, thick smoke streams from his lips into the air above him.

"It isn't something I haven't thought of before," I admit, "long before she pulled this stunt with Hamburg, long before she gave me the ultimatum. I want her with *me*, Niklas. I want to teach her. I believe she is capable of succeeding. And she refuses to be babysat. By anyone. Particularly me."

"And what if she *doesn't* succeed?" Niklas looks upon me, sincerity and concern hardening his features. Concern for me and not necessarily for Sarai. "Victor, you're setting yourself up for a lifetime of pain. Falling for a woman." He laughs derisively, though more at himself, I know. "I fell for a woman once—you remember—and you see what it got me. What it got *her*. She ended up dead and I ended up destroyed because of it." He shakes his head. "And do I need to remind you what happened when Fredrik fell in love? No, I didn't think so."

He stands up, snuffing the cigarette out in the ashtray.

"I'm sorry, Victor, but I think this is a really bad fucking idea."

"But it's the only idea," I say calmly. "And I hope that you will respect it enough that we don't have a repeat of Los Angeles."

I knew my words would sting him, using the incident when he shot Sarai in a hotel, an incident that he thought we had gotten past. Niklas looks down at me, resentment and pain in his eyes.

"*Really*, brother?" he asks with disbelief, propping his hands on the edge of the table and leaning forward. "After everything I've done all these months to help *protect* her? After I gave you my word, as your brother, as your *blood*, that I'd never do anything to harm her again? If I wanted her dead, I could've killed her a thousand times over. You *know* this, Victor. I thought we were over this."

I lower my eyes, letting the guilt of my accusation do what it wants with me. Niklas is loyal to me. He always has been. When he shot Sarai in Los Angeles and tried to kill her, it was only because of his love and loyalty to me. Because he knew that the way she had compromised me was going to be my undoing, that it was going to get me killed. And while although I don't excuse what he did and I will never forgive him for it—and he knows this—I understand why he did it, just the same.

In our kind of life sometimes terrible things must be done to those we love to clear a path for new beginnings. My brother, as intolerable as he may be, is no exception. In fact, he is a prime example of that rule.

And today things are different. He will not kill her, but he will not hesitate to kill *for* her.

"I do trust you, Niklas," I say. "I hope you believe that."

He nods slowly, forgiving me, appearing absorbed in deep thought.

"I'm not asking you to prove it, Victor," he says, "but there's something that needs to be done. For the sake of our business. For the sake of our lives." He begins to pace, back and forth near the length of the table.

"What is it?" I ask, looking up at him from my chair.

He stops at the center of the table, crosses his arms and looks down at me with a look of uneasiness on his face.

"If Sarai is going to be involved in our operations in any way whatsoever," he begins cautiously, "you know she must be put through the same level of tests that anyone else working for us would be put through. Because you have feelings for her doesn't make that rule any different."

"What are you saying?" I ask.

I know precisely what he's saying, but what I really want to know is how far he wants to take this. Niklas has never been known to half-ass anything.

"I'm saying," he goes on, "that I know you don't want to go through what Fredrik went through with Seraphina. And I know you don't want a repeat of Samantha. Sarai's loyalty to you must be tested. I'm not saying this because I have some kind of underlying vendetta against her, or because I want her to betray you so that I can prove a point." He puts up his hands. "I only want to know that she can be trusted, that if she's ever compromised, that she can't be broken and compromise the rest of us."

"I trust her," I say. "I know she wouldn't betray me. I trust her."

It doesn't matter how many times I say those words aloud or in my head. *I trust her. I trust Sarai. I trust her.* I know that Niklas is right. There is too much at stake. Our black market business, our lives and the lives of the many people who work under us. And with Vonnegut and the Order incessantly in search of me, I cannot take any chances.

"What do you propose?" I ask, accepting the truth.

Niklas nods, relieved by my cooperation and understanding.

He takes a breath and prepares to explain.

"I will approach Hamburg," he begins. "I will gain his trust by falsely selling you out to him. He'll believe that I'm just an unforgiving brother who has been commissioned by my own Order to kill you since you went rogue and betrayed us all. All for the sake of one girl. A girl who, it is no secret to people like me, Hamburg wants dead now more than ever."

I'm already nodding in agreement before he's done explaining, a vivid image of the scenario playing out in my mind.

"When the time is right," he continues, "I'll lead Hamburg's men straight to Sarai…"

Niklas goes on about the plot to initiate Sarai and at the same time, get Hamburg and Stephens where we want them.

"But I don't want her hurt," I say. "If we do this, you have to give me your word that you will not let anyone go too far. That *you* will not go too far." I narrow my gaze on him.

"How much can she take?" he inquires.

"She can take a lot," I say. "She is strong. But before it goes down, I want her to train as much as she can. I can take her to Spencer and Jacquelyn in Santa Fe. The experience will toughen her up some more. Let me prepare her as much as I can in the little time we have before we do this."

"OK," Niklas agrees.

"You know she's going to hate you even more when this is all over," I point out.

Niklas nods. "Yeah, I imagine she will. But I don't care how much she hates me. I'm not the one who has to sleep with her." He laughs lightly. "It's a risk I'm willing to take for the sake of everything. The real concern is, how much will she hate *you* once it's all over?"

I look away, staring off toward the wall. "It's a risk I'm also willing to take," I say distantly.

"Maybe she'll understand," he says, trying to ease the worried thoughts written all over my face. "If she's going to be a part of us, to be a part of *you*, she'll need to know how and when to separate your working relationship from your emotional relationship."

"Yes," I say, "she will need to learn that."

He slaps his hands gently against the table.

"And if she's as strong as you say she is, then she'll understand and be able to get past it."

I say nothing more.

"So then it's settled. I'll head to Los Angeles tonight. I have a meeting with Fredrik, anyway."

"I take it he still hasn't mentioned anything about me to you?" I ask.

"Nope," Niklas says. "The guy is as solid as a Catholic behind a confession booth. He's not going to betray you, Victor. Why do you still worry that he will?" Niklas grabs his cigarettes and car keys from the table. "He passed your test months ago. How long did they have him in that room for? Six days? Fredrik is loyal. He can't be broken."

"I'm not so sure," I say, staring down at the wood grain in the table. "You seem to forget what Fredrik's specialty is. He brutally tortures people and quite enjoys it. I think if anyone can get through an interrogation without breaking, it's Fredrik Gustavsson."

Niklas looks at me in a sidelong manner.

"What are you thinking?" he asks, intrigued by my train of thought.

I look up at him.

"I have one more test to put Fredrik through," I say. "If I leave him alone with Sarai, he will believe that I trust him fully. It will seem as though I've let my guard down." I stand up and walk toward the bookshelf, thinking long and hard about this new plan that I've only just devised. "If he contacts you and tells you that he has Sarai, then we'll know that his loyalties truly lie with the Order. Sarai is the perfect bait. What better way to allow Vonnegut to lure me than to use the girl I…,"

Silence ensues. I feel Niklas' inquisitive eyes on me from behind.

"The girl you're falling in love with?" he says.

I pause. "Yes…," I whisper.

CHAPTER TWENTY-EIGHT

Sarai

I haven't spoken to Victor in hours. Three at least. I've let him undress and bathe me and tend to my wounds. I've listened to him 'explain himself', though in a manner only someone as relationship-challenged as Victor Faust can be. He didn't resort to pleading with me to speak to him, to stop giving him the silent treatment. He just talked. As calmly as any conversation he's ever had with me, though this time it was very one-sided. But I did detect the worry in his voice, although he masked it well. I did sense when he touched me, brushing my hair, cleaning the debris from the wounds on my back, that he had wanted to touch me more affectionately. He wanted to pull me close and hold me there in his arms. But I knew he didn't want to cross his bounds.

And he was smart not to, because I would've punched him in the face.

By nightfall, although exhausted and still in pain from my head to my feet, I'm well enough that I can walk about the house on my own, though carefully because my back is pretty messed up. Victor had left me to be alone in the bedroom of his Albuquerque house. I needed time to myself, to think about everything that happened, about what he and Niklas put me through. I needed time to take into consideration Victor's reasons. I could give a shit less what Niklas' reasons were or what part he played in it. Niklas isn't worth my time much less my thoughts. Victor, on the other hand…A part of me wants to feel betrayed, as if it's the normal thing to do. I feel like I should curl up on the floor and cry, to beat the walls with my fists, to dwell in my own self-pity, also only because it seems the normal thing to do. But that's not me. And I'm not normal. And nothing about my life or Victor's life even comes *close* to normal.

I know Victor wonders what I'm thinking. He worries about how deeply my anger towards him runs, if it's so deep that I'll never be able to pull myself to the surface long enough to forgive him. I know he's probably convinced that my silence is the only answer I'm ever going to give.

But he's wrong.

I stop him before he leaves the bedroom after coming in to get something from his briefcase.

"Was it Niklas' idea?" I ask from the bed.

I hope like hell that it was.

Victor stops in front of the door with his back to me, and instead of opening it the rest of the way, he shuts it. He sets the black file folder he took from the briefcase down on the tall chest of drawers near the door, and comes over to me. His black dress shirt hangs untucked over the top of his pants. His long sleeves are pushed up against his elbows, exposing the masculinity of his forearms and the strength of his hands.

I raise my shoulder from the headboard and sit on the edge of the bed, dropping my feet onto the floor. I'm dressed in a thin, loose red top that doesn't rub against my back too much, and a pair of jogging shorts.

"Yes, technically it was," he answers.

"*Technically*?" I ask with a scowl.

He sits down beside me, his arms resting atop his dress pants, his hands touching his knees.

"No one is exempt from the trials," he says. "Niklas simply had to remind me of that when it came to you. It's all about trust—"

"You didn't trust me already?" I counter.

"Yes, I trusted you," he says evenly, looking ahead. "But what we put you through was necessary, Sarai. You wanted in. *I* wanted you in. If that was going to happen it had to be done by the book or there would always be conflict among the rest of us. My judgment would constantly be questioned. You would always be held in suspicion. No one is exempt. Fredrik wasn't. That man at the back of Hamburg's restaurant who helped you get away. The man who carts Mrs. Gregory around to safe-house locations."

"Amelia?" I ask. "She didn't know anything about what you and Fredrik do, according to what you told me. Or, was that a lie, too? Was *she* beaten like I was beaten?"

"No," he answers and looks over at me. "It wasn't a lie. And no, she didn't go through anything like you did. Amelia and others like her, those who know nothing about what we do, we test their reliability in other ways. But for those of us on the *inside*, who know as much as *you* know about any of us, the trials are more…extensive."

I look away.

"Did you send Stephens to Amelia's house?" I ask quietly.

"No," he answers and I turn to look at him on my left, distrust in my eyes.

"Then how did they know about her? How'd they know Dina had been staying with her?" Anger rises in my voice. "Did you put Dina at risk? Please tell me the truth!"

He's shaking his head before I even finish the question. "It is the truth. We may never know exactly how Stephens found out about Amelia or that Mrs. Gregory had been hiding out there. The one who could answer that question is now dead. But I can assure you neither I nor Niklas, or even Fredrik had anything to do with it. It could've been a number of things, Sarai. Mrs. Gregory might've contacted a family member at some point while staying there." He gestures his hands now as he speaks. "She could've accessed her bank account and it triggered her general location."

"Stephens could've *killed* me," I say bitterly, jumping back and forth between topics. "He wanted to kill me bad enough that he'd have done it if Niklas hadn't shot him first. What if he'd have killed me days before? What if Stephens had beaten me to death?" My chest rises and falls heavily as I try to contain my anger.

Victor sighs and looks down at his hands as he uneasily brushes the fingers of his right hand over the knuckles of the left.

"I'm sorry for that," he says regretfully and then slowly raises his eyes. "Yes, it was possible that Stephens could've killed you, I won't deny it, but I knew Niklas would do everything to make sure that didn't happen."

I laugh with contemptuous disbelief. "*Niklas?*" I say incredulously. "The same man who *shot* me? You're telling me that you put your faith in someone who has wanted me dead from pretty much the moment he set eyes on me?" My voice is beginning to rise and Victor is beginning to show signs of discomfort.

"I may never be able to make you understand," he says, still composed, "but I know that Niklas will never hurt you. He and I have been through a lot since I left the Order. We have come to an understanding. He accepts you—"

"I don't *need* to be accepted by him!" I shoot upright from the bed and stare down into his face, my hands clenched into fists at my sides. "Niklas is the last person on this Earth who I need any kind of approval from! He tried to *kill* me!"

Fraught with resentment, my body stiffens as I bring my fisted hands up in front of me and hold my breath, gritting my teeth.

Victor stands up, placing his hands on my shoulders. Hesitantly, I let the breath out and calm myself, but I can't look him in the eyes. Just like before, when I wanted to feel betrayed because it's the normal thing to do, right now I want to hate him because of the same reason. But I don't. I may not understand why he trusted Niklas, of all people, with my life, but I think the only reason I don't understand is because I don't want to. I *want* to be angry. I *want* to be unforgiving. Because it's easier than accepting the unthinkable truth, that Niklas deserves a chance. Because if I were him, and I were trying to protect my brother from the Order, I probably would've shot me, too.

Victor brushes my hair away from my face, tucking it behind my ears. He looks at me for a moment as if he's recalling a memory that I'm sure includes me in some way. How could it not? That thoughtful, admiring look in his green-blue eyes, the way he made sure to brush along the sides of my face with his fingertips when he moved my hair behind my ears. I want to scream at the top of my lungs at him, but all I can do is stand here and watch his darkly beautiful gaze sweep over me.

His hands fall away and he stares out into the room.

"The night I found you in my car," he says, not looking at me, "I instantly saw you as a threat. I wanted to get rid of you. Quickly. To take you back to the compound, or drop you off on the road somewhere. I very much wanted to kill you."

Already knowing all of this, it doesn't come as a surprise, but I'm curious about why he's bringing it up now, just the same. I remain quiet, folding my arms over my breasts, grimacing a little as the skin is stretched on my back.

"I could've, and often thought that I should've killed you many times over," he goes on. "I had every opportunity. But I couldn't do it."

"You needed me," I remind him. "As leverage. Maybe if I hadn't given you the idea, warned you about how Javier did business, you might very well *have* killed me."

"No," he says quietly, shaking his head subtly. Then I feel his eyes on me and I look over. "I didn't need to use you as leverage, Sarai. I knew when I left that meeting with Javier Ruiz that after I reported the payoff Ruiz offered for me to kill Guzmán, that in the end I'd only be commissioned to kill Ruiz. Because Guzmán's offer was higher than his. Whether or not I ever received the other half of the money from Ruiz was irrelevant. I didn't need to use you as leverage at all."

"I don't understand what you're getting at," I say, and it's the truth.

Victor inhales a breath and looks away from me again.

"That morning when Izel was on her way to pick you up from that motel, before you woke up, I had every intention in handing you over to her. I had even gone as far as telling them where we were. But when you woke up...," he stops mid-sentence and raises his eyes to the ceiling momentarily, letting out another concentrated breath. His chin comes back down and he looks right at me. "If you hadn't woken up, you'd still be with Javier Ruiz right now."

With my arms crossed, I take a few steps toward him, tilting my head to one side thoughtfully.

"What are you saying?" I ask. "I'm here with you now because I woke up before Izel got there? I don't understand."

"I couldn't do it," he says. "Like shooting an innocent person, anyone with a conscience can't do it if they're looking at them. When you woke up, I couldn't hand you over."

Still not exactly sure what Victor is trying to say, all I do know is that it wasn't because of something as ridiculous as love at first sight. But as I study the unsettled look in his eyes, I slowly begin to understand that he is learning something extraordinary about himself. I let him speak, as it seems that he needs to get it out, to let it go so that maybe he understands it fully himself.

"I fought with myself," he says, "every step of the way while you were with me, I told myself I needed to get rid of you. You were a threat to me, to my job, to my life, and later you threatened the relationship between me and my brother. I knew it the moment I saw you through the rearview mirror when you had that gun at the back of my head, that desperate, scared look on your face. You threatened *everything*. But for the first time in my life, I went against everything that I was: a trained killer with a repressed conscience...." His eyes harden and he steps up to me. "...I could've let you go a long time ago, but I didn't. I didn't want to let you go then and I don't want to let you go *now*."

A shiver moves along both of my arms as he rubs the palms of his hands against them, up and down.

"I am sorry for what you went through," he says softly. "I want you to stay, more than anything, but if you want nothing more to do with me, I'll understand." He presses his lips against the top of my hair and walks toward the door, taking up the black folder from the chest of drawers.

"Victor?" I call out softly before he reaches for the door knob.

He looks back.

I start to say, "I'm glad you didn't let me go," but I stop myself and swallow the words. As much as I want to tell him that his words touched me, to let him know that I can never imagine a life without him, I'm still angry about what he did to me and I can't excuse it. Not yet. Not that easily.

"Was that it?" I ask instead. "The test I went through? Was that the last of it? The only time I'll have to go through something like that? Because I have to be honest, I don't want to wake up every morning thinking I'm going to be abducted, or beaten, or drowned. I don't want to *not* trust you…"

He places his hand on the knob and turns it. The door cracks open.

Looking back at me he says, "No, there's just one more thing."

My heart hardens like a hot stone in my chest. I didn't expect that.

"The bigger trial is whether or not you can work alongside my brother," he says. "But you can trust me. And you can trust Niklas. And you'll never be put through anything like that again."

He pauses and says, "I hope you'll stay," and then leaves the room, closing the door behind him.

Some time passes while I'm left alone again to think about everything. I know that *right now*, not yesterday, or the day I escaped the compound in Victor's car, but *right now* is when the rest of my life begins.

And I know there's only one right choice.

I leave the bedroom and join Victor, Fredrik and Niklas in the den. They've been going on about how Fredrik never knew a thing and how he passed all of Victor and Niklas' tests. I've been listening to them, mostly Fredrik and Niklas talking, as Victor seemed quieter than usual.

The three of them look up at me when I step into the room, their conversation halted mid-sentence.

"Ah, there she is," Fredrik says with a big, gorgeous smile. He waves his hand toward him. "Come and join us. We were discussing what's next on the agenda for the four of us." I can tell that Fredrik isn't as confident about my mindset as he's pretending to be.

Niklas simply nods at me.

Victor stands up and holds out his hand, offering me to sit with him.

"I need to say something first," I answer.

He puts both hands behind his back and then steps to the side, waiting patiently.

I look at all three of them, one by one, and then I stop on Victor.

"If I'm going to be here," I say, "there are a few things I need to make very clear."

A flicker of hope moves through Victor's greenish-blue eyes.

I look over at Fredrik and Niklas again and continue, talking to all of them:

"I do what the hell I want to do," I say. "I'll follow Victor's orders like either of you would, I'll train until I bleed and I can't walk straight. I know my place. But not because I'm a girl or because I'm younger than all of you. Or because you think I'll get 'hurt'," I quote with my fingers. "Of *course* I'm going to get hurt, but I don't need any of you," my eyes fall on Victor again, "running to get a goddamned Band-Aid every time I fall down."

Fredrik laughs lightly. "Hey, no argument here," he says, putting up both hands and then dropping them back on his knees.

My eyes fall on Niklas. Still, I show no emotion on my face while looking at him. I think I'm just not sure yet which emotions they should be.

He smirks at me, though I know it's entirely innocent.

"I think you know better than to expect *me* to come running after you every time you fall," he says.

I just roll my eyes and turn to Victor.

"Sarai—," Victor says, but I hold my index finger up at him.

"That's another thing," I say. "Sarai Cohen died a long time ago. She died when I was fourteen-years-old and spent my first night in that compound in Mexico." My finger folds back toward my hand and then I lower it.

I glance at each of them.

"I want to be known from here on out only as Izabel Seyfried."

All of them look to one another and then nod, looking back at me.

"Izabel?" Victor asks, picking up where I had cut him off.

I look into his eyes.

"I'll understand if you never forgive me, but—"

"Would you forgive *me* if it was the other way around?" I ask, trying to make a point that he instantly gets. "Victor, you did what you had to do, just like the night I manipulated you into—." I stop myself before revealing too much about our personal relationship to Niklas and Fredrik. But I can tell by the look of understanding in Victor's eyes that he knows what I'm referring to.

"But that's hardly the same thing."

"It doesn't matter," I say. "Let me just say for the record, right here in front of Pretty Boy and the Devil's Advocate, the hell I went through is not only forgivable, but was absolutely necessary. I *know* what I'm involved in. We *kill* people, some of us for a living, some of us for revenge. I'm not working at a *bank*. A lot more than a background check and my credit score has to be taken into account if I'm going to be a part of this. And to be honest, I feel a lot safer around all of you knowing that you will go to such extremes to make sure that everyone in this room can be trusted. That anyone who joins us later will be put through the same hell."

My eyes fall on Victor once more. "There's nothing to forgive," I say and his face softens.

Niklas stands up from the leather chair.

"Sar—*Izabel*," he corrects himself, stepping up closer to me. "Look, I do need to say one thing to you. I'm very sorry for shooting you in Los Angeles. I really am. I won't ever try to hurt you again."

"I believe you," I say, and by the looks on all of their faces, none of them expected it. "I think it's safe to say that I'll have a hard time even being in the same room as you, Niklas. I'm not enjoying it right now. Honestly, I'd rather not have to see you much. I think you're a dick, and a crazy psychopath who belongs in a prison mental institution. I'll never fucking like you and I doubt I'll ever have any respect for you. But you're Victor's brother, and when I begged him not to kill you, it was for a reason and I don't regret it. But I'll never like you and I'm warning you to stay-the-fuck-outta-my-way."

He raises both hands out at his sides in a surrendering fashion, and takes a step back. "All right, all right, I get it. Out of your way." He laughs lightly.

It's mostly for show. I know he still has his issues with me—he's as bullheaded as I am—but for Victor's sake, he'll tolerate me as much as I'll tolerate him. I despise that constant cocky look he wears. I despise his confidence and his arrogance and I anticipate that Niklas and I will butt heads a lot. But for Victor, I'll endure it.

Niklas turns his back to me and starts toward the chair.

"Niklas," I say, and he stops to look at me.

I move closer.

"There's just one more thing I want to say to you."

"Yeah?" He turns around fully and watches me curiously, waiting.

When I'm in arm's reach I pull my fist back and then bury it against the side of his face, right along his jaw. The force of the blow sends a painful tremor through my hand. I try shaking out the pain by spreading and wiggling my fingers, but that just makes it worse.

"*Owww, shit!* What's your damn problem?" Niklas holds his hand over the corner of his mouth. "Never mind. I get it. I shot you and now we're even. I deserved it." With his hand still over his mouth as if he's trying to pop his jaw back into place, he moves the rest of the way toward the chair and sits heavily into it.

"That wasn't because you shot me," I snap. "That was for killing Stephens. He was *mine*." I point at him. "And the only way we'll *ever* be even for you shooting me is if I shoot you back. So like I said before, stay out of my way."

Niklas looks across at Victor standing behind me, giving him a look that reads *Is she for real?* Victor doesn't say anything, but when I glance back at him briefly, I notice he's smiling.

Fredrik is lounging against the sofa with his arm across the back and a big grin on his face.

Finally, I take Victor's hand and his offer to sit down. I'm too sore to stand up on my own for too long. He walks me to the sofa and helps me onto the soft cushion, holding my hand until I'm all the way down. And then he sits beside me.

Fredrik leans over and looks at me on the other side of Victor, his dark, charming smile in-tact.

"I'm glad you're with us," he says. "Of course, you have a lot of training ahead of you, according to Faust here." He nods in Victor's direction. "But something tells me you're a natural." He winks. "Stubborn. Reckless. Mouthy. *So* unladylike. But I probably wouldn't like you much if you weren't all of those things."

"Thank you, Fredrik," I say with sincerity *and* a smirk.

Niklas leans back in the chair, propping his black military-style boot on his knee. I don't know why, but I make note of that. Military boots? I look the rest of him over. Dark jeans. Plain gray t-shirt that fits tight around his bicep muscles. Disheveled hair.

I look to and from him and the always-sophisticated Victor, and I can't help but wonder if I'm missing something. I glance around Victor at Fredrik to his right, and like Victor, Fredrik looks the same as he always does, in expensive dress shoes and a refined suit.

"Why is he dressed like that?" I ask Victor, indicating Niklas with the tilt of my head.

Victor glances over momentarily, but it's Niklas who answers.

"Because I prefer it over those ridiculous suits," he says. "And since I'm no longer with the Order, I feel like I can dress however the hell I want."

Surprised, my eyes fall back on Victor without moving my head.

Victor nods a few times, confirming what Niklas said.

"He left days ago," Victor says. "Fredrik is the only one still on the inside."

"But...why?" I ask. "I mean, wouldn't it be better if Niklas was there keeping tabs on Vonnegut, especially where *you're* concerned?"

"I left because I had to," Niklas says. "It was taking me too long to kill Victor."

"And as expected," Victor adds, "Vonnegut was beginning to question Niklas' loyalty. Vonnegut may not know that Niklas and I are brothers, but we've had a close working relationship for many years. It was taking too long and it was getting too risky."

I let out a worried breath and start to lean against the couch until I remember my back.

I look at Fredrik. "What about you?" I ask. "Does the Order know about your relationship with Victor? Or Niklas, for that matter?"

Fredrik smiles at Victor. "See, she's already hard at work," he says with light laughter and then looks back at me. "The Order knows I worked with Victor a few times in the past, but not anymore than anyone else he's ever worked with. As far as Niklas, when Victor went rogue, I was approached by Niklas—now we all know why—to help him find Victor. I was under the impression that I was to report to Niklas from now on."

"But Vonnegut never knew of my involvement with Fredrik," Niklas speaks up.

"So for now," Victor says, "Fredrik is safe in the Order."

"And I'm their only eyes and ears left on the inside," Fredrik adds.

"Wow," I say, shaking my head, trying to take all of this in and what it means for us.

"Getting scared?" Niklas asks with a grin on his lips.

"Not at all," I answer with a smirk. "Just trying to figure out which job is more imperative, the compound in Mexico, or taking out the Order and getting them off our asses."

Niklas grins and it seems that once he realizes it, he averts his eyes away from mine.

"I think I'm in love with your woman," Fredrik says to Victor in jest.

"Somehow I doubt you're capable," Victor says nonchalantly.

He looks at me. "I know which job is more imperative." He smiles slimly and places his hand over mine.

CHAPTER TWENTY-NINE

Izabel

The footsteps carrying through the hallway are faint as guests walk back and forth every so often. Tall heels. Tasteful dress shoes. Rich voices pretending to be intrigued, overdramatizing the insignificant things in life. Artificial laughter. Classical music—Bach, I believe—plays downstairs, so crisp and elegant and distinguished that it makes me feel like I'm attending a party for the Queen of England rather than sitting patiently in a dark room with my favorite knife in hand. I call her Pearl.

This room smells no different than it did the last time I was here, like too much cologne and sweat and stale potpourri and dryer sheets. A heavy, square marble table sits across the room. I remember that table. I will never forget the way Victor bent me over it, or the disgusting pig who watched as my panties pooled around my ankles.

It's dark outside, just after nine o'clock, and the moonlight bathes much of the room from the walk-out balcony behind me. I've made sure to leave it open so that I can feel the night air on my skin. It's incredibly warm in these tight clothes. Black from the neck down. Boots dress my feet, much like what Niklas prefers to wear except mine have daggers sheathed within the leather. A gun is holstered to my hip, but it's only there in case I need it. I like my knife.

I sit in a chair near the center of the spacious room, just out of the soft gray light pouring in from the balcony. My right leg is crossed over the left. My hands rest carefully within my lap, the pearl handle of my knife fitted firmly in my fist. I tap the thin silver blade against my thigh.

Twenty-six minutes have passed since I sat down. But I'm patient. I'm disciplined. As much as I can be, I suppose. I promised Victor that I'd wait. That I'd sit here just like this, practically unmoving, until it was time. I said that I could do it, that I could get through it without marching my way downstairs and taking care of business there. I intend to prove it. Though, I admit it's hard.

I glance over at Niklas standing in a dark shadow near the balcony doors with his hands folded together down in front of him. He's grinning at me, taking pleasure in my growing frustration. I smirk back at him and look toward the bedroom door across the room.

Thirty-two minutes.

I hear the voices of the two guards always stationed outside of the room. They're talking to Arthur Hamburg.

Seconds later, the door opens and a blast of light from the hallway shines into the room. But it doesn't touch me. And just as quickly, the light is shut out as the guard closes the door after Hamburg steps inside. He doesn't notice me when he walks past the large bed and then the marble table.

"What do you think of the hair?" I ask.

Hamburg stops cold in his tracks.

I lean over forward in the chair, pushing myself into the path of light.

"Jet black," I say so casually. "Do you still think I'm stunning no matter what kind of wig I wear?" I reach up with my free hand and touch the short cut carefully to show it off.

The overhead lights in the room come on when Hamburg says, *Lights on*.

"How did you get in here?" he asks desperately, his gaze bouncing about the room, looking for the answer and for signs of anyone else.

When he notices Niklas and Victor both standing near the balcony entrance behind me, guns in their hands down at their sides, he starts to call out to his guards. But then a loud *thud* sounds just outside the door. And then another. Hamburg stops feet in front of the door, no longer sure it's safe to open it.

He looks back at me.

I smile and tap the blade against my leg some more.

The door behind him opens and Fredrik is standing there with two white collars clenched in his hands. He drags the bodies of the guards across the marble floor, releases his grip and their heads hit the marble with a *thump*.

Hamburg stares at Fredrik, wide-eyed like a fish, his overweight body frozen in the same spot, his sausage-like fingers barely moving against his slacks, nervously, as if he's absently searching for a weapon that he normally keeps on him and he doesn't want to believe that it's not there when he needs it most.

Fredrik shuts the door and locks it. He walks back over to the bodies, taking them up by the collars again and dragging them across the room. There's no sign of blood on them. He must've used his weapon of choice, a needle filled with something deadly and untraceable.

I look at Hamburg.

"Y-Yes…the black looks good on you," he says uneasily. "W-Why are you here? Willem is missing. I-I don't know where he is. I swear. I haven't seen or heard from him in over a week."

I smile and tilt my head to one side. "That's because he's dead," I say matter-of-factly.

Hamburg looks behind me at Victor. And then at Niklas. And then back at Victor again.

"Look, I-I told him to leave it alone," he continues to stutter. "I didn't send him. I-I specifically told him not to look for either of you."

Sweat beads from his chubby face, glistening on his double-chin. The armpits of his white dress shirt are wet with stains, the moisture spreading quickly across the fabric. The collar of his shirt changes color as it soaks up the moisture like a cheap paper towel.

I stand up. "You're a liar." I walk slowly towards him. "But it doesn't matter. I'm not here because of Willem Stephens. I'm here because of you."

Hamburg takes the same amount of steps backward that I take toward him, his bloated, wrinkled face twisted by trepidation, his thick hands feeling behind him for a door or a wall.

Fredrik steps in front of the door, blocking Hamburg's path and Hamburg stops. I watch as his throat moves when he swallows. Fear is ever-growing in his eyes.

He keeps looking behind me at Victor and Niklas, always focusing his attention on Victor last.

Victor steps away from the balcony door and stands beside me.

"Look, I held true to my word, goddammit!" Hamburg shouts, the lines around his eyes deepening. He points his fat finger at us, dressed in a thick gold ring. "I never went looking for either one of you after you killed my wife! I kept my word!" He points directly at me. "*You* were the one who came looking for *me*! Y-You started all of this!"

I shake my head, smiling across at him, at how desperate and afraid he is. It alone gives me some satisfaction, seeing him squirm, the way he's begging for his life without outright begging.

I step a little closer.

Hamburg doesn't move because he can't. Fredrik is behind him.

"Oh, this has nothing to do with me," Victor says to Hamburg. "I kept my word. I never came after you. But Izabel, on the other hand," Victor taunts in his trademark casual manner, "well, you didn't make any deals with her, unfortunately for you. And I don't own her. I never did. She's here of her own accord and there's nothing I can do about it."

Hamburg looks right at me, the anger shifting in his face to something more pathetic.

"P-Please…I'll do whatever you want," he begs, "give you anything you want. My money. My house. Just ask and it's yours. I'm worth millions."

I step right up to him and I can smell the stench of his sweat. He stares into my eyes underneath a shrinking gaze, one filled with hatred and horror. His large frame trembles inches from me and I know that if he thought he could get away with it, he'd grab me right now and choke me to death.

Suddenly, his expression changes to better fit his scathing words. "You won't do it," he taunts, sneering coldly as he looks straight into my face. "You don't have it in you, to kill in cold blood. You killed my guard out of self-defense. You won't kill me. Not like this." There's humor in his eyes.

I stand poised in front of him, my index finger fixed against the blade of my knife pressed against the side of my leg. I don't say anything, I just watch him, smiling with faint, yet obvious amusement, at his wasted attempts to save his own life.

He steps to the left and starts to walk away. I let him.

"I'll get you all a drink," he calls out, raising his finger up beside him. He removes his oversized suit jacket and lays it over the back of the leather chair next to the marble table. Then he starts undoing the buttons of his dress shirt.

I'm behind him like a ghost, sliding the blade across his throat before he has a chance to take his fingers away from the last button. A chilling gurgling sound fills the space, followed by Hamburg choking on his own blood. Both of his hands come up as if he were trying to fight his way out of a plastic bag. Red splatters from the side of his throat, and he falls to his knees with his hands pressed over the cut. Blood pours from between all of his fingers and drenches his shirt.

I watch him. I watch him not with horror or regret or sadness, but with retribution. My eyes feel wider as the air from the balcony hits the backs of them. I can't stop looking. I can't turn away. But I can feel Victor, Fredrik and Niklas' eyes on me, watching me revel in the moment of my first official cold-blooded kill.

Hamburg chokes and weeps, tears dripping from his eyes as I move around in front of him and crouch down to his level. I study him, the way his face contorts, the way the blood-red is contrasted so starkly against the white of his shirt. I watch the terror in his eyes, the fear of the unknown overshadowing him so quickly.

A small smile creeps up on one side of my mouth.

Hamburg falls forward onto the floor, his heavy body jerking and convulsing for only moments until it goes completely still. He lies with his cheek pressed against the marble tile, his mouth open as well as his eyes. They stare out at nothing, filled with nothing. Blood pools around his head and his chest, soaking up within his clothes.

Still crouched in front of him, I lean over on my toes toward him, my forearms propped on the tops of my legs.

"That's how those people felt when you strangled them to death," I whisper to his corpse.

I rise into a stand and take one step back before the blood pooling on the floor inches its way to my boot. One by one I look at Fredrik, Niklas and then Victor and all of them give me the same silent approval. But it's in Victor's eyes that I see so much more. An everlasting bond between us not created by this moment, but by that night we crossed paths in Mexico. Thrust into each other's lives by a twist of fate and held there by our rare similarities and our need to be together.

We are one in the same.

CHAPTER THIRTY

Izabel

One year later...

Victor comes into the bathroom of our New York house to find me relaxing in a bubble bath. I look up at him casually as he pulls his gun from the back of his pants and sets it on the counter. My hair is pinned to the top of my head in a sloppy bun. I lay against the tub with my arms laid out along the sides, one knee drawn up from the water, partially covered by bubbles. It's been a long day. I killed John Lansen, the CEO of Balfour Enterprises and rapist extraordinaire, and still have his blood under my fingernails.

I close my eyes and relax.

"Where have you been?" I ask Victor without raising the back of my neck from the tub.

"Cleaning up your mess," he answers calmly.

Compelled to look at him after his accusation, I open my eyes again to see him looming tall over me.

"What do you mean?" I ask. "It was a clean kill."

He cocks a brow and looks down at my hands.

"Is that so?" he says incriminatingly. "Clean means no blood at all. No fingerprints. Nothing left behind, not even your scent."

I sigh and close my eyes. "Victor," I say, waving my fingers above the side of the tub dramatically. "I didn't leave anything behind. I cleaned up after myself. Spotless. Ask Fredrik. He was there. He double-checked everything."

I feel Victor's body hovering closer as he sits down on the side of the tub.

"But what order did I give you, Izabel?" he asks, as calmly as before. "Before you set out on that mission with Fredrik, what did I ask of you?"

"No blood," I answer, still with my eyes closed. "Poison the man so that it looks like a heart attack."

I open my eyes again and look up into his dominant gaze, the green of his eyes darker than usual.

"Poison is Fredrik's thing, not mine."

"You defied my orders," he says, "and it will be the last time."

I smile at him and drop both of my hands underneath the water just to feel the bubbles on my skin. I know Victor isn't truly upset with me. This has become a game we play with each other: sometimes I do the opposite of what he says and he punishes me for it. It's the kind of game we both win. I would never have defied his orders on a mission of importance. John Lansen was just a loose end and another one of my training missions.

"What are you going to do to me, Victor?" I ask with a seductive gleam in my eyes. I bring my left leg out of the water and prop it on the side of the tub, just behind where he sits. "Are you going to punish me?"

With his sleeve already pushed up past his elbow, his right hand moves across the length of my leg slowly and then falls beneath the water. I gasp when his fingers find me.

"I'm taking you out of the field until you learn to control yourself," he says, two of his fingers slipping between my nether lips.

The back of my neck presses harder against the tub and my legs fall farther apart.

"And what if I can never control myself?" I ask breathily, barely able to concentrate on him talking while his fingers continue to move between my legs like that.

He's such a bastard. And I fucking love him for it.

Two fingers slip inside of me and my legs begin to tighten and tingle when the pad of his thumb moves in a hard, circular motion against my clit.

"Open your eyes," he says softly, but demandingly.

I do, just barely, as it's becoming increasingly difficult to control my lids. I whimper and moan and bite down so hard on my bottom lip that it hurts.

"If you can't control yourself, then I'll have no choice."

"...No choice...than to what?" My bare chest heaves. I reach beneath the water in search of his hand, coiling my fingers halfway around his strong wrist and then trailing them down toward his own fingers as they continue to move in a circular pattern.

Then he stops.

He pulls his hand from the water, stands up and dries his arm off with my towel hanging over the shower door.

I stare up at him blankly.

He walks out of the bathroom and leaves me sitting here, alone, unsatisfied and sexually frustrated.

"Hey!" I shout out to him. "Where the hell are you going?!"

No answer.

"*Victor!*"

Nothing.

I growl under my breath, shoot up from the water and step over the side of the tub. I grab Victor's gun into my wet, soapy hand as I storm out of the bathroom and into our bedroom. He's standing with his back to me next to our king-sized bed, taking off his dress shirt with a casual, uninterested grace, which only frustrates me further.

I step up behind him, soaking wet, water and bubbles dripping onto the floor, and I go to shove his gun into his back. But he's too fast and he whirls around at me, taking the gun from my hand and shoving it under my chin, all in two swift seconds that pass me by in a blur.

The barrel is cold against my flesh. The intensity in his eyes sends a shot of heat through my body and between my thighs. My breasts are shoved against the hardness and warmth of his chest, his free hand positioned in the center of my back, his long fingers splayed.

"No discipline, Izabel." He studies my face with a hungry and calculated sweep of his eyes. He licks the side of my mouth and shoves the gun deeper into my throat. "You will never learn."

I try to kiss him, searching for his mouth with my own, but he refuses me, teasing me with the distance of his lips barely an inch away.

He licks me again. And then he shoves me down on the bed and crawls between my naked legs, still dressed from the waist down in his black slacks. I shudder when I feel his hardness pressing against me through his pants. My body breaks out in shivers as he drags the tip of his tongue upward between my breasts.

He kisses one side of my jaw, and then the other.

"Maybe you should get rid of me," I whisper onto his lips.

"Never," he says, kissing me once softly. "You're mine for as long as you breathe." His mouth covers mine ravenously.

~~~

That was how I became what I am, a sex slave turned killer. And that was the beginning of not only a love affair between Victor and me, but of a new underground assassination ring that is so secret it has no name.

Four became five six weeks ago, when we welcomed the blond-haired, hazel-eyed devil, Dorian Flynn, into our group. And while although there are many who work for us, spread out over several countries, the five of us are central to the entire operation, with none other than Victor Faust at the head of it all.

Niklas is still an intolerable bastard who loves money and women and pissing me off. Indirectly, of course, but he knows what he's doing. Even after a year, he and I still pretty much despise each other. Maybe I despise him a little more than he does me, but we manage for Victor's sake. For the most part we stay out of each other's way. I still have yet to make things even with Niklas by shooting him. But I'll get around it. Eventually.

As for Fredrik, the women still love *him*, but I grew bored with trying to figure him out a long time ago. Why women practically drop their panties when they see him. I figured the only way to know that is to sleep with him, and since that will never happen, I decided to leave it a mystery. But Fredrik is like a brother to me, and, like Victor, I can't imagine not having him in my life. Without realizing it, he does try to run after me with those damn Band-Aids every now and then, whether it's after a brutal training session with Victor, or the night I was stabbed in the shoulder while on a mission. I have to remind Fredrik, in my most unforgiving Izabel Seyfried voice, not to treat me like a frail little girl. But deep down, I like that he's so protective of me. I'll just never tell *him* that.

Dina, the mother that I should've been born to twenty-four years ago, now lives in Fort Wayne, Indiana. We set her up in a safe-house as small and humble as her house back in Lake Havasu City had been. Victor tried to get her into something large and immaculate because he wanted her to have the best, but she refused. "I like things simple," she said that day.

Dina still doesn't know everything about what we do, but it's safer that way and she accepts that. And as far as her safe-house, it's open only to Victor and me. I visit her once a month. But her health is failing. I worry more about her than I do about myself or Victor. But she's a tough old woman and I think she still has many years left in her.

And as far as Amelia McKinney, Fredrik didn't kill her. Killing innocent women isn't his style. He set her up in another safe-house on the other side of the country, somewhere in Delaware. New identity. New everything. But he never visits her. The last thing he wants is for some woman to think he's interested in something other than sex.

That's the story of Fredrik's life.

As promised, after we were done with Hamburg and Stephens, we started devising a strategy to kill Javier Ruiz's brothers and to free the girls imprisoned in the Mexican compound. I went through six months of grueling training, *real* training, not being dropped off somewhere to let strangers teach me, before we set out on the mission.

Unfortunately, most of the girls at the compound who I had known had already been sold off, or were dead by the time we got there. I killed Luis and Diego Ruiz, slit their throats just like I did Hamburg, after Victor, Niklas and Dorian took out the guards around and inside the compound with a barrage of bullets. I'm not as good with firearms and still have a lot of training ahead of me. Years of it. But I get the job done with my ever-growing collection of blades. And I'm learning more every day.

When the mission in Mexico was over and we saved who we could—a total of six girls who were so broken that although they are free, I don't expect them to make much of their lives—we went on to the men who did the buying. And still today, just as it will be tomorrow and next year, we seek them out and we eliminate them. It will be a long road, tracking them all down and giving them what they deserve, but I'll never stop until it's done.

But more important than anything, to me especially, is taking out the Order. It'll be a long time before I can truly sleep soundly at night, knowing that there are men looking for Victor every hour of every day. It's a much more dangerous and complex feat than probably any mission we'll ever take on.

The Order is massive, with thousands of members and it is one of the oldest assassin organizations in existence. It will take some time. But it will be done if it's the last thing I ever take part in.

Victor is my life and I will die helping to protect him.

Though that mission will continue to be a difficult undertaking now that Fredrik had to leave because of suspicion, and we no longer have dependable eyes and ears on the inside. We have new moles placed within the Order, but they have yet to prove they're trustworthy like we know Fredrik had been.

And Victor...Victor is still all business. All cold-blooded killer-for-hire with little to no conscience when it comes to fulfilling a job. He is still seemingly emotionless, ruthless and deadly by all accounts. But behind closed doors, when it's just me and him alone, he is a different man. He loves me without having to say it. He cherishes me without having to prove it. When he touches me I know what he's thinking, how he truly feels beneath that mask he wears in the face of others. I'm the only soul he's ever let into his life completely. And the only one he'll never let go.

He became my 'hero', after all. The other half of my soul who could never let anything bad ever happen to me. I trust him with my life, no matter how often he tells me to always trust my instincts first. The truth is that everything we do is risky. Taking a step out a door. Making a phone call. Eating a bagel in a café. Everyone we come across is a threat until proven otherwise. Either one of us could die at any moment. But at least I know that Victor will always put me first and do everything in his power to keep me safe, just as I will always do for him.

Staying one step ahead of death, it is our way of life. It is *my* way of life, and I believe it was always meant to be this way. But as strange as it may seem, I feel perfectly safe in the company of killers.

Check out a sneak peek of J.A. Redmerski's upcoming New Adult novel, SONG OF THE FIREFLIES.

~~~ ~~~ ~~~

SONG OF THE FIREFLIES
Coming February 4, 2014

Elias

Anthony leaned forward between my and Bray's seats. He reached out and touched the bracelets on Bray's left wrist. I didn't like that much.

"Did you make those?" he asked. He peered in closer and tried to finger the bracelets individually, but she snapped her hand away.

"Ummm, no I bought them," she answered.

I could sense the nervousness in her voice. He had made her uncomfortable. Not. Fucking. Cool.

With my hands still on the wheel, I turned my head slightly to look over at him. I thought I was going to have to tell him to back off, but he saw the look in my eyes and fell back against the seat before I could say anything.

"Hey, sorry," he said, smiling. "I didn't mean anything by it."

Whatever. By now, I wasn't feelin' it anymore, hanging out at his place. It wasn't just that he touched her bracelets, it was something else, a vibe, the way Anthony seemed to go from helpful, smiling party guy to creepy backseat hitchhiker in such a short time.

"How much farther is it?" I asked, glancing at him in the rearview mirror.

"Just a few more minutes," he said.

A few minutes came and went. I thought we would probably be getting off at the next exit, but when he didn't say anything about it ahead of time, I flipped on my blinker anyway and planned to take it, if not for any reason other than to drop them off at the nearest convenience store.

"Where are you going?" Anthony asked. "We don't get off here."

"Well we're getting off here anyway," I said and proceeded to veer onto the exit ramp.

The sound of a gun cocking at the back of Bray's head and the shiny black glint of the barrel in the corner of my eye caused my heart to jump into my throat.

"Don't take that fucking exit," Anthony demanded with a threatening edge in his voice. "Stay on the freeway."

At the last second, I remained in the same lane and watched helplessly as the exit ramp flew past my car.

"Elias?" Bray said from the passenger's seat, her voice filled with fear.

"Elias, huh?" Anthony probed. I saw him push the gun against her head harder. She closed her eyes momentarily. I was white-knuckling the steering wheel. "Thought your name was John."

"What does it matter?" I asked. "What the hell is this?"

"What the fuck do you think it is?" Anthony said, laughing.

Cristina was still passed out against her door.

"Look, man, I know how this goes," I said, but I could hardly look at him. I was far too preoccupied with the gun against Bray's head. "I've got cash on me. Whatever you want. Just please don't hurt her."

Bray's lips were trembling, the only part of her stiff body that was moving. I wanted to pummel this motherfucker to death.

"Pull over up there," Anthony demanded with the nod of his head, indicating the side of the road.

"All right. All right." I tried to keep calm. It took everything in me, but I had to keep my head clear. Hopefully he planned to rob us and run off into the woods. But if I even for a moment got the feeling that he was going to shoot us down, I would make a last, desperate attempt. I wasn't about to let this fucking lowlife shoot Bray without at least trying stop him.

The car came to a stop and I put it into Park. And I waited.

I was hopeful when I saw headlights blazing toward us from behind, but the lone semi drove right past us, pushing wind against the car.

"Empty your pockets. Wallet. Anything you have on you. Put it on the dashboard."

"I take it you don't have a beach house?" I said sarcastically as I did what he told me to do.

"Fuck no," he said and laughed. "And that car in the parking lot wasn't mine, either." He barely looked away from me long enough to say to Bray, "You too. Whatever you have put it on the dashboard."

I thought about using that split second he looked away from me to grab for the gun, but I couldn't risk it. It likely would've gone off and killed her right there next to me.

There was no saliva left in my mouth. My whole body was stiff and sweating. Aside from getting that gun away from Bray's head, all I could think about was beating the fuck out of this guy. All I could see was red. I wanted so badly for him to slip up and give me the opportunity to take him down and cave his face in with my fists.

"Now get out," he demanded, looking right at me.

My heart dropped into my feet then. Was he going to take off in the car with her in it?

"Take the fucking car," I said, raising my hands up in front of me. "Just let her out."

"Get. The. Fuck. Out." He moved the gun to the back of my head now.

I only felt slightly better about that. At least it wasn't on Bray anymore.

I placed my hand on the door handle carefully, popped it open and stepped out, keeping my hands raised up, my fingers level with the top of my head.

From my peripheral vision, I noticed another set of bright headlights coming toward us off in the distance. My eyes darted to and from it, then to Bray, still sitting in the front seat. Cars sped by on the other side of the freeway, but it was too dark for anyone in them to see what was going on.

"Let her out," I said as I stepped around to the grass on the side of the road. "Please just fucking let her out."

Cristina's red-blonde head raised up from being pressed against the window. She rubbed her eyes and dragged the palms of her hands over her face and head like she was trying to wake herself up.

Then she noticed Anthony getting out of the backseat with the gun in his hand, pointed right at me.

"What—Anthony? What the hell are you doing?" Her voice began rise with alarm as realization set in. "What the fuck! Anthony, no!"

"Shut up!" he yelled at her from outside the car, his eyes still on me as well as the gun. "Now get your girlfriend out. I don't need more than one bitch flapping her fucking jaws at me the whole ride."

Without a thought, I swung Bray's car door open and grabbed her by the arm, pulling her out faster than she could get out herself. The car coming toward us was so close. I pulled Bray against me and then pushed her around behind me. I looked up as the car neared.

"Don't even think about it," Anthony said, pointing the gun at me through the side window.

And just like with the last exit ramp, I watched as our last hope for help sped by at seventy miles per hour. Bray was shaking behind me, her fingers digging into my ribs.

"Thanks for the ride, man!" Anthony said just before he jumped behind the wheel and sped away with Cristina screaming curses at him from the backseat.

I watched until what were once my brake lights became tiny red dots in the distance and then blinked out.

"Son of a fucking bitch!" I punched at the air in front of me, wishing it was more than air. Then I turned to Bray. "Oh shit!"

She stood there trembling with her face buried in her hands.

I dropped the anger and became the comfort she needed. "Baby, come here." I tried to pull her toward me.

"Leave me the fuck alone!" she roared, her hands falling straight down at her sides. She took several steps back farther into the grass. I followed. Tears shot from her eyes. "Just…just leave me alone."

I knew she wasn't mad at me. She just needed a moment. She just had a goddamn gun pointed at the back of her head.

She sat down against the grass, her hands shaking as if she were freezing. I crouched in front of her and rested my hands on the tops of her knees.

"What the fuck are we doing, Elias?" She looked up into my eyes, tears glistened on her cheeks in the bluish dark. "What the fuck are we doing here?"

I sat down fully and held her hands. "We can go home if that's what you want. Bray, all you have to do is say the word."

She shook her head no. She wasn't sure of anything, just as I wasn't. She asked me what we were doing here, but it was only a moment of realization. She knew that things were so much worse than getting robbed and left on the side of a freeway hundreds of miles away from home. I knew Anthony had little to do with what was going through her mind at that moment. He was just the messenger, a small and insignificant piece of a much larger picture that we were lucky enough to have forgotten all about for just a little while. This situation only brought back to reality the gravity of the bigger situation surrounding it.

"I don't want to go back," she said, raising her eyes. "I want to keep going. I just want to keep going."

"Then that's what we're going to do," I said.

I pulled her over into the throne of my lap and covered her with my arms.

To see more of the characters in REVIVING IZABEL, visit the author's Pinterest page:

PINTEREST.COM/JREDMERSKI/IN-THE-COMPANY-OF-KILLERS/

~~~ ~~~ ~~~

OTHER BOOKS BY J.A. REDMERSKI

THE EDGE OF NEVER
THE EDGE OF ALWAYS

SONG OF THE FIREFLIES
(COMING FEBRUARY 2014)

-IN THE COMPANY OF KILLERS-
#1 – KILLING SARAI
#2 – REVIVING IZABEL

DIRTY EDEN

-THE DARKWOODS TRILOGY-
#1 – THE MAYFAIR MOON
#2 – KINDRED
#3 – THE BALLAD OF ARAMEI

ABOUT THE AUTHOR

Born November 25, 1975, J.A. (Jessica Ann) Redmerski is a *New York Times*, *USA Today* and *Wall Street Journal* bestselling author. She lives in North Little Rock, Arkansas with her three children, two cats and a Maltese. She is a lover of television and books that push boundaries and is a huge fan of AMC's The Walking Dead.

www.jessicaredmerski.com
www.facebook.com/J.A.Redmerski
www.twitter.com/JRedmerski
www.pinterest.com/jredmerski

Printed in Great Britain
by Amazon.co.uk, Ltd.,
Marston Gate.